Bernice Rubens won the Booker Prize for Fiction for her fourth novel, *The Elected Member*, in 1970. She was also short-listed for the same prize for her ninth book, *A Five Year Sentence*, in 1978. Her most recent novel is *Brothers*, which is available in Abacus.

I Sent a Letter to my Love has been filmed with Simone Signoret and also made into a stage play in America.

In addition to numerous novels, Bernice Rubens has written for the stage, television and films. She lives in North London.

Also by Bernice Rubens in Abacus:

BROTHERS
THE PONSONBY POST
MADAME SOUSATZKA
BIRDS OF PASSAGE
I SENT A LETTER TO MY LOVE
SUNDAY BEST
FIVE YEAR SENTENCE

and under the Sphere imprint:

THE ELECTED MEMBER
SPRING SONATA

Bernice Rubens

MR WAKEFIELD'S CRUSADE

First published in Great Britain by
Hamish Hamilton Ltd 1985
Published in Abacus by
Sphere Books Ltd 1986
27 Wrights Lane, London W8 5SW
Copyright © 1985 by Bernice Rubens
Reprinted 1988
Published in the United States of America by
Delacorte Press 1985

Printed and bound in Great Britain by
Cox & Wyman Ltd, Reading

CHAPTER ONE

My name is Luke Wakefield, and I am a failure. All my life, almost forty years of it, I have been a loser. My ability to miss out, to fall short, to come to grief, amounts almost to a talent. So singular is this gift of mine that I have tried on occasion to exploit it, to make of it a virtue, to set its scene with humorous production. But I have failed in that too. Even my failure is a failure. My life has lurched from one catastrophe to another.

It all began on the day of my birth. I was born a loser, since my parents had wished for a girl. And from that day, it was downhill all the way. My schooling was disastrous. Every September saw me at another establishment of education. Not that my parents were itinerant. On the contrary, they were stolid working-class, immovable from both dwelling and opinion. Except towards the end, but I won't go into that. They lived in a terraced house in North London, went annually to the same west coast resort and the same boarding-house for the first two weeks of August, voted Tory in every election, and never strayed from telly and take-away. Except towards the end, but I won't go into that either. No, for the most part, they were a thoroughly and boringly dependable pair; it was their son-who-should-have-been-a-daughter, who was wayward, and I passed from one school to another with reliable regularity.

But despite my lack of formal education, I pulled myself up by my frayed bootlaces, as working-class lads are often wont to do, much to the confusion of those who have achieved unearned station in life. Thus it was that I turned to books to enlarge my vocabulary and to tailor myself in syntax and style. I turned, too, to the study, if not the practice, of good foods and wines, a knowledge of which is passport to any decent drawing-room. In those respects I make, as they say, my way.

I now move on to the heading of marriage, on which I shall not dwell overlong, for it is painful. That episode of my life was a failure of a specialised sort. When a marriage fails, it is usually because one of the partners finds another more suitable. That was so in my case. Ah, if only that had been *only* so. My wife did leave me, and indeed for a more suitable partner, but not for another man. That would have been painful enough, but in time it would have been palatable. No. Connie left me for a woman, one Stephanie, a rather large apparition that loomed from down under, where they now together besport themselves in antipodean ways. I suppose that the fact that she did not opt for another man might have been some source of solace to me. But on the contrary. Her flight to Stephanie seemed to me to be a desertion, not only of myself, but of the whole of mankind, and I felt weighed down with the responsibility of having failed my entire gender. The episode left me an angry man, and I am that still, and with no intention of forgiveness. So I don't want to dwell on it.

The final item in my catalogue of failures concerns my working life, on which I shall later elaborate for it is pertinent to my tale. But for the moment, let it suffice to declare that it followed the same monotonous pattern of dismal inefficacy.

Yes, I am without doubt, a failure. Moreover, from time to time, I go round the bend. But of all the things that I don't want to go into, this latter is the one that bears the least investigation. Forget that I ever mentioned it.

But even failure has to be organised, and in that respect I am a man of action and routine. Part of the latter is a visit every Tuesday morning to my local post-office, for I am familiar enough with the side-effects of failure to know that lack of communication is very dangerous indeed. And it was on one such Tuesday morning, a year or so ago, that I took myself to the post-office and found, as I had expected, a very long queue. Now I do not work in any employment, and I am in a position to attend the post-office at any time. But I like the business of waiting. In such business lies expectancy and a margin of hope, and there is little of either in my present way of life. There is the promise, too, of contact with other people.

6

Perhaps some words might be exchanged. That too, is an event that figures rarely in my life-style. I know that Tuesday is pensions-drawing day, for senior citizens, parents with children, and those with special disabilities, so there is every likelihood of meeting a variety of claimants. In view of all these bonuses, I would not dream of going to the post-office on any other day.

I joined the end of the line and waited. I had little hope of conversation with those who stood in front of me for they were so intent on their turn that they were unlikely to turn round and find me a target for dialogue. But I, on the other hand, having all the time in the world, was not eager to reach the counter, and I was already turning my head in anticipation of the claimant who would follow me. She was a young woman wheeling a capacity-filled twin-pram and, as if that were not enough, three other children tugged at each side of her skirt. She clearly would have no time for communication outside her own immediate family. I did a quick reckoning. With her five progeny, she was due to collect well over £30 a week and, my God, she deserved every penny of it for her endurance, for they were squalling and dribbling about her harassed person in a manner that looked suspiciously like organised punishment. I blessed myself that I had no children. I turned my head and inched myself a little forward in the line and, for want of something better to do, I studied the man in front of me. He was taller than I, so that I had to stand a little to the rear, knocking over the fertility symbol behind me, in order to measure him precisely. Over six foot, I thought, a man who carried his height with ease. He was well-dressed, and that helped of course. His coat was of cashmere and I was tempted to reach out with my fingers and to touch it. But I refrained in fear of how such a move would be interpreted. His fair hair curled over the collar of his coat and, though a sartorial expert might have shuddered at the style, I myself found a touch of class in it. I longed for him to turn round, but though I willed it, staring at the covered nape of his neck, his head remained firmly fixed. He moved forward slightly, and I was able to step a little sideways and view his profile. That too had class, and a certain beauty. The nose was long with a teasingly flared nostril, the chin square and resolute. His neck was covered with a silk cravat so that his age was difficult to determine. Late thirties, I surmised from the small wrinkles under the eye, and the lightly-veined hand that he now withdrew from a suede glove in preparation for his turn at the grille. He had an air of total unapproachability, and I dearly wished to speak to him. But shyness stilled my tongue and, as we approached the counter, I moved a little closer so that I could eavesdrop on his request and thus learn to know him better. Very shortly his turn arrived and I inched towards him. His request was simple. One first class stamp. He drew a letter out of his pocket and affixed the stamp to the envelope. Then he did an extraordinary thing. Quite simply, he fell down dead. It was as if he had gone to the post-office for the express purpose of mailing himself to heaven. My eye caught the man's final epistle that still lay on the counter and, for no reason that I could think of, I put it in my pocket. Then I looked at the body of the man whom I thought, from the back and profile of him, could have been my friend.

It lay on the mock-marble floor, disturbing the careful symmetry of its diamond-shaped tiling. I sensed an air of annoyance about the office, a sense of shame almost, as if it were not done to expire on government property. It seemed a sideways blow to the establishment. I suppose it was akin to dropping dead in the House of Commons, an act which would reflect a total disenchantment with the democratic system. I viewed once more his serene profile and I shivered like a mourner. Then out of nowhere a stretcher appeared, and two solemn-faced bearers. They lifted the body onto the canvas and covered it with a blanket. I noticed how they hesitated as the cover reached the dead man's chin. Both men knew without doubt that their passenger was dead, but they knew too that it was not within their authority to pronounce him so. So they turned the blanket into the shirt-collar, loosely and with little care, for they must have known that, at a doctor's glance, they could cover him entire. For a split second I caught sight of his bare neck as they lifted the man's scarf. It was less wrinkled than I had envisaged. Perhaps he was nearer thirty. Even so, I wished him as a friend. The men picked up the stretcher, took a moment to balance the weight between them, then they strode out of the post-office.

I noticed how some of the customers had taken advantage of the hiatus in the service and were jumping the queue. An ill wind will always blow well for some. But I held firmly to my place which was now at the head of the line, my poor predecessor having been well and truly served. The clerk returned to his business as if nothing untoward had happened, and he looked at me questioningly from behind the grille. My mind was elsewhere, still dwelling on that shattering event that had been so swiftly glossed over, and wondering whether it was perhaps a figment of my own imagination.

'Sir?' the clerk said.

What does he want, I wondered.

'Stamps?' he suggested. 'Postal order?'

I stared at him.

'Air-letters?' he tried again.

This last rang a distant bell, tolling mournfully from Connie in Australia. 'That's right,' I said quickly. 'Two air-letters.'

I knew I'd need two. I always did. Connie is a correspondent with whom I always have second thoughts. My first are always penned in the belief that they are the final draft. Then, on reading them through, the sheer misery of those thoughts stun me. And I know they are too stark and too painful to relay down under. I'm damned if I'll give Connie the pleasure of my misery. I don't know why I write to her at all, for she rarely writes to me except for a postcard or two from some exotic place with which to needle me. I suppose I write to her to nurture my resolve never to forgive her, to feed my anger in weekly missives, for indeed I do not know what else to do with it. So I write her a second draft, each sentence a lying declaration of my good health and cheer, and it is this draft that wings its cheery mendacious way towards Melbourne.

I slid the exact change under the grille in exchange for the air-letters and, as I left the post-office, I slipped my hand into my pocket. I fingered the letter that I had purloined and wondered what on earth had possessed me to pocket it. I was aware that I was committing a felony. Interference with the mail is an offence that the courts view with little favour. I could of course have simply posted it, as its late sender had clearly intended. But had he known he was going to die, I wondered, would he still have sent that letter? Perhaps it was a missive of anger, reproach or insult, that later perhaps, had he lived, he might have regretted. Or was it a letter of love or forgiveness, which offering, if withheld, would vex his ghost for ever more? With such thoughts, I was seized by a sudden sense of responsibility towards the deceased. I would effect a compromise, I decided. I would go home and steam the letter open and, according to its contents and my own judgement which I trusted implicitly, I would post it as would any upright citizen, or I would tear it into pieces as if it had never been. I suffered a small nudge of conscience, but I was excited, too, and that excitement overcame all scruple. I hailed a passing cab, anxious to get home and quickly savour what would be an event, an occasion, in my humdrum daily existence. For I have to tell you that humdrum it was.

I suppose I could say that I am a man whom life has passed indifferently by. When on occasion it has touched me, or rather, when I have accidently collided with it, it has been an encounter which has promoted nothing but failure. That I have already made clear. I have spoken of my disappointing birth, and my even more hopeless marriage. Nor, I must admit, can any thread of success be traced in my working life. I have tried my hand at a number of trades, and have come to grief with them all. In the last, an attempt at printing, I had come a complete cropper. I had declared myself a bankrupt, and had gone into voluntary liquidation. That was my accountant's phrase, and for some reason I savoured it. It was like opting for a swim in the warm Mediterranean. In its mellifluous sound, I heard a faint undertone of success. I remember repeating it to myself several times. 'I shall go into voluntary liquidation.' I had kept singularly quiet about my failures in birth, education and marriage, but it was in my working-life, and for the first time, that I was able publicly and legally to declare myself a failure. There was a certain euphoria in it. But it was short-lived. The memory of it, however, still lingered, and as I rode home that day in the taxi, clutching the dead man's letter in my hand, I had a premonition that that euphoria would return, and that the contents of the letter would be a key to a brighter future.

The door-man stood to attention as I entered the block of flats.

'Good morning, Mr Wakefield,' he said, knowing no more about me than my name, but thinking that enough to assure me of his personal attention. I acknowledged his greeting as I do every day, both coming and going, though I know that he knows the name of every single resident and greets them likewise.

I passed by the lush sofas in the foyer, the tropical plants and the ornate fountain, and I remembered how, in the beginning, I had thrilled to all those lavish appointments. Three years or so ago, I had moved into this luxury as a consequence of an event that radically changed my life-style. And to that event, you shall be privy.

I had returned from the bankruptcy court to my single bed-sitter in Camden Town, whence I had repaired after Connie had left me. I found a letter waiting. It was from a firm of solicitors and signed by one of its three partners. Brown, Brown & Brown, the letter-heading read, and not surprisingly a Mr Brown had signed it. I was not impressed by the multi-partnered company, for I have an unerring nose for failure. I have, after all, had some experience in that area. It occurred to me immediately that Mr Brown was a man of deep insecurity, and that he had so little confidence in a single-identity persona that he had to proclaim it in triplicate. I felt rather sorry for him. And I warmed to him, too, for his message was of stunning report. It informed me that the letter contained the contents of my mother's will.

I sat down on my bed that did for a sofa, and occasionally a table, and tried to digest that piece of information. For that opening sentence was the very first indication I had that my mother was no longer alive. Not that her death gave rise to mourning or melancholy of any kind. It had been almost twenty years since I had seen my mother, and that had been at my father's funeral. We had parted bitterly, and since that time there had been no communication between us. I sat there on my bed and wondered how I felt, or more precisely, how I *ought* to be feeling. But I could conjure up no remorse, no guilt, nor even relief. I read the opening sentence of Mr Brown's letter once again, and I registered it with disturbing indifference. But I was curious to discover what she had left me. At my last sight of her she had been poor enough, and I expected little beyond her belated blessing, and that, I thought, was hardly worth the stamp the third or possibly whole part of Brown, Brown & Brown had invested. But the phrase *a substantial sum* caught my eye, and I read further with unashamed appetite.

In the terms of your late mother's will, the letter read, *you stand to inherit a substantial sum of money. I would be glad if you would contact me as soon as possible in order to arrange a meeting, so that I can read to you the full contents of the will, and answer any queries that may arise.*

I read the letter over a number of times and still found it hard to believe. I was tempted to ring Mr Brown immediately, but I did not want to appear too anxious. I considered that anxiety, in such circumstances, spelt greed. So for a few days I avoided the pay-phone on the second landing, a simple enough evasion, since I lived on the first floor. On the third day of my anxious procrastination, my landlady called me to the 'phone. 'A Mr Brown,' she shouted from the upper floor.

I bounded up the stairs, suddenly assailed by pangs of negligence, an accusation far less excusable, I then thought, than greed. I apologised profusely to whomsoever of the Browns was calling, and in triplicate too, with respect to Mr Brown's presumed paranoia. I would have 'phoned earlier, I improvised, but I had only recently returned to London after a few days in the country. I caught sight of my landlady's unbelieving eye through the crack in the door and I turned my back on her. I promised Mr Brown that I would go to his office that very morning. As I put the 'phone down, I heard my landlady muttering behind me, 'In the country, indeed.' I turned and put out my tongue, for I knew that I could soon be disobliged to her.

It did not take me long to reach Mr Brown's office and to confirm my earlier judgement of the man's lack of self-esteem. For despite the triple legend on the door, I noticed that the Brown partnership sported only one office and a small annexe for a secretary. The meeting was brief. I learned that my mother had died in America, in Eugene, Oregon, where she had lived for twenty years with her second husband who had pre-deceased her. That husband was the owner of a chain-store business and, childless himself, had left all his wealth to his wife. And much wealth it turned out to be. Over a million dollars of it, and net to boot, and I, Luke Wakefield, time-honoured failure, was the sole legatee.

'How was her husband called?' I asked, for I wanted to know to whom I was indebted.

'Your mother was a Mrs Curtis, so I presume that was her husband's name.'

'Thank you, Mr Curtis,' I muttered under my breath, and it is a name that till this day sings in my ear, for it allowed me, if not happiness, then a certain freedom.

My first act was to discharge myself from bankruptcy. I was tempted to send some money to Connie, just for old time's sake, but I feared she might construe the gift as an act of forgiveness, and I was by no means ready for that, and doubt that I ever shall be. So with what I had left of my inheritance, I made investments as a provision for my future, and acquired a beautiful penthouse overlooking Regent's Park. But I have to confess that I no longer thrill to my surroundings. I am become indifferent to the marble foyer, the exotic plants and the fountain. Nor do I relish the porter's subservience. Over the years it has begun to irritate me. My life's pattern of failure has changed, but only because I no longer have to try. The respect and freedom that money can buy has made me not one jot happier than in my former years of penury. For still my life has no aim, no purpose. Every day is so like another that I no longer sense a week-end, or even a new season. This purpose-less meandering is reflected too in my thought-patterns, as must be already clear to the reader. I have written of my childhood, my schooling, my marriage and my work, with no respect to chronology. But that is a consequence of a life of failure and idleness. One makes detours, one goes off the point all the time, skirting the issue with seeming irrelevancies, until the point itself, when one returns to it, is sorely blunted. So I will delay and meander no further, for that visit to the post-office, over a year ago, and my reading of that letter, wrought a change in my life which merits some little recording.

I took the lift to my penthouse, fingering the letter in my pocket. I let myself into my apartment and trod the deep pile carpet that covers the total expanse of my quarters. And such was my sense of expectancy that I broke with routine, and I did something that I had not done for many years. I took off my shoes and sank my feet into the woollen pile, sinking each step into its velvet depths. I was pleased with the gesture, for I saw it as one of hope, as a declaration almost that thenceforth my life would take on change, as evidence that I was prepared to avail myself to new experience. I fingered the letter once more, but now with reverence, as if it were a talisman.

I took it straight to the kitchen and boiled the kettle and waited for the steam to rise. Then, holding the envelope flap into the steaming jet, I watched it slowly curl from its mooring, until a gentle easing with my thumb freed it entire. Then I took it to the living-room and laid it on the coffee-table. I tip-toed to the drinks cabinet and poured myself a large whiskey from my Waterford cut-glass decanter. I was setting a scene for the discovery I was about to make. I settled myself into an armchair, sipped at my whiskey and wiggled my toes into the carpet pile. Then I picked up the envelope and turned my face away. For despite my earlier rationales, I still harboured a small scruple as to what I was about to do. I put two fingers into the envelope and withdrew the letter. Only then did I turn my face and confront what I had done.

It was neatly folded, and in four equal parts. The pleats were knife-sharp and had clearly been ironed by thumbnail. The meticulous folding indicated that the sender was a man of patience and order, and I recalled his proud profile and knew that I owed it to him to treat his final missive with reverence. I held the letter at a formal distance from my eyes and, since I hoped for a drama, I read it aloud, starting with the sender's address. It was a crescent in Hampstead, one familiar to me, for I passed it every Tuesday on my visit to the post-office. But familiar for another reason too. Had I not seen that address before, and quite recently? I reached quickly for the envelope, and found that the addressee, one Mrs Marion Firbank, lived at the same abode. I was puzzled. Perhaps it was another flat in the same building, in which case a mere trip up or down the elevator would have saved a stamp. I was excited. It was certainly a promising beginning. I read further.

Dear Marion Firbank. That form of address surprised me, too. The use of the full name is a strange method of addressing a correspondent, unless perhaps it is a formal business letter, in which case it is typed. But this missive was written by hand, and moreover in an enviable calligraphy with meticulous attention to every pothook and hanger. The plot thickens, I thought, and I read on.

Thank you, dear Marion, for your letter. I note your advice that I should try to settle myself into a relationship of sorts. But you know as well as I, my dearest, that I am by now, addicted to living alone.

I paused then to savour his words. I sipped again at my whiskey, then continued to read aloud.

I am so seduced by my own company, Marion. Not that it is in itself seductive, but that it is safe and knowable. So ensnared am I by my own company that occasionally I get down on my knees and beg myself not to leave me. For from time to time, myself threatens to up and go. For it is foolish, it says, to live the way we do. Indeed, my dear Marion, the dialogue and argument I have with myself resemble that of any married couple, and I should know, for it was such dialogue that I had with you, and which led to my present solitary state.

I paused yet again. I warmed more and more to the writer of this epistle. Of such a man I could have made a friend and, as a might-have-been-friend, I began to mourn him. I toasted his memory with another sip of whiskey. Then I returned to the letter.

But this discussion of my solitary state is not the purpose of this letter. I write expressly to ask your forgiveness, forgiveness for the monstrous act that I perpetrated against you. After so many months of our correspondence, often so bitter, I am now able to say with all my heart, that I am sorry. And that I beg your pardon. I have done to you what no human being should do to another, and perhaps it is only God who can forgive me. But I beg your forgiveness, too. This letter must be short, for I am not feeling in the best of health. Perhaps I should see a doctor. And so you should have, my friend, I thought to myself. The letter was coming to a close, and I regretted it, for my curiosity had been aroused and I could see no way to satisfy it. But I was eager for the signature, and so I read to the end. *Please write soon,* he had written. *With all my love and remorse, Sebastian Firbank.*

I lifted my glass once more, and noticed how my hand was trembling. Then I read the letter again, quietly to myself and in my mind I recapped the scenario.

A Mr and Mrs Firbank lived in the same house in Hampstead and had been corresponding with each other for some months, and using the government postal service to do so. That in itself was intriguing. But of greater interest to me was the monstrous act that Sebastian Firbank had perpetrated against his wife. I was glad that he had lived long enough to ask her forgiveness, but I knew that I could not rest easily until I knew the sin for which he had begged her pardon. I did not know that I could sleep that night, to say nothing of the nights to come, while that mystery, on which I had so accidentally stumbled, remained shrouded in darkness. Was it possible that Marion had done a Connie on him? That was an act monstrous enough to merit the most monstrous revenge. Oh, how I mourned that melancholy profile. I was tempted to go out forthwith and to haunt that Hampstead crescent. I saw this mission of mine as a long and patient investigation, a search which in itself would enrich my life. I was so excited that I poured myself another whiskey to complete my euphoria.

I looked around my apartment, and thrilled once more to its lush surroundings. It was as if I was seeing it for the first time. In my shoeless feet, I moved from room to room, marvelling at the luxury of my life-style. I even ventured onto my roof terrace, and the roof garden that I had long since ceased to frequent. Now only my gardener went there, and weekly reported the growth of the plants and the shrubs. I felt ashamed now that I did not avail myself to the sight of all that beauty, and I stayed there for a long time, viewing the rolling acres of parkland below. I saw them as a laird might view his estate, for I was in that condition of excitement that proclaims the world as one's own and, as a corollary of that ownership, the ability to change the world according to one's will. It was a feeling of tremendous power. I leaned over the balcony railing and savoured it, while I considered my next move.

CHAPTER TWO

I knew I could not make an official visit to the crescent until after Sebastian's funeral. I reckoned that, in view of the circumstances of his death, there would be an autopsy which would delay the burial. I considered that two weeks would be an adequate time to deal with all the formalities, after which time I could begin my investigation in earnest. But two weeks was a long time to restrain myself, and the following day, and almost every day afterwards, I took a walk on Hampstead Heath passing the crescent on my way. I told myself it was by way of reconnaissance. I had begun to look upon my mission almost as a military manoeuvre that needed the most careful preparation. On my first visit I walked on the other side of the street and barely slowed my steps as I passed by number 62. On subsequent visits I became more daring and I actually stopped opposite the house and viewed its entrance. But nothing could be gleaned from the exterior. By the end of the week, I made so bold as to walk up the driveway, and there I was able to ascertain that the house, large as it was, was not divided into flats. This was evidenced by the single brass bell in the centre of the door. It was clearly a one-family residence. Mr and Mrs Firbank did not even have separate quarters.

On the sixth day of my reconnaissance, I turned the corner of the crescent and was surprised by all the paraphernalia of funeral. I considered it premature, and was faintly irritated by the thought that Sebastian's nearest and dearest should wish to dispose of him so quickly. I would not allow myself the temptation to join in his funeral, though it was hard to resist. So I crossed the road swiftly and took up my vigilant stance obliquely on the opposite side, half-hidden by the privet hedge of one of the houses. And there I waited.

There were but two black funeral cars parked outside the house, chauffeurs at the wheels. Clearly there were no expectations of a large funeral. The hearse was already dressed, and the coffin barely covered with four wreaths. There was no sign of activity around the house and I took advantage of this lull to cross the road and peer inside the hearse. I was anxious to discover the names and inscriptions of the funeral cards. Once at the hearse, I took my time, as if I were a browser in a book-shop. The chauffeurs eyed me with disdain. But there was no crime in what I was doing. I could be accused only of poor taste.

The central wreath was neatly inscribed with condolence and sympathy from one Richard, clearly so close a friend, he did not need to identify himself in full. To the right of it, there were chrysanthemums from Aunt Chrissie and Uncle Ted. The third wreath, that of roses, was inscribed, in a shaking hand, 'From Mother', and that circle of remembrance moved me unutterably. It was possible to fail in death as well as in life, by outliving one's own seed. I crossed the road again. I was shocked that there was no wreath from Marion, and I was quickly assailed by pangs of guilt. Would she have sent flowers had she known that Sebastian had begged her forgiveness? I resolved that, whatever the outcome of my mission, I would create the opportunity to appraise her of his plea.

I kept my eye on the front door of the house, and after a while it opened. A man dressed in shabby mourning, clearly the usher from the hearse-cab, was the first to emerge, and on his arm a frail old lady whom I took to be Sebastian's mother. An oldish couple followed who, according to the wreath register, would answer to the names of Chrissie and Ted. The last mourner, a tall gentleman, not unlike Sebastian in appearance, I presumed was Richard, and he closed the front door behind him. That was the whole cortège. No Marion. Once again I felt guilty, responsible for her absence. I waited until the small procession drew away and, as the hearse passed me by, I doffed my hat in memory of a man who might have been my friend.

*

I let some days pass before I made my initial move. I decided on my best suit and I took some time with my dressing. My intended manoeuvre was chancy and, if humiliation were to ensue, or downright failure which, in view of my history, was far more probable, an immaculate turn-out would be bound to give me a small advantage, and withdrawal, though bloody, might be unbowed. I took a taxi to the crescent in order to make an impression – on whom, I couldn't imagine – but my attire was not that of a pedestrian. I asked the cab-driver to stop exactly outside number 62, and obliged him to linger there for a while, while I fumbled for my change. Then I shut the door loudly, took a deep breath, and walked up the drive. I rang the bell straightaway, to give myself no opportunity for second thoughts, and almost immediately the door was opened, giving me little time to assemble my first into some kind of order.

'Good day,' I said. 'Quite like summer,' I added, knowing that as a good phrase for temporising, for it can lead to all manner of meterological discourse, and gives one time to marshal one's thoughts. I put on a cheery face too, for I was not to know it was a house of bereavement. The woman bid me 'Good day,' in her turn, and was clearly going to give the weather short shrift. For her expression was business-like, as if her time were valuable.

'Bit cold, though,' I pursued. 'Might even turn to snow.' I waited for her opinion on that forecast, but she was plainly not interested.

'Can I help you?' she asked.

Her accent was not of the crescent. It had ridden on a 20p. bus-ride from the outer edges of Kilburn where the Irish hold court in splendid if reluctant immigration, and the duster she held in her hand marked her as Sebastian's 'treasure'.

I steadied my voice. 'Can I see Mr Firbank?' I said.

She raised her eyebrows.

'Mr Sebastian Firbank,' I clarified.

'Who are you?' she said, on her guard.

'I'm an old friend. I've been abroad. I haven't seen him for a while.'

She leaned forward and her face almost touched mine. 'You'd better come in,' she whispered.

I noticed a glint in her eye, that glint of a foul-weather

friend. She ushered me in to what looked like a study, and sat me down in the most comfortable armchair, then she placed herself directly in my line of vision, setting the scene as it were, for her performance. Whatever news she had to impart, that news to which I was already privy, she was going to make a meal of it. She licked her dry lips and took a deep breath and, in doing so, she put down her duster, as if that were not a suitable prop for the matter of her speech. 'He's gone,' she breathed.

'Abroad?' I asked innocently. I was happy to help her spin out her tale.

'No,' she said, and almost angrily as if I were an idiot. 'He's gone. Dead,' she said.

I feigned shock, and after that, distress. She warmed to my reaction and possibly regretted that she had so quickly broken her news. For now she was bent on back-tracking a little, on giving me particulars of Sebastian's demise, the manner of his departure, which items, had she had style, she would have used as precursors to the dénouement of her tale. But style was not the woman's forté. She picked up her duster again, and took a chair opposite mine. No doubt she had conversation in mind, or more probably, a monologue, since it was she who held all the cards, and I could only offer my grunts and sighs, in shock and sympathy. But I was glad to be a listener and collect any clues she might offer.

'There was nothing the matter with him,' she was saying. 'He was healthy as a young boy.'

I noted her first lie. Sebastian had clearly stated in his last letter that he was out of condition. The woman was an unreliable witness and I wondered whether any of her testimony could be depended on.

'It was Tuesday,' she went on. 'I know it was a Tuesday because that was my day for Mr Firbank. I did for him, you see. Once a week. Tidied up the place, though I'll say this for him, he was not one to make a mess.'

I made a mental note of that clue to Sebastian's character. Trivial as it may seem, a man's concern or otherwise with neatness can be a reliable pointer to his personality. Very often, one who keeps his house in excessive order and cleanliness betrays an inner spirit of chaos and mismanagement. I remember myself, when Connie left me, how I would end-lessly wipe down the surfaces of my kitchen. And not only of the kitchen. Any surface would do. Wipe and shine. Wipe and shine. I am a surface man. I dared not look inside me, below the surface, for I was not willing, and certainly not able to attempt any spring-clean therein.

Sebastian's treasure droned on, itemising her late employer's fastidiousness. 'His wife was the same, he used to tell me.'

My ears pricked uncomfortably, not so much at the information, but at the tense that she employed. Her demise must have been very recent, I thought, since Sebastian's letter of ten days ago was written in reply to one of his wife's.

'Was?' I whispered.

'Oh, I forgot you've been away. You wouldn't have known,' she said. 'I never met her myself. I came shortly after she died. About six months ago, it was.'

I felt slightly faint. I swivelled in my chair and leaned my head on the desk alongside me. In doing so, I caught sight of a pile of letters neatly fastened in an elastic band, and I recognised Sebastian's writing on the top envelope.

'Are you feeling all right?' she asked. 'It's been a terrible shock for you, I'm sure. Shall I be getting you a glass of water?'

I nodded feebly, and as soon as she was gone I grabbed the package of letters and slipped them into my inside pocket. Then I hugged my head again and feigned distress. My heart was fluttering, not but with faintness, but with that former excitement that had followed my theft of Sebastian's last epistle. I was a filcher without scruple, and it struck me that perhaps theft was the sole profession in which I would not have failed. For indeed I had some skill in it, and lately, not a little practice. But I had other things on my mind. I was anxious now to get away from the house, leaving no trace of my name or person behind, and quickly too, before the gap, where the letters had been, was noted and wondered at. I was on my feet before she returned. 'I think I ought to be getting home,' I whispered. I took the glass of water that she offered and avoided her look of concern. Such a look has always unnerved me, for it threatens intimacy. I do not wish to be known, not even by myself, for there are things about me that I am obliged to think are unknowable. But I won't go into that. I leaned against the desk to hide the letter-gap and I gulped the water quickly. Then I took her hand to offset the rudeness of my swift departure. 'Thank you.' I offered my invalid whisper, and I made for the door. 'His mother,' I said, having an instinctive feeling that I would need her for further investigation. 'Is she still alive?' I asked, though from the wreath I knew she was still with us.

'She'll be here this afternoon with the executor. Shall I be giving her a message?'

'No,' I said quickly. 'I'll ring her. Is she still at the same number?'

'It's in the book,' she said. 'Hampstead Lane. Just round the corner.'

'I have it,' I said, and I fled before the woman could ask for my name.

Outside the house, I stumbled down the drive in case Sebastian's treasure was watching from the window, but once out of sight of the frontage, I hurried to the main road to find a cab, patting the package of clues in my inside pocket.

I was tempted to take them out straight away, but the need for mise-en-scène was predominant and nagged at me, so I allowed myself only to finger them as a child will explore a present-wrapping, guessing at the mysteries therein. There was no sign of a taxi and I was obliged to walk, my appetite increasing on the way. By the time I reached my apartment block, my fingers were fairly raw with exploration. The porter greeted me in his usual fashion, and I even paused to indulge in some weather exchange. Moreover I lingered at the exotic plants in the foyer, and studied the tank of tropical fish. I was torturing myself with delay.

'The lift, sir,' I heard the porter say, and turned to find him standing by the open door. He bowed slightly as I entered. I pressed the penthouse button and saw how my hand was trembling.

When I arrived in my apartment, I set the scene in much the same way as I had prepared the backdrop for Sebastian's last missive. When it was all set, my whiskey in my Waterford glass, my stockinged feet nursing the carpet-pile, the packet of clues fairly charring the bird's-eye maple of the coffee-table, I stretched out my trembling hand to discovery. I lifted the whole package – at a guess, there were about a dozen letters – and I freed them from the band. I intended to read them in chronological order and, on looking through the separate postmarks, I saw that they had already been arranged in such order, probably by Sebastian's own fair hand. I laid them out separately on the table, dealing them as if they were a pack of Tarot, for I fully expected omens of prophecy from the letters' contents.

From my reckoning, the correspondence had started some six months before. The date-stamp marked a fortnight between each letter and indicated a certain regularity. But my attention was more drawn to the location of each postmark than to its timing. For, although each letter was addressed to the same house in the crescent, those in Sebastian's hand were franked *Hampstead*, while what I assumed was Marion's writing hailed from Wimbledon. This threw me a little, I confess. Wimbledon lies across the river, a terrain which most professional Londoners consider abroad. It is a state of mind rather than a location, and not to be taken over-seriously. Perhaps Marion simply worked in Wimbledon, in which case, unemployment being what it is, she might be forgiven for a daily journey across the water. Yet I could not understand why they were obliged to write to each other at all. Was it possible there were no spoken words between them? I would delay no longer, I decided, and I reached for Sebastian's first letter. The envelope had been neatly sliced with a paper-knife, as had all the others, I noticed, and it was possible that both Marion and Sebastian used the same letter-opener, and probably in front of one another, I ventured to think, for there seemed no limit to the lunacy of their relationship. And the opening sentence of the very first letter amply confirmed that Mr and Mrs Firbank dwelt in banana-land.

Dearest Marion, Sebastian had written. *I have just returned from your funeral.*

I read that sentence again, convinced that I was dealing with a madman. But when I ventured on the second sentence, it seemed I was dealing with much more.

I killed you, my dearest, as gently as I was able, and I buried you where no-one will ever find you.

I put the letter down. I had a murderer on my hands without a shadow of doubt, and a Broadmoor candidate at that. I wondered whether I should read any further, whether I could accommodate all the disturbances that the letters would undoubtedly burrow into my life, and whether my dull, boring and uneventful but peaceful existence, hitherto, was not preferable. And then I recalled that Sebastian was dead. I my-self had seen him expire. He was beyond justice now, or any reproach of mine. But Marion? Her friends, her parents? Children, perhaps? Brothers, sisters, aunts and cousins, and all funeral attendants who had been denied a body for their mourning. It seemed to me that ignorance was truly bliss, for knowledge always entailed responsibility. Yet it was too late now to withdraw. I already knew too much, and certainly all there was to know about Sebastian and Marion Firbank. The rest was mere trimming. But it was the trimmings that aroused my curiosity, and I was faintly ashamed of my appetite. I took a long draught of whiskey and picked up the letter once more. I found myself holding it at a distance, as if there were some contamination in the print. I confirmed that Sebastian had been to his wife's funeral, had killed her gently, and had buried her in an unfindable grave. And, as if that were not enough, he was actually writing to his dead wife to put her in the picture.

Was it his conscience that nagged at him, or did he honestly expect her forgiveness from the other side of the tomb? I was itching to read her imagined reply, and I was glad that Sebastian's letter was a short one, for there was only one page to it. Besides, I was beginning to dislike him a little. It is, after all, hardly a gentlemanly thing to bump off one's wife even with the extreme provocation of having perhaps done a Connie on him. I must confess I have often wished my Connie dead, together with her concubine, but I doubt that I would ever have killed them, partly from scruple but more from fear of failure, for I would have bungled it as I have bungled most things in my life. I returned to Sebastian's letter. *My dearest*, he went on, *I do not know that I regret what I have done. Not yet anyway. But you became too much for me. I could no longer tolerate your invasion. I grew to hate you because you made me live a lie, and the self-deception became unbearable. I recall our early days together and how much hope I had of our future. I would like to re-live those times in recollecting thoughts, for thoughts, as long as they do not materialise, do not threaten. You will write to me I'm sure, my dearest one, and together in absentia, we will learn to love each other once again. Sebastian Firbank. P.S. I am sorry that your interment was such a lonely one. I am sure there would have been many mourners, including those friends of mine whom you could not help but alienate.*

*But in the criminal circumstances of my offence, I could hardly invite
witnesses.*

I put the letter back into its envelope and laid it aside. My
mind was in turmoil. I recalled that alternating postmark.
Wimbledon. It was not that poor Marion *worked* in Wimbledon. She was simply in the business of being dead there. I
thought I must go straight to the police, and I began to
rehearse my bizarre story. 'Excuse me, Officer, but you see
. . . well there's a dead body somewhere in Wimbledon. A
woman. Her name's Marion Firbank. No Officer, this is not a
hoax. I've got proof. There's a letter. Oh . . . oh I just found
it.' I realised then that I could not incriminate Sebastian
without admitting to my own felony, and I was not prepared
to sacrifice myself even in poor Marion's memory. No. Going
to Scotland Yard was clearly no solution. If Marion's body
were to be found and restored decently to her kith and kin,
then I, and I alone, the sole guardian of the proof of her
murder, only I could discover it. But Wimbledon, for God's
sake. Countless square miles on the London map, half of
which was common-land, and eminently suited for burial. To
say nothing of the tennis courts, that annual venue for scream-
ing fans and pouting players. Was it possible that poor Marion
was being tossed about in her grave beneath the interminable
deuces and tie-breaks? It would be folly to attempt a search.
Yet I could not shuffle from my mind the image of poor
Marion, wasting in her Wimbledon winding-sheet, unhon-
oured, inglorious and unsung. How had Sebastian explained
her disappearance to her family and friends? Perhaps he had
claimed that she had gone and left a note that requested that he
should never contact her again. In any case she had left no
address.

I picked up the second letter, Marion's first posthumous
epistle, and I marvelled at the postmark. So great was Sebastian's guilt, that he had to take atonement with as much
realism as was possible in the circumstances. He had actually
made the long and tedious journey from Hampstead to
Wimbledon every single week in order to authenticate his
penance. Poor Sebastian. Once more I warmed towards him,
and I found it hard to think of him as a murderer.

I opened Marion's letter. It was short, which did not
surprise me. There were few enough words that Sebastian

could dictate to her pen in such dire circumstances. Neverthe-less he had found some apt phraseology that suited his need for punishment at the time, a need no doubt he would feed in further letters, until he could, with all his heart, ask her pardon. Having read the ultimate letter of their correspon-dence, I presumed that that was the point of it all. I was glad he had written it before he died.

Dear Sebastian Firbank, Marion's letter read. I noticed that it was penned in a distinctly feminine handwriting, evidenced by the slightly pathetic frills and furbelows. Moreover it was written with a common biro, as opposed to the fountain-pen which Sebastian used for his own communication. *You have not asked for my forgiveness, so I do not give it to you. You do not even say that you are sorry. Do you want me to write to teach you to regret what you have done? Must I tutor you in repentance? Would you have me itemise each stage of our marriage and prove how you wronged me from the beginning? Shall we mull it over, you and I, I the victim, you, the torturer, until it is I, who have been so wronged, who will beg your forgiveness? Is this what you wish, Sebastian? Then you must give me clues, signposts to my own calvary. I suggest that you start with our picnic on the river, that day you proposed to me for the first time. For you may well remember that you offered many proposals. I took a little persuading, did I not? But then, I was but a simple girl from the provinces, Merthyr Tidfil, deep in the Welsh valleys, frightened of that great London of yours, and your art and your books and your music. You would school me in life, you said. But you did not mention death, and that was the only lesson that you managed to teach me.*

Here the letter ended and Marion's curly signature crawled beneath it. I was delighted with the clue that Sebastian had given me. I had a sudden and vivid picture of Marion in my mind. She was short, I was sure, and possibly dark-haired. I pictured her father as a coal-miner – my imagination is poor and could not stretch further, but it did for the time. Her home was a poor one and her education sadly neglected. Yet she had a thirst for knowledge and Sebastian had appeared like a ministering angel. It was a stereotyped picture that I drew of her, but the cliché is an apt companion to pedestrian thoughts and I make no apology for it. I even had her poor Dad die of silicosis in his prime, and I had to stop thinking to stem the tears that threatened my eyes.

The more I felt sorry for Marion, the angrier I felt towards her murderer and I was at pains to recall that gentle profile to recapture my erstwhile affection for the man. He had a bit of a nerve, I thought. The style of the letter he had penned on behalf of his late wife was one of sheer arrogance. And that he could have been concerned with style, at all, was a fact that faintly unnerved me. For Marion's letter had, without doubt, a certain mannerism that must have been the result of painstaking thought and arrangement, and I found it offensive that Sebastian should concern himself with such irrelevant niceties while his hands were covered with blood. As my distaste of Sebastian increased, so did my crusader-intents on poor Marion's behalf. And I resolved, there and then, to give the letters a rest for a while, for I was not interested in Sebastian's one-sided recapitulation of his marriage, and to set to work forthwith on the one shining clue that Marion had provided for me. That of her own birth-place. I would insert an advertisement in *The Times*. I grew quite excited with my decision and the possible clues it would uncover, and once again I went out onto my balcony to savour the content that had newly entered my life, and all the possibilities of change.

*

It was some days before the advertisement was due to appear. It was a Tuesday, my post-office day, but since my theft of Sebastian's letter I had happily forsaken that routine. I heard the rustle of paper in my letter-box, and I rushed to confront what I considered my first practical step in my search for poor Marion's body. I turned at once to the classified and read it aloud. 'Information sought on the whereabouts of one Marion Firbank, last heard of in Merthyr Tydfil in the '50s. Reply in confidence to Box No. 806.' I had hazarded a guess at poor Marion's age, presuming that she was younger than Sebastian and that decade of the '50s would have governed her girlhood in the Welsh valley. I had been aware that the advertisement might only reach those who would have known Marion in her London and more privileged times, and, conscious of that limitation, I had inserted the same advertisement in the *South Wales Echo*, a paper, I was told, that appealed to a larger cross-section of society. I had been very thorough, and I was impatient for replies. I wondered how I could spend my waiting time in other avenues of fruitful search.

I decided to have a go at Sebastian's mother, though I did not quite know what I meant by that phrase. I could easily discover her address and, from my recollection of Sebastian's funeral, I knew what she looked like, if that frail lady was indeed Sebastian's mother. But beyond that, I had no means of addressing her. But such paltry hurdles do not deter me. I have always been a man of great resolve, even though most of my pursuits have ended in failure. But until my advertisements elicited replies, I had to seek clues elsewhere. I would leave no stone unturned. Mrs Firbank, unrewarding as she might be, was an obvious quarry. I decided to make meticulous preparations for the hunt.

CHAPTER THREE

But, as was my wont, I made no preparations at all and, as I entered the gates of 25 Hampstead Lane – I had checked the address in the 'phone-book – I was no more prepared for the encounter than I had been in that fateful moment at Sebastian's door. I rang the bell without hesitation, no doubt depending once again on meteorological discussion to get me over the threshold. So I was pretty well clobbered when the door opened and a duster appeared, quickly followed by the hand of none other than Sebastian's Irish 'treasure', who clearly did for the whole family. I was about to stammer my pathetic weather forecasts when I recalled that she had heard them before, and had been distinctly unimpressed even then. The prospect of rain dribbled down my chin, and I said, with more resolve than was perhaps merited in the circumstances, that I had come to offer my condolences to Mrs Firbank and, so determined was I to spread my sympathies, that I actually put one of my educated brogues in the door. But this time the 'treasure' was not interested in my company, having no more bad news to impart, and she moved the door ever so slightly so that the jamb brushed against the leather of my carefully-buffed left shoe. I looked her straight in her challenging face and raised my eyebrows. It was the most strategic defence I could muster at the time.

'Mrs Firbank's away,' she said. 'She's off with her sister and her husband. They took her to Florida for six months, to help her get over her terrible tragedy.' Her r's rolled like thunder.

'Aunt Chrissie and Uncle Ted?' I ventured, as if with a life-long familiarity with the whole of Sebastian's kin.

'Mr and Mrs Ewbank,' she corrected me, with a tone of censure.

'Aunt Chrissie and Uncle Ted,' I repeated, not so much to spite her, but out of my own frustration, for I saw, in the temporary emigration of my three wreath-signatures, the closing of all avenues of search. Then I recalled the remaining wreath and funeral attendant, one Richard.

'Is Richard around, d'you know?' I asked with the non-chalance that covers a total ignorance of what one is talking about.

'Richard who?' she asked warily.

I saw the beginnings of suspicions in her eye.

'Oh you know Richard,' I squeaked. 'Everyone knows Richard,' I added, with the inference that those who didn't were sadly lacking in learning. I felt a slight squeeze on my left foot, which clearly conveyed that Sebastian's 'treasure' had better things to do with her time. There was malice in her eye. I withdrew my foot with unconcealed haste in order to avoid amputation. I left her agape in the doorway without even a gesture of farewell. I did not think that I was likely to run into her again. Sebastian's family, for whom she did, had with-drawn themselves from my jigsaw as if they had never been part of it at all.

I walked back to my flat in a mood of total desolation and, as I took the lift to my penthouse, I felt myself slowly invaded by that old almost-forgotten feeling of negativity and uselessness that had scored my life in pre-Sebastian days. There was one letter for me in my postbox, too soon, I thought, to be an advertisement reply, then I winced, when, through the grille, I caught sight of the Australian post-mark. I was puzzled as well as incensed. A full-blown sealed envelope from Connie was a rare event. Her sporadic communications consisted mainly of 'Glad you're not here' postcards. A letter signified something more serious than sheer malice, and might even, within its carefully sealed manilla, betoken a change of heart. The thought excited me and my mood of despondency lifted almost at once. Not that I was sure that I wanted Connie back. The only advantage of such an arrangement was that I could have her in front of me and could punish her face to face, and note from day to day how my revenge was wearing her down. I found such a situation highly seductive. I would delay answering her letter, I decided. I would withold my forgiveness. I was by now wholly convinced that her letter contained such a plea. I would wait for her to write yet again, and beg my pardon once more. In any case, I was not yet ready to allow her the luxury of my penthouse even though I would fashion it as her prison. Let her rot for a while down under, alone and penitent, biting her nails for my postal amnesty. I already felt much better and I poured myself a neat whiskey, eased off my shoes and settled into my leather arm-chair. The letter was bulky as if it contained much matter, and I relished the thought of her atonement and breast-beating that had required so many pages for its accommodation. I slit the envelope very slowly with my paper-knife as if I were preparing her neat neck for the scaffold. The weight of the letter on my hand quickened the knife a little and I could hardly wait to unfold its many pages. So I was furious, to say the least, to discover that the envelope contained but one small sheet of paper, not even large enough to merit a fold, and I realised that the bulk of the missive consisted of the envelope's quilted padding. But I contained my anger. I told myself that atonement needed but one word to express itself. 'Sorry,' or, stretching it a little with respect to grammar, two words. 'I'm sorry.' Or even, 'Mea culpa,' which expression would disguise the embarrassment of repentance. For a foreign tongue will often lighten the load of confession. I began to favour the laconic statement, for the fewer the words, the more reliable the sincerity. Indeed, an apology that was couched in 'style', and elaborate explanation, already seemed to me no real apology at all, but an ego-trip of self-reproach. No, the small scrap of paper heartened me, and I withdrew it from its padding with a surge of gratitude.

So I was pretty well unhinged to read its contents. Connie, as was her wont, came to the point straight away. She was not one given to preamble, innuendo, or anything that might pass as style, and she informed me in her very first sentence that she and Stephanie were about to have a child. She, that is, Connie, my erstwhile wife, she who had eschewed maternity as if it were the plague, that very same had now, down under, become some kind of earth-mother, according to the string of tightly-packed clichés that followed this shattering announcement. *Children are our future*, and such phrases curled with shame on the page, and I wondered by what miracle this man-hater of mine had conceived. The following sentence provided the answer. *I have been artificially insemminated.*

Now Connie had always been an irritating speller, but I found that misplaced double 'm' offensive in the extreme. For it seemed to compound the obscenity of her act. God knows who of those thousands of pot-bellied beer-swilling studs had fathered the child. I had to stop reading, so acute was my disgust. I noticed that there was but one more sentence to the letter, and I wondered what further insult she could now hurl in my direction and, when I finally gathered strength to read it, I found it injurious enough. With crass nerve and insolence, she actually had the gall to invite me to become the child's godfather. She even expressed the hope that I would be honoured to accept such a role, and that she had no doubts of a prompt and affirmative reply. I shivered with rage, and was about to hurl my whiskey glass against the opposite wall, but I remembered in time that it was Waterford, and that Connie and her bastard were hardly worth the cost of its replacement. Yet I seethed with rage at the sense of impotence the letter had wrought in me. For the three or so years we were together, was I not capable of fatherhood, and by natural, non-artificial means? Now it was clear it was my money she was after, and only that, and through my own inheritance, her bastard's future would be assured. I'd die sooner than give her a penny. I downed what was left of my whiskey. Then I took one sheet of my headed notepaper, and with all my boiling rage I told her exactly where she could put her offer of sponsorship. The paper fairly sizzled under my seething hand, yet when it was done, I felt no relief. My mood was even more desolate than before, for now it was laced with anger, an emotion that I have always kept by me, which, when released, I have never learned to deal with. Except to go on a bender of rage. To this end I rummaged in my desk drawer where I kept all Connie's missives, all those irritating picture-postcards she had sent me since her departure. I read and re-read them; I studied meticulously each exotic landscape, feeding my envy and my rage. And still I was not satisfied. For anger is like a tape-worm, self-feeding and self-starving at one and the same time. I read her latest letter once again. I was doing myself no good. That I knew, for as I read it, I experienced a positively physical pain in my groin. Her announcement of maternity, by whatever

32

devious route, was her final gesture of castration, and the thought crossed my mind that I should fly forthwith to Melbourne and kill her. I slipped my stockinged feet into my shoes and stormed out of my apartment. The lift was mercifully waiting – I don't think I could have cooled my heels on that landing for very long – and I pressed the down button as I entered and, hissing, I urged its quick descent. Once in the street, I was unnerved by the speed of my gait. My feet barely touched the asphalt. I seemed to levitate in my rage and, in such a state, I was immune to any obstacle. So it was hardly my fault that a young woman was making her unconcerned way in my direction. When our bodies made contact, mine with more velocity than hers, I cursed with annoyance and, looking down, saw her spread-eagled on the pavement, her skirt hooked up around her thighs. Her lay-out sickened me, and I kicked her none too gently on her shin and went on my levitating way. At the corner of the square I had to pause to still my trembling body and, in pausing, I came down to earth. Then I broke into a run of such terror that the sweat poured through my shirt and my knees melted. But I dared not stop. I made my galloping way round the back of my apartment block and took the service-entry to the large non-passenger lift reserved for furniture and the like. Its ascent was painfully slow and gave me unwanted time to reflect on what I had done. I began to fear for myself. I did not trust myself to be abroad, and by the time the lift had creaked its weary ascent to my floor, I had decided that I must stay indoors for a while to keep myself out of harm's way.

It was thus that I took to my bed and, apart from short excursions for my natural needs, there I stayed, and would stay, I intended, and wait for the post. For answers to my advertisements, and the clues I hoped they would offer, were now the only reasons that would drag me from my bed. My life seemed to have returned to its old pattern of aimlessness, and I turned my face into the pillow and tried to block out Connie-thoughts. And there I remained for many days, my ears cocked only to the sound of the postman's rattle. Every morning I viewed his delivery with despair, the sparse impersonal post of a failed, rich and idle man. Appeals from numerous charities, offers of teaching courses in writing/dressmaking/pottery, sundry bills and announcements of private catering. Nothing personal. Why, some of the envelopes were even addressed to a Miss Wakefield, so ignorant was the whole world of my identity. Each morning I crawled back into bed, and the days passed, including a Tuesday, and I was almost tempted to rise on that day and go to the post-office, and thus resume my erstwhile humdrum routine. But I chained myself with little effort to my bed. There was no point in making a retrograde step. Besides, a visit to the post-office would only confirm my pattern of failure, how yet again, in my life, another hot-footed pursuit had ended in fruitless fashion. I had set such store by my Sebastian adventure, by my Marion crusade, I was loathe to give up the chase, though my enthusiasm was threatening to wane. I prayed that someone, somewhere, would answer my advertisement. And God is occasionally good.

The first reply came on a Thursday, just over a week since the advertisement had been placed. It came from the Welsh source and, to my disappointment, it was singular. Just one reply. I had expected the *South Wales Echo* to elicit a larger response, but after my days of despondency I was happy to settle for just one dim light on my horizon. Once again I decided to give the letter-reading some manner of production. I dressed myself for the first time in many days. It was too early to hit the bottle, so I made some filtered coffee, and boiled a couple of eggs. My appetite had suddenly returned, and I tried to restrain my excitement in fear of yet another disappointment. But a reply was a reply, even though it was so singular. It indicated that somewhere in the Welsh valleys the name of Marion Firbank, *née* whatever it was, had rung a distant bell. As my toast was browning, I eyed the envelope and tried to guess at the gender of its hand. It struck me as female, and I was pleased with that, for women are far better at purveying information than men. They are, on the whole, more accurate. I pulled myself up sharply on that thought. How could I stray into such stupidity? There was nothing in which women were more than men, nothing at all, for they lacked the imagination and sensitivity. I was so outraged with myself for having a thought of such misplaced generosity, that I allowed my eggs to overboil, a fact which did not improve my temper. I looked at the letter again and, though it probably offered the only clue I was likely to receive, I already felt hostile towards it, for it was by now so clearly in a woman's hand. I downed some coffee to calm myself. Then I took my prepared tray to my dining-table, together with my paper-knife, and I availed myself to discovery.

The letter was written on lined note-paper in a spindly handwriting that lost confidence as each sentence neared its end. It was strong and sure on its capital letters, and had the writer spoken it aloud her voice would surely have dwindled to a whisper as it stumbled towards the full-stop. Whatever the matter of her letter, her calligraphy inspired little confidence.

Dear Box Number, she wrote, an appelation that did little to boost my waning ego. *Regarding your advertisement in the* Echo, *I am writing to tell you that I am the Marion Firbank you are looking for. Because that's my name see, so I must be.* I heard the Welsh lilt behind her declaration, and a faintly veiled threat in her certainty. *My whereabouts are in Merthyr Tydfil, like you said, and my address is written on the top of the page. I wrote it in capitals so that you could read it nice and tidy. Now I shall wait for your reply, and then, if you want, I shall come on the bus to London, so long as you will meet me mind, at the bus-stop. Oh and yes, you'll have to send me my fare see, because I'm a bit short like. Well it's not as if I'm asking for the train fare, which is twice the price. Anyway, I'd rather go by bus, and see a bit of the country. Now you write quick and let me know what to do. Yours faithfully, Marion Firbank.*

Her signature, too, like the address, was capitalised. I threw the letter onto the table. I was deeply disappointed. And vaguely frightened as well, because I could not help but smell a slight sniff of blackmail in her words. I decided to write to her forthwith and put paid to all her expectations. Which I did, and on my headed notepaper, in order to give it some authority. I told her that the fact that she was called Marion Firbank was sheer coincidence, for she was not the Marion I sought. I could hardly tell her that the only positive thing I knew about my Marion was that she was dead. Thus there was no point in looking for her. It was her relatives I sought, to appraise them of their loss. I needed to share the burden of what I knew with others. I needed their help to give poor Marion a decent burial. So I cobbled a story that told how I knew from reliable evidence that the genuine Marion had left Merthyr Tydfil in her 'teens, and had gone to India. I thanked her for writing and apologised if it had put her to any inconvenience. I posted the letter without re-reading it and, as it dropped into the box, I realised that I had volunteered my address, and I cursed myself for my stupidity. But there was nothing I could now do about it, and I returned to my flat more disconsolate than ever.

I did not know where to turn. Marion's undiscovered body nagged at me. I was possibly the only person in the world who was aware of its existence, or certainly by now, of its decomposition, and it would be a gross failure of justice were I not to discover it for, although her murderer was dead and beyond punishment, the world did not know that Marion Firbank had once been and was now no more. That was my present mission.

For want of anything better to do, I turned to the bundle of Sebastian's correspondence and opened the letter that was Sebastian's reply to Marion's first epistle from the grave.

My darlingest Marion, he wrote.

His wife's death had clearly given Sebastian the freedom to love her, a feeling he'd not been able to express during their marriage.

Merthyr Tydfil, he wrote. *The sounds of those words are etched into my ear. I remember how beautiful those sounds were in the very beginning and how, as time passed, they began to jar with discordant cacophony. But now once again I hear them with joy. As it was in the beginning, when you were everything I wanted, everything of which I had dreamed.* The letter went on in this vein for two whole paragraphs and was beginning to bore me. Old Sebastian was a humourless sod, I thought, and I couldn't understand how one could murder one's wife and lack a sense of humour. But I ploughed through the paragraphs searching for a clue. And then, at the bottom of the first page, it came. Richard. That name again. And in the following guise.

I was sorry that Richard was with me, but when we set out from London I had no idea that Merthyr Tydfil would hold treasures other than Brian's paintings.

I dug my shoeless feet into my carpet, for the plot was threatening to thicken.

But Richard had always advised me in my purchases, and I have never bought a work of art without his sanction. But when I saw you for the first time in Brian's studio, I wished I were alone. For in acquiring you, I needed no mentor, no assessor of your worth or durability. As it turned out, I misjudged the latter, but even Richard could not have foreseen that error. In any case, it was no misjudgement at the time, for you were then the embodiment of all my needs. But a woman is not like a painting. She changes, blurs, fades, and ceases to please. Richard would have advised me against you, I think. He did not even notice you when we entered Brian's studio. But I looked at you even before I viewed the paintings. And I envied Brian that you should be his servant, and the thought crossed my mind that you might serve me instead. As I write these words, I long for you once again. Nowadays I notice how my hair begins to grey. And has been I suppose, for some time. But when we were together, I never noticed it. Now it troubles me. You have left me with my age to deal with, Marion, and that was unkind.

A pretty unfair judgement, I considered, since it was he who had bumped her off. He was a rum bugger all right, old Sebastian, but I was grateful to him for the clues he had provided. But before acting on them, I decided to read Marion's reply, as much for the sake of chronology as curiosity. For I like order in my life. Loose ends bother me.

Dear Sebastian, Marion had written. *You were right about my frail durability. You loved and wooed me as a servant-girl, and would have me always so. But over the years I acquired ideas above my station. I was no longer the picture you had bought with such joy. But there was more to it than that. When I expressed ideas of my own, you patted me on the head with benign tolerance. When I consulted Richard, who would never be my friend, even that you tolerated. But it was more than that, Sebastian, but I cannot bring myself to say it. . . . Besides these are your words, and in this case, you are too mean to give them to me. You want them all for yourself. Keep them. For your letters. Not mine. Marion.*

Well, I could hardly stop there. I had to know those words that Sebastian regarded as his very own, that he jealously guarded for his own hearing. I opened his next letter.

Dear Marion, you are right. That wasn't all. There was more than that. And here it is. You got fat, Marion. Fat, d'you hear? And that was unforgivable. D'you remember when I first saw you? You wore trousers and a loose shirt. Nothing about your attire indicated the shape that it clothed. Except that the armature was lean, for the clothes hung on you, and moved almost with a life of their own. I ached to see that frame. I imagined it frail, unfed, unlearned. More like a boy's perhaps, with innocence retained. Easier for a boy. A

37

baby-girl loses innocence on the first sight of her father. Yes Marion, you got fat. Men have murdered for less. Sebastian.

I had perforce, by virtue of my sense of order, to read Marion's reply. It was short.

Dear Sebastian, she wrote. *I never knew my father.*

I put the sheaf of letters aside, in case I was tempted to read further. For I was determined to read the correspondence in instalments, to serialise it, as it were, and thus prolong my excitement. I intended to gather clue after clue, to pursue them and, if they led nowhere, then I would read another instalment. I was determined not to read the last of the letters until I had discovered Marion's body.

I recapped on my newly-gleaned information. Sebastian has gone to Merthyr Tydfil in the company of one Richard, in order to view and possibly buy a painting by one Brian somebody. In the studio he had met Marion for the first time. Marion was presumably Brian's maid-servant. And probably illegitimate. Richard was presumably Sebastian's art mentor. It was quite a body of information, and I decided that a short trip to Merthyr Tydfil would clear the decks a little. Once again, I caught that old excitement that had nudged me on that fateful Tuesday at the post-office, and all memory of my so recent depression evaporated.

*

On the following day, I took the train to Merthyr Tydfil. I had never been to Wales before, and I was not exactly sure where it lay on the map. But my interest in the location was by no means geographical and, as I rode in the train, I tried to imagine Sebastian's thoughts as he journeyed unknowingly to his love. The enigmatic figure of Richard was at my side. I could distinctly remember his face from the funeral, but I could read no character in it. I sensed that Richard played a key part in the Firbank drama, and I toyed with the idea that Marion had had an affair with him, her husband's trusted friend, and that it was for this demeanour that she had forfeited her life. I did not buy that fat story. One did not kill for fat, unless the victim were a turkey or a goose, force-fed for that purpose. I found it difficult to put myself in Sebastian's shoes. His person puzzled me. He was cruel. Of that I was sure. Murder is not a gentle pursuit. Yet he was capable of loving, and the occasional turn of phrase in his letters revealed great tenderness. I felt on the whole that he did not know himself. and that his letters were an exploration of the enigma that he could not fathom. That enigma that had led him to murder.

I looked at the passing countryside, and I wondered whether we had reached the border, for I regarded Wales as a foreign country, much as I regarded South of the river Thames. Shortly we passed through a tunnel, which I had read was the entrance gate to Wales, and I began to grow excited. I had high hopes of my Merthyr Tydfil mission. I did not feel I had in any way to prepare my entrée into the community. It was a small enough place, I had heard, and not a popular venue for artists. Brian was possibly one of the very few painters who had made their homes there, and in respect of this scarcity, it did not worry me that I didn't know his surname. I would simply drop into a central pub, and make the acquaintance of the landlord. Having learned of Brian's whereabouts, I would make formal and polite enquiries about his work, but only as a preamble to my main line of questioning. That of the Marion who did for him, and were any of her family and friends still resident in Merthyr Tydfil. I saw no hurdles in that line of enquiry. In such a small community Marion would be remembered, and no doubt character-assessment would abound. Perhaps Brian himself was still around, and with luck he would have painted her, as artists, I am told, are often wont to do with their cleaning-ladies. I think it has something to do with the concept of the 'noble savage', a notion entertained by those who, for reasons of their own, seem to feel they have to make amends to the working-class. Gauguin was such a painter, though he took this notion to the extreme, for his models were not only poor, but foreign to boot, but I suppose it's because everyone else's working-class is always more exotic than one's own. Still, I was not interested in Brian's moral standards. Artists on the whole do not rate highly in that area. Connie knew an artist once, and he was no exception. This sudden thought of Connie took me by surprise, not for the thought itself, but that it did not rouse me to anger. I ascribed my calm to the fact that I was busying myself in other matters, and so engrossed was I in my present pursuit that Connie-thoughts had retreated into a manageable distance. It should have been a lesson to me. But I knew that I would not learn from it. That the moment my Marion-pursuit threatened to fail, Connie would loom yet again, and oblige me with my fury.

The train was slowing down. My directions were to leave the train at Cardiff and then to take a bus into the valley. As I walked along the platform, I felt suddenly nervous. My optimism began to bother me. Habituated as I was in my life to failure, I wondered why I had ever entertained any hopes of success in my mission, and I was suddenly overtaken by such a depression that the thought crossed my mind simply to cross the platform and take the next train back to London. I felt Connie loom large. It was almost as if she were nudging me over the railway tracks, urging me to go back home, the useless failure that I was, and there to seethe in Connie-anger with no outlet for my spleen. Such a prospect terrified me, so much so, that even failure in a one-eyed hick town like Merthyr Tydfil was preferable. I rushed out of the station and crossed the road to the bus-depot. Of all the buses assembled in that yard, I sniffed out the right one with a desperate survivor's instinct. I could not bring myself to verify my choice. If it were the wrong bus, it would have to do. Because I had to go somewhere. Anywhere. I had to *travel* with my anger. I had to air it, shift it, bestrew it, dispel it, and finally turn it adrift. And all that called for motion, and the direction of that motion was irrelevant. In any case, I had no idea of how to pronounce Merthyr Tydfil, and I was damned if I was going to make a fool of myself in front of these foreigners. I was beginning to hate this principality and I resented that it was so physically joined to my own. I now saw it as a setting for a further chapter in the weary catalogue of Luke Wakefield failures. I knew that if the bus remained stationary for much longer, I would begin to weep, but mercifully, it very soon throttled itself into motion and, as a bonus, the conductor actually shouted 'Merthyr Tydfil' down the aisle.

I clenched my fists and tried to calm myself. I told myself that if I did not take a strong hold on my feelings, Connie would finally destroy me. I dared to take a look at the foreigners around me. One, a man on the opposite aisle, actually smiled at me. I had perforce to shape my features into some form of response, or else appear very rude. At my smile, his mouth opened slightly as if he intended conversation, and I quickly turned my face away, because I did not yet trust my voice for decent conversation. I might well have cursed him for no reason, in much the same way as I had mindlessly kicked that innocent passer-by in the street outside my house. The memory of that incident frightened me, and I shivered with its recall. That, too, had been the outcome of a Connie-thought. I wondered if I would ever be free of her and, not for the first time since she left, I wished again that she were dead. But I knew that death does not ease rejection. Indeed it compounds it. Because for the survivor, death is the greatest rejection of all. I squirmed in my seat and turned my face to the window, trying to accept the impact of the scenery on my eye. I must pull myself together, I told myself. I shall go to Merthyr Tydfil and put my best foot forward. If my mission fails there, there will be other clues. There was much of the Firbank correspondence as yet unread. For a moment I was filled with hope once more, and I shut my eyes to fix that moment in my time, while the bus, in its own time-capsule, made its way into the valley, and came to a stop at my promising quarry.

CHAPTER FOUR

I was surprised and a little discomforted by its size. Marion had
spoken of herself in village terms, unschooled in the ways of
the world. I had expected a cluster of dwelling-places, a few
shops, a school, one or two public houses perhaps, and all
nestling in a valley overshadowed by the winding-gear of a
coal-mine. But there was no pit in sight, leave alone a valley.
The town, for such it was, sprawled, with little sense of
planning, as far as the eye could see. I stood in the middle of the
bus-depot and, frankly, even with my best foot forward, I did
not know where to turn. I began to hum to cheer myself a
little, for the temptation to get back on the bus was overwhelming. I moved away quickly and into what looked like a
main street. I jogged down the pavement, because I sensed
once again that movement was all, for my anger threatened to
return. I slowed down at the end of the road, and surprised
myself that my breathing was still steady and that I panted
hardly at all. I was in good physical condition and this thought
cheered me a little more for, when one is not too sure of one's
mind, it is reassuring to know that, somewhere about one's
person, a small corner of health is hiding. I went straight into a
public-house that was near at hand, not for the purpose of
enquiry, but to quench a thirst I had acquired in my jogging
and quietly to toast myself to success.

There were only three or four people at the bar, and I was
tempted to make some off-hand enquiries since, with a small
audience, failure is less humiliating. But suddenly I was aware
of how city-like Merthyr Tydfil was, how metropolitan
almost, and I realised how stupid my questions would sound
in their city-ears. One might as well walk into a pub in London

and enquire the whereabouts of a common enough Christian name, and expect some measure of intelligent response. I quickly ordered a double whiskey to fend off the pessimism that threatened to flood me. As I downed it, I decided to begin my enquiries further afield. No serious artist in any community would choose the city-centre as his watering-hole, and Merthyr Tydfil seemed a large enough city to have an artist's quarter. The problem was to locate it. I decided to take the bull by the horns, and I turned to my neighbour at the bar.

'I've never been to this town before,' I offered him. I still was wary of pronouncing its name.

'A one-eyed town, this,' he said. 'You're not likely to want to come here again.'

'I was looking for the artists' quarter,' I said, undismayed.

The man laughed and turned to his neighbour. 'He's looking for the artists' quarter,' he said and I noticed that he took up my accent as if to mock me. The air was distinctly unfriendly and I was anxious to be gone. I turned from the bar and watched as my neighbour put his hand in my arm. It felt like an arrest.

'What would you be looking for an artists' quarter then?' he asked. 'You an artist?'

He was leering now as he took his hand from my arm. It was clear that his notion of 'artist' had nothing to do with painting. I made for the door.

'This is a man's town,' he shouted after me, as if as a warning never to ask that question in his precious Merthyr Tydfil again.

I found myself outside the pub, shaking. It was not a good beginning, and once again I was tempted to make my way back to the bus-depot and return to London. I saw a local bus approach and stop at the traffic-lights. I ran and quickly boarded it, knowing that any vehicle would do to satisfy my need for movement, for that need was surely creeping upon me now, with Connie-thoughts in its wake. I ran up the stairs to the top deck and took a seat up front by the window, from which vantage-point I could see the streets and the people, and note how each area changed. I had been to Paris once or twice and had visited the Latin quarter. I was also familiar with the Hampstead and Chelsea areas in London. I was thus not unschooled in spotting the 'artistic' clues to a neighbourhood, and my eye was skinned for them now. As I settled in my seat, I caught sight of a young girl carrying a violin-case, and my hopes soared. Merthyr Tydfil, however it was pronounced, was not a town totally without artistic merit. When the conductor came for my fare, I took a ticket to the end of the line. I could then alight when the fancy took me.

The bus trundled along. From my view-point, Merthyr Tydfil was a dull sort of place, rather like Pinner or any trivial suburb of London. The violin promise was not repeated and again I started to hum to myself to revive my hopes. Then suddenly I spotted an alley that led off the bus-route. At the end of it was a small all-purpose store with racks of green grocery outside, and from where I sat I could spot the exotic fruits and vegetables that hailed a million miles from Merthyr Tydfil. A promising sight. More promising still was a group of people about the racks. Not so young in their years, but laughing like children, with an air of such total irresponsibility, that I could not help but equate that air with artistry of a sort. Besides, one of them, a woman, was actually carrying a vast portfolio under her arm. I rose quickly from my seat, and bounded down the aisle and stairs, and jumped off the bus as it slowed down at the lights. Then I made my way back to the alley.

The small group of people had dispersed by the time I reached the shop, but I caught sight of the portfolio'd one as she turned right at the end of the narrow street. I decided to follow her. As I turned the corner, I found myself in a small tree-lined lane. On either side were workmen's cottages, obviously tied dwellings of railway-workers, for the line ran behind them on one side. This sight heartened me. It was a common enough pursuit for impoverished aritsts to move out of the cities and find some quaint and cheap accommodation in small towns and villages, where silence and a north light could be bought for a minimal rent. And, as on all corners of most streets in the valley, a pub stood and, no doubt, my quarry. I sat on a stone wall and viewed it. It was now afternoon and the pub was closed. But I was glad to wait until opening time. I fully expected Brian whoever, or at least an acquaintance of his, to grace the bar in the course of the evening. Meanwhile I would stroll along the streets and acquaint myself with what I was now quite sure was once poor Marion's neighbourhood. The street signs were all in a foreign tongue, Welsh, I presumed, and sub-titled in English for the benefit of tourists. And I do believe, for the natives as well. For in all my wanderings that afternoon, I heard not one word of Welsh spoken. True, their English was heavily sing-song, and jarring I thought to the ear. I had heard about the Welsh Nationalists, but clearly they did not hold much sway in the South. Its proximity to the Severn Bridge, that easy visa to England's green and pleasant land, was probably the cause. The Welsh of the South were clearly cool on Home Rule, their one eye cocked enviously over the border, where the rose smelt far sweeter than the leek. The leek, for God's sake, I thought to myself. How lacking a nation must be in self-esteem to choose for themselves such an emblem. I began to feel very superior indeed and, what with a possible discovery in sight, my good temper was fully restored.

I wandered through the maze of little streets and came across a square with a garden at its centre. I entered by a gate on the one side and found myself in a children's playground, where children swung on swings and slid on slides, totally un-attended by a clutch of mothers who sat chatting and laughing in a bench alongside. My good humour threatened to sour. I am not over-fond of children, but the sight of their swinging and sliding began to depress me, probably because their mothers were so patently negligent. I could not help then but think of Connie, and the news she had sent me of her perverse pregnancy. I passed an empty bench but dared not sit on it, for the anger that was creeping upon me once more required movement and I quickened my pace and skirted the park. As I passed the mothers' bench, I looked at their faces, and each and every one of them looked like Connie. I threw them a look of such hatred that I feared their violent response, and I practi-cally ran out of the park with terror in my heels. I did not stop walking, and I retraced my steps down the same tree-less streets over and over again, until my anger abated. Which it did, mercifully enough, towards dusk and opening time.

I made my way to the corner pub. It was already pretty full and my spirits lightened. I eased myself into a place at the bar. My neighbours seemed friendly enough, shifting themselves to give me space. One of them even smiled at me, and I gladly returned his silent greeting for I knew that conversation was at hand.

'Visitor, is it?' he said.

'From London,' I told him. I ordered a beer and asked my neighbour to join me.

'I'll have the same,' he said, pointing to the glass in front of him. 'And thank you. Never been to London myself,' he said. 'Only to Reading, then on to the airport like. Every summer we go to Spain. Costa Brava,' he said. 'Or Costa Plenty, my wife calls it.' He laughed and downed the beer that he himself had paid for. 'No,' he went on chattily, 'you can keep your London. Merthyr's my place. Born and bred here. I'll die here, I suppose,' he laughed.

'Then you must know it very well,' I said, hope springing in my heart.

'Like the back of my hand,' he said, displaying it on the bar. It was gnarled like oak, with flat-topped fingers. His nails, though, were surprisingly manicured and the cuticles shone like half moons. 'Every street, every house, every family, bar those that come from your parts, like. Artists, they call themselves. Come down here, buy a piece of land cheap, take a perfectly good cow-shed and turn it into what they call a studio. Gypsies more like,' he said.

I paused to take breath on his behalf. I had not expected such a windfall, and so soon. I decided to come to the point straight away.

'I'm looking for one of those,' I said. 'He may have left by now, but he certainly lived here for a while. I'm not even sure of his full name.' I shrugged my shoulders, willingly offering him my ineptitude. 'Brian something or other,' I added. My heart paused for his reaction.

'Masters,' he shouted. 'Brian Masters,' he announced to the bar. The name was greeted with laughter, but it was not of mockery. Rather it rang with affection.

'Say what you like,' a man at the end of the bar donated, 'he brought a bit of life to this place. Duw, d'you remember that night with the piano? When Evan Jones wanted to sing? You was there that night, Dai,' he turned to his neighbour, and within minutes the subject of Brian Masters and his exploits was being aired from all corners of the pub. I was pleased that I had seemingly fallen into such a mine of possible information but, at the same time, I was disturbed by the tone of their reminiscences, which was distinctly one of mortality.

'Where is he now?' I dared to ask.

'Pushing up the daisies, poor bugger,' my neighbour said.

From time to time during my life, I have suffered bereavement, but none of these deaths, not even that of my father, affected me as sorely as did the passing of Brian Masters, a man whom I had never met. My clues, such as they were, had an uncommon habit of emigrating or dying on me. But I pinned what was left of my former optimism on the memories of these men and the information they could impart.

'How did he die?' I asked, injecting concern into my voice.

'Drink, how else?' one of the men said. 'All that posh lot that kept coming down from London. Bringing him whiskey. That's what got him started. The hard stuff it was. Sold his paintings for whiskey towards the end. Poor bugger.'

'People from London?' I asked.

'Dealers they were,' my neighbour said. 'Oh but he could paint lovely. Lived hard, worked hard. I'll say that for him.'

'What sort of things did he paint?' I asked. It was one way of moving towards the subject of Marion.

'Still-lifes, they called them,' another man said. 'Oh but he did them lovely. Remember those peaches, Jack? Could have plucked them from off the plate. So real they was.'

'And that cauliflower, mun,' another recalled. 'Eat it, you could have. Duw, he was clever.'

Marion was slipping away, lost in an avalanche of fruit and vegetables.

'There was a Marion,' I said, rinsing my voice of any urgency. 'She worked for him. What happened to her?' I tossed off the question as nonchalently as I was able.

'Marion?' they said, practically in chorus.

'He had so many like,' my neighbour explained. 'One of them must have been called Marion. They didn't stay long. He was a bit of a lady's man, was Brian. But one of them *must* have been a Marion,' he said, seeing the disappointment on my face. 'It's a common enough name in these parts.'

'Thousands of Marions,' another man consoled me. 'Bettys, Gwyneths, Myfanwys, he had them all.'

I tried to hide my desperate disappointment. But I would not lose hope. 'Did Brian have friends? Any who still live here?' I asked.

'Well there's us,' my neighbour laughed, 'and we're here all

47

right. But if you're meaning other painters like, well no. There wasn't many round at the time, and he never went out much. Just to the pub. And sometimes days would go by, you wouldn't even see him here. Working he was. Sometimes he would go up to London, on business, he said. But he always came back quick. Couldn't stand the noise, he used to say.'

'Where did he live?' I asked in some despair. I could not accept that this one clue that had been so full of promise, was leading so swiftly to nowhere.

'A few streets away. Mynnedd Street, it's called. But the cottage is gone. Pulled down a year ago it was. Fire risk, they said.'

I suddenly saw my whole Marion pursuit go up in black smoke, and the thought crossed my mind that I should give it up altogether and, with that thought, came another. Connie. As if the two of them were indissolubly linked together. Failure and Connie. I knew in that moment that there was only one way to get Connie off my back for good. But with my history, the road to success was unknown, untrodden. But I would try. There were clues to come. Of that I was sure. Much of the Firbank correspondence was still unread, lying on my chiffonier in my London study. I had to get back quickly. I had to travel once again.

'I have a train to catch,' I said, downing my glass. 'Got to get back to that place you have no room for,' I laughed. They had offered me such spontaneous friendship that I felt obliged to offer a reasonable excuse for taking my leave of them. But they seemed unperturbed.

'Thanks for the beer,' my neighbour said.

'Back to London is it then?' The man at the far end of the bar was walking towards me, his hand outstretched. 'Sorry you never met old Brian, then.'

I took his hand.

'It'll be the milk-train then,' he said. 'Missed the last express you have.' He looked at his watch. 'Going just about now,' he said. 'Milk train 'll get you in in the morning though. Nice and early.'

I cursed my bad timing. The prospect of a journey on a milk-train, shunting from station to station, and stopping interminably for milk and paper loads, appalled me. But it was travel of sorts, enough to propel my anger and disappointment. I took my leave, thanking them for their company, complimenting them on their city, and debasing London for their sakes. 'One must live where one has work,' I said helplessly, glad that they were ignorant of my state of total and unearned unemployment. They cheered me on my way, and no doubt after my departure gave me not another thought.

I picked up a bus on the main road and alighted at the bus-depot. It was still early evening and the bus that took me to Cardiff deposited me at the station with twenty minutes to spare for the last express back to London. I could not believe that my companions had lied to me. It was a ploy, I thought, to keep me in their company. Or perhaps they were truly ignorant of the railway time-table and could not imagine that any train for any place would take the trouble to leave Merthyr Tydfil after opening time. I was heartened by my good luck. My needs in life are simple. It takes very little to lift my spirits, and I settled myself in the train as it throbbed almost non-stop to London. I looked forward to my future without acknowledging that that future held nothing in store.

By the time I reached home, I had lost all appetite for the Firbank correspondence, for I feared yet again that it would reveal no clues. Such disappointment could wait. Life is long and art is short, whatever the pundits might say. So I went straight to bed, my optimism unimpaired.

The following morning, my spirits were still bright, though for no apparent reason, and I had a premonition that, very soon, some cause would present itself. As it turned out, I was right, for on opening my *Times* that morning, while I breakfasted on my terrace, I found reason enough for optimism. For my eye had caught the name of Brian Masters, in large and bold type. It sang out of the column that announced gallery exhibitions. It was a well-known house in Cork Street which showed distinguished painters of some repute. This Masters exhibition was a retrospective one, to commemorate the first anniversary of his death. I fairly whooped with joy. The Merthyr clue had turned out not to be so dead-end after all. I noted the date of opening. It was a week hence. I knew from some small past-Connie-experience – though I would not allow that thought to trouble me – that the preview of an artist's work usually took place one day before the official opening. Such occasions were easily gate-crashed, and I immediately made a note in my empty diary, underlining it with a red pencil, for I had high hopes of the event and the leads it might offer. Above all, I had hopes of meeting that shadowy figure of Richard, who had clearly played a large part in the Firbank drama, especially as it impinged on the person and work of Brian Masters. As a Masters follower, and possibly a friend, he would surely be at the opening, and it would be a matter of little difficulty, in the atmosphere of bonhomie, to approach him and make idle conversation. But that was not till a week hence, and I had to find some way of occupying myself until that event.

I decided that I would spend the time in an art-gallery crawl, acquainting myself with the medium, eavesdropping on the odd comment, so that by the time of Brian's opening I would be well-versed in authentic critic jargon. I would start on that very day. There were enough galleries advertised in *The Times* column to see me through till the end of the week, to say nothing of the National and the Tate, where I could while away the surplus hours. I showered, put on what I considered a gallery suit, and made my way to the West End to the first site of my reconnaissance.

It was a small gallery, but of some repute. It lay parallel to Brian's gallery, which was in a street I intended to avoid until the opening. The window was dressed with a few sculptures with names like 'Wind', 'Sea', and 'Fire', though I could find no clue in the figures that pointed to these elements. Art was a blank in my worldly view of things, and I intended to fill that gap in the coming week. An arrogant thought no doubt, since people spend lifetimes in such pursuit. But fundamentally I suppose, I lacked respect for what I considered to be airy-fairy, and the province of dubious persona. I would have felt infinitely more at home had Brian been a businessman good and proper.

I entered the showroom and was unnerved to find that it was empty of spectators and that I was wholly available to the assistant's concern. She lost no time in approaching me, eager for company if not for a buyer. She handed me a catalogue.

'Would you like to sign the visitors' book?' she asked, guiding me to the central desk.

I was wary of signing, but I dearly wanted an eyeful of its signatures. I was eager for Richard's. An art-lover, he was surely likely to visit galleries to keep himself au courant. I idly flipped the pages of the book, ignoring the pen that the assistant held at my side. And then I saw a Richard, the only one in the two short pages of signatures, discounting a number of mere 'Rs', evidence too flimsy to consider. Cobham was Richard's surname and I mentally noted his Kensington address. A mews in SW3.

The pen hovered below my nose. I hesitated, scratching in my mind for some alias that would look authentic enough on paper. I was haunted by the sense of being discovered. I'd noticed this feeling had dogged me ever since I had left the post-office on that fateful day. I knew that my paranoia was groundless. No-one on earth knew that I was in the business of rehabilitating Marion Firbank. Even if someone had seen me filch Sebastian's letter from the counter, no-one, apart from myself, was privy to its contents. Yet the feeling of being watched persisted, and the thought crossed my mind that Sebastian's ghost had returned to haunt me to warn that I must uncover no evidence as proof of his homocide. With that thought came another, and an angry punitive one, that I would write his name in the visitors' book, and thus exorcise him once and for all. I took the pen she offered me, and wrote 'Sebastian Firbank' on the thin black line. I was strong in my resolve. Even so, my hand trembled, and I felt the assistant staring at me as if she were aware of my forgery.

'A little Parkinsons,' I offered her in my defence.

She blushed with embarrassment and I was delighted to have so fazed her.

'Oh I'm sorry,' she said, reviewing her initial assessment of my character. She now clearly found me honest and upright to a fault and berated herself for having ever thought otherwise. She put out her arm to steady me. I think she had it in mind to lead me round the exhibition, but I drew the line at that form of sympathy.

'Walking's all right,' I said. 'It's only in my hands.'

She took the pen from me and scanned my signature. 'Address?' she asked with a smile. 'We like to have that so that we can put you on our mailing list.'

I took the pen again. What the hell, I thought. Might as well go the whole way, and, with a shaking hand, I wrote the address in Hampstead Crescent. That letter-box had been the receptacle of enough lunatic post in its time. By the end of the week, I intended to have left Sebastian's signature like a snail's trail in all the private galleries in London, and to fill his letter-box for ever more. I returned the pen with a shaking hand, and set out on a round of the exhibition. From time to time, I consulted the catalogue like a connoisseur, though my interest in the figures was quite minimal. Indeed, after I left the gallery, after a tour of superficial scrutiny, I realised I had not even noted the name of the artist.

My next port of call was a gallery in an adjacent street which displayed a collection of abstract paintings. There were a handful of spectators inside, and I made straight for the reception-desk and scanned the signatures in the visitors' book. I was glad to note that Richard Cobham had preceded me, and probably on opening day, some pages back, and from the same mews in Kensington. I Sebastianed myself on the newest page, and had a distinct feeling of euphoria. Sebastian's ghost might well be trailing me, but I was certainly in pursuit of Sebastian's accomplice in crime. I giggled, then quickly stopped my mouth when people turned and looked at me.

I would happily have skipped the viewing part in all the galleries I visited that week. All I wished was to dash from one visitors' book to another and sign in Richard's shadow, but for form's sake I turned to look at the pictures. There seemed to be no catalogue available, which in any case would have been of little help. For no matter how abstracts are titled or priced, such tags give no clue as to the picture's import. Indeed, they tend to compound it. But I decently dawdled around the show, drawing close to other viewers, in the hope of picking up a comment or two. But nothing of value was forthcoming. One of them commented on the beautiful colouring, a fact that I could see quite clearly for myself, but as to meaning they were silent, and I suspected them as ignorant as I. When I had completed the circle of the exhibition, I did the round once more to show my sincerity, then I left the gallery and sauntered down the street, where, a few doors away, lay my next port of call.

Thus did I spend the whole of my first day of reconnaissance. Out of the ten galleries I visited, Richard's name figured on six of the visitors' books, and I could clearly visualise the mews in which he lived. But that was a clue that I would keep in reserve, for I hoped to meet him face to face at Brian's show. That week in my life passed very quickly. And enjoyably too. I had few Connie-thoughts during that time and, when they did graze my mind, I found I could dismiss them, so intent was I on my cultural pursuits. But I must confess to have learned very little about the nature of painting, and I own with complete honesty that during that week, it had not enriched my life in any way. But it was wonderful to rise each morning with a purpose in view. There were times too of complete euphoria; that moment of signature in the visitors' book, that frequent discovery of Richard's name, for I entertained no doubt that Richard Cobham of Kensington Mews was one and the same as the lonely attendant at Sebastian's funeral.

I stayed at home on the day that preceded Brian's opening. After my week's sorties, I was weary and I needed to gather my strength to confront the sundry clues that I was certain would present themselves at the exhibition. Through discreet enquiries I had checked on the date and time of Brian's opening and, on that day, I took time with my toilet, wishing to look my best, to appear as a figure of some authority, an aura, I thought, that would off-set my gatecrashing status, should that be discovered.

The show opened at 6.30. I thought a 7 o'clock appearance would be seemly. Anything earlier would betray a greed for free drinks, and a later arrival would betoken a lack of interest in Brian's work as well as a certain rudeness to one's hosts. So the stroke of seven, sounding distantly from Liberty's bell, found me descending from a taxi outside the Primrose Gallery in Cork Street. From the opposite pavement, I could view the crowd through the plate-glass windows. I was glad of their number, for a multitude is a good subterfuge, should such a cover prove necessary, and ticket-less, I made my bold entry into the foyer. I looked around as one is supposed to do at such times, ostensibly seeking familiar faces, but only one I sought, that of Richard, whose funeral features were still vividly imprinted on my mind's eye. But the small foyer was not a good vantage-point for such observation, for it was on a slightly lower level from the main gallery. So I wound my way to the drinks table, took what appeared to be a glass of white wine, and boldly took the few steps into the exhibition. From that angle, I viewed the room again but, in all that sea of

53

faces, I found none that resembled Richard's. I made my tortuous way back to the foyer again, and to the reception desk. I had no intention of signing the visitors' book, but I wanted to discover whether Richard's name was inscribed. There were only two short pages to cover, so my inspection did not take long. But in the whole list there was no Cobham.

I would be patient, I decided. It was possible that Richard was delayed. I decided to while away the time looking at Brian's paintings. Not easy at an opening, for the walls were hardly visible, lined as they were with revellers who did not, even in their merry-making, have the grace to face the pictures. I was envious of their comradeship, and that made me hostile, and in that hostility, I bulldozed my way through the crowd, and allowed a space for myself before one of the larger paintings. The man in the Merthyr Tydfil pub had been right. Brian was clearly into fruit and veg. and, on this canvas, both were displayed in full splendour. A red cabbage formed the plate's centre-piece, looking uncommonly like a rose, and as if to support this illusion a few green leaves of artichoke were strewn around it. A cluster of black grapes leaned on one side of the plate with such an authentic texture of velvet that one was tempted to touch its bloom. A single apple and a common-or-garden potato completed the picture, and the whole canvas was labelled by what it exactly was. 'Fruit and Vegetables'. After my weeks' meanderings among Fire, Earth and Water, and blobs and circles and lines of meaningless design, it was a relief to my simple reasoning to discover a spade that was called a spade. I noticed that the picture had a red sticker attached to its frame. After my week's cultural orgy, I had learned that sign for sold.

I made a further attempt to elbow my way round the exhibition, but it was like an obstacle course, and when I was able to catch sight of a picture, or the lower part of a frame, that same red sticker was attached. I applauded Brian's success, for although he had as yet yielded no clues, I felt well-disposed to him, since he had known and possibly loved poor Marion. I managed to circle the gallery once again, and I took up a vantage-point to view the newcomers. But still no Richard. Once again I fought my way to the visitors' book. There were four pages of it now, but still no Cobham. I looked at my watch. It was almost 8 o'clock. The gallery was actually emptying now, and more and more pictures were visible. I had nurtured a wild hope that, among the fruit and veg, Brian might have found space to paint the girl who peeled and cored them, but there was not a single portrait, either of man or woman. I could not but acknowledge my disappointment. I moved towards the door, and stood there, isolated and brazen, watching the faces of those departing guests, checking on them once more, and waiting hopefully for the late arrivals. And there I stayed until only half-a-dozen or so were left in the gallery, and it was clearly closing time. I was depressed that the evening had yielded such negative result, but I tried to keep up my spirits by reminding myself of Richard's Kensington mews. It was a stone worth turning. I looked at my watch. 8.30. It was still early enough to make a call.

I left the gallery quickly and hailed a taxi and gave the driver Richard Cobham's address. The house was one of a cluster in a courtyard, and inaccessible by car. I paid off the driver and walked down the mews, preparing myself for the encounter, but without any preparation. I suppose I was still dependent on my weather forecast to gain access to Richard's rooms. I looked at the weather and decided that it would answer to the description of 'cloudy'. I rang the bell of number 21 without a moment's hesitation, took a deep breath, which I was on the point of exhaling when the door opened wide. A man stood there, tall, white-haired and distinguished looking, a little stooped perhaps with age, and wearing a brown silk smoking-jacket that matched the cigar in his hand. He smelt very rich indeed. He looked at me and raised his one eyebrow. I have noticed that the English upper-class are often contemptuous of words. It's as if they're rich enough not to need them. A gesture will do. So he raised his eyebrow, and it was a direct enquiry as to my business at his white-painted Georgian door. To such an unspoken question, I could hardly offer my cloudy weather-forecast.

'Could I speak to Mr Richard Cobham?' I said, loud and clear, and I heard my voice squeak a little with over-confidence.

'You are speaking to him,' the man said, with a regal third person distance.

My knees melted a little both with fear and fury. The man was lying. Of that I had no doubt. He bore absolutely no resemblance to my funeral Richard. More likely than not, this was his father. Then the thought struck me that both father and son had the same name – that too, an upper-class folly – and I smiled at the old man in token of my forgiveness.

'I mean Richard Cobham Junior,' I said.

The eyebrow took off once more, though not in questioning, but in ripe indignation.

'There is no Richard Cobham Junior,' the man said. 'I am unmarried. I think you have made a mistake, young man.'

The door closed ever so slightly. He was too well bred to slam it in my face. I saw my one remaining clue evaporate completely and, in my fury, I raised my fist to him.

'You're a liar,' I shouted. 'You've got a son all right. Why are you hiding him?'

The door slammed neatly in my face and I heard the rattle of a chain. I was trembling and I leaned against the door to steady myself. My ear was against the jamb and from inside I heard the dialling of a telephone. Then Richard Cobham's voice informed the police that a dubious character was loitering in the mews. I took to my jelly-heels and I fled. As I turned out of the mews, I heard the siren of a police-car, and slipped into the driveway of a house. I heard the car pull up outside the mews and a banging of doors. I waited for the scurry of feet to fade, then I fled to the taxi rank on the square. Mercifully one was waiting. I climbed inside, hiding my haste and whispered my address to the driver. As we drove out of the square, I dared to turn and look out of the rear window, fully expected a flashing blue light. But only an innocent cyclist followed up our rear, and I leaned back in my seat with enormous relief, that relief that is close to euphoria for, despite the futility of my evening's explorations, I counted myself lucky to be in the clear. But the euphoria passed, and by the time I reached my penthouse apartment, my mood was black with despair.

*

I do take a drink from time to time, but by nature I am not a drinking man. Whatever that means. But that night I lurched over to my drinks cabinet like a drowning man seeks a raft. I did not bother with a Waterford glass. I took a large cheap tumbler from the cupboard and filled it to the brim with neat whiskey. I did not sip it. My mood did not call for elegance. I suppose I must have gulped it rather, for I remember re-filling it to the brim. I recall little of that night but that gesture of totting up. I must have fallen into a comatose stupor for, when I opened my eyes that morning, the empty bottle lay on my lap and the room undulated like a sea at high tide. And the letter-box was rattling. Or so it seemed. I was unsure of my whereabouts, of my sight and my hearing. I closed my eyes again and I thought I heard the morning-paper drop onto the tiled hall floor. I could not understand it. I firmly believed it was still evening. Then why the too-bright light that filtered through the curtains, and the sound of the early morning traffic through the park? With infinite effort I raised my right hand, and with it I lifted my wrist and viewed the face of my watch. 8.30. It was indeed morning, and with that realisation came a reminder of the dreary events of the night before, and my black mood returned. I must get a hold on myself, I thought. A Connie-thought could descend at any time and could well shatter what was left of my equilibrium. I would make myself a fullsome breakfast, collect my paper and what little post I expected, take myself onto my terrace, and pull myself together.

I prepared my tray, and carried it to the shady part of the terrace, for the sun was already high in the sky, and its light and heat were too intense for my lingering sense of displacement. Then I went into the hall. *The Times* lay folded on the tiled floor and, on top of it, a single letter. The envelope was white and square, the address handwritten so it was clearly no bill or common circular. I grew excited at the prospect of some personal communication. I did not examine it, but carried it unseen to the terrace. I returned to my desk for my paper-knife for I intended to squeeze the last drop of pleasure from an event so rare in my life. I returned to the terrace, poured some coffee, buttered my toast, cracked my egg, and slit the envelope in one resolute flick of the wrist. Then, for the first time, I looked at the postmark, and my heart, so lately lifted, now sorely sank at the sight of its provenance. Merthyr Tyfil. And below the postmark the familiar handwriting of Marion Firbank, that Marion who was certainly alive and very kicking. I opened the single folded sheet with a faint dread.

Dear Mr Wakefield, I read. *Well look now. It's all very well for you to say that I am not the Marion you are looking for. I'll tell you for why. Marion Firbank is* not *a common name, so there's no question of coincidence like you say. You only* heard *that she'd gone to India. Well there's a lot of rumours flying around about everybody, and she no more went to India than I did, which I didn't, 'cos I'm the Marion you're looking for. Look now Mister, get this straight. My name is Marion Firbank, and I live in Merthyr Tydfil. Won't I do?*

I put the letter down. Poor unwanted Marion Firbank. I felt enormous pity for her. But no, she wouldn't do at all. I imagined her life as uneventful as my own in my pre-Sebastian days. That nothing had probably ever happened to her, and her non-journey to India was the least of it. I decided not to reply. A letter from me, or anybody for that matter, would be a happening in her life and she would exploit its meagre potential for the rest of her days. Poor Merthyr Marion. I tore the letter very carefully into eight equal parts. I piled them neatly on my tray and took a large gulp of coffee. As I downed the cup from my lips, a slight breeze rose up from the south, and lifted the dismembered Marion from my tray, and she wafted, quite gracefully I thought, but sadly disjointed, over my terrace and down into the square below. Rest in peace I thought, and not so much for her sake but for mine for, empty as my life was, I could live without the Marion who simply wanted to *do*. As if that were enough in life. Just to fit, however awkwardly, into the drab monotonous scheme of things. Count me in, poor Marion bleated from Merthyr. Daily she would hover for my reply, never abandoning hope, until that hope itself became an event, an illusion, a faith by which she could live, that might even lighten the burden of her load. Yes, I thought to myself, I would do her a favour not to reply. I leaned over the terrace and watched her as she landed on the footpath of the park. A jogger paused to pick up a piece of her. 'Won't I *do*?' he must have read, for he crumbled her plea in his hand and, with a health-fiend's intolerance, he chucked it into the trees.

I returned to my table and my breakfast, for which by now I had very little appetite. I did not know where to turn. Again I was assailed with a sense of futility in my search. Was I the only person in the world who cared about Marion? Had she not yet been missed, enquired after, and searched for? And in any case, was it any of my business? But such self-questioning I knew would lead to Connie-thoughts and despair. I resolved then to return to the Firbank letters and hope for further clues. After all, in a hunt of any kind, there were bound to be leads that led nowhere. And the longer my search, the more time I could give myself to understand Connie and perhaps, in the end, forgive her. But for that pardon, I knew my search would have to last a lifetime.

CHAPTER FIVE

I am a great believer in procrastination, There is never any
point in doing today what could, with no loss, be accom-
plished tomorrow. The Firbank correspondence could wait.
I picked up *The Times* and turned at once to the Deaths
Column. This is a daily habit of mine, as it is the wont of other
people to turn to the Crossword. Both are the pursuit of the
alone and the frightened, and both are pertinent to survival. I,
for my part, prefer to confirm the survival of my body rather
than that of my mind. I am a tolerant man, so each to his own,
though I have known the most mindless people who are able
to finish *The Times* Crossword. Now the body is something
quite different. It is pedestrian, prosaic, reliable. It has no
nuances. It is either dead or alive. And every morning, with
my live body, I refresh myself with those who are no more.

I have noticed that people who die in *The Times* tend to be
rather old and, apart from the odd accident or two, are well
into their three-score and ten years. *Times* readers are well-
heeled, I suppose, and do not risk malnutrition or lack of
medical attention, two factors which are not conducive to long
life. Besides, the simple fact that they are noted in *The Times*
points to a larger than average income. The popular press does
not carry an obituary column at all, for there would be no
profit in it.

That morning, the Column was quite short, and I had
already finished it while still eating my boiled eggs. Much as I
enjoy it – the column I mean – there is no relish in reading it
twice over. A man dies but once in his life and, like all
mundane matters, the tale does not bear repetition. I marma-
laded my last piece of toast and poured myself another cup of

coffee. Obituary notices always give me an appetite. I turned to the front page. For unlike crossword fanatics, I do actually *read* the paper. The main headline concerned itself with the astonishing results of a bye-election, where a safe government seat had been upturned. There was a mournful picture of the candidate who had had his come-uppance, and his failure pleased me. The rest of the front page was devoted to the economic collapse of the world in general, an area of speculation that holds no interest for me, so I turned to page two for the home news.

And in that turning, I entered heaven. No more, no less. For a headline struck me in the eye. *Body found on Wimbledon Common.* I slammed my hand on the notice. My whole being shivered with excitement. I teased myself by keeping my hand firmly on the paper. Then I slithered it down an inch or two, and allowed myself to read it again. For there is nothing mundane about such a headline, and it can be relished many times over. But did I really relish it? Was it not all over too soon, my crusade, and by another's hand? I had a fleeting hope that it was not my Marion who lay buried there, so that my life could continue to have some purpose. I lowered my hand for further evidence. *Early yesterday a body of a woman was discovered buried on Wimbledon Common. According to the pathologist's report, she was in her early thirties and had been dead for 6–8 months.*

I stopped reading. There was now no doubt in my mind that my quarry had been unearthed, and I had a desperate feeling of let-down. I read on, but now with little appetite.

The body was discovered by a young boy who was exercising his dog on the common. He told the police that his dog, an alsatian, kept returning to one spot, and started to claw the earth. Police are making enquiries.

I have never liked little boys, especially of the boy-scout kind, those prigs of busybodies who, all the time, are up to doing good. This one had queered my pitch, and not by any diligent research or reconnaissance, but simply by boy-scout accident. I could have killed him. Marion was my exclusive business and, in token of that sense of priority, I decided to make my way forthwith to Wimbledon, there to make my own personal investigation.

I showered and dressed, relieved to have something to do with my day. I put on my walking clothes, for Wimbledon

Common is not the reserve of clever little boys. I took the long tube ride to Wimbledon station, and from there set out for the heathland. I had never been there before, and that in itself was an adventure of a kind. Or so I told myself in order to keep up my spirits. Besides, I kept telling myself, although Marion's body had been discovered, I was the only person in the world who knew who had put it there. But I had no intention of helping the police with their enquiries. I reached the outskirts of the Common and found a vantage point from where I could view it almost entire. A few hundred yards from where I stood, I spotted a police-cordon. The boys in blue were out in strength, and a small cluster of people wandered around the site of the discovery. I decided to take a stroll in their direction, then to pause for a while and pick up what information I could.

A small tent was erected inside the cordon, no doubt the area of tell-tale evidence that might lead to an arrest. I stood on the edge of the cordon and, in all my private knowledge, I felt vastly superior. Let the police scan the list of missing persons, dig up records, and scour fingerprints. I knew the victim well enough, and I knew equally well that her murderer was dead. I knew, too, that after months of investigation they would have to conclude that the woman, whoever she was, was murdered by person or persons unknown. This terrible shroud of anonymity depressed me for it struck at the very core of my crusade: that Marion should be known by name, and by her kin who could decently bury her. I hung around for a while. I saw one or two bold spectators approach the police with questions, but there was a wall of silence around the cordon. I looked around the common and found it much the same as my own local Hampstead Heath, and I wondered why Sebastian had chosen Wimbledon for Marion's interment. After all, if he had to bury her, the Heath was his local bone-yard, a mere stone's throw from the crescent where he lived. Or if that were too close for comfort, he could have transported her to Epping Forest, a favourite dumping ground for all manner of remains. There must be some significance in Wimbledon, I decided, and the only source of such import would be found in the letters. I was a fool not to have read at least one more pair before I'd left my apartment. There was nothing for it, except to go back and do my homework properly.

I decided on a cab. I could not face that tube journey again. I cannot bear to be a witness to so many people who are going about their business, for I envy them that they have business to do. I do not mind that the taxi-driver has business to attend to, for that business, as long as I am in his cab, concerns my needs. I crossed the Common swiftly and hailed a cab on the outskirts. The driver seemed delighted with such a fare, for it promised, because of its distance and posh destination, a fine tip at the end. But he was mistaken. There is no man meaner than a rich man, as he would eventually learn to his cost.

When I reached my apartment it was lunchtime, and I welcomed another excuse to postpone the Firbank letters. Once again I sat on my terrace, and lunched on smoked salmon and a chilled chablis. Then I took out the next pair of letters from the folder, and decided to give them my full attention. As I recalled, Marion's last letter had claimed that she had not known her father, and that therefore she had retained her innocence. I myself did not fully understand that premise. Fathers are convenient scapegoats for dissatisfied daughters. It's a woman's world, whatever Connie and her like may say. But I knew I must not think of Connie, and I took out Sebastian's next letter with a certain fury.

Dearest Marion, he had written. *I do not want to quarrel with you, so early on in our correspondence. Of course you got fat, but I am happier when I recall the lean times. D'you remember the night of our first anniversary? You wanted me to take you to the Mirabelle. You knew it was my favourite restaurant. You wore white, I remember. It was summer and there was gold on your skin. People turned their heads when you walked into that restaurant, and I was so proud. The Martins were there, d'you remember, and the Webbs. It seemed all our friends' night out at the Mirabelle.*

I put the letter down. Two paltry clues. The Webbs and the Martins, of whom there were hundreds in the telephone directory. Perhaps he would speak of those Webbs and Martins in a little more detail, so I picked up the letter once more. Sebastian went on at length about Marion's beauty and the pride he'd felt in showing her off. He'd gone with some detail into the meal as well, which he had been allowed to order for her, a fact which seemed to give him a great sense of power and pleasure. The letter ended with a request for Marion's reminiscences of the same evening. I put the letter down. I found it all rather boring. I had no interest in Sebastian's need for atonement, which I felt in any case was faintly insincere. I was not interested either in Marion's echo of his sentiments. This one-sided correspondence I considered sick in the extreme. It seemed that Sebastian had an ego of narcissistic proportion, and that he had married Marion simply for the purpose of showing her off. My initial affection for him had waned considerably, but my zeal for my Marion crusade was not abated. Indeed it was intensified by Sebastian's conceit and ill-treatment. I put the packet of letters aside and wished that I had stayed in Wimbledon hot on the trail, which, cool as it might turn out to be, could not have yielded less clues than the Firbank correspondence. I scuffed my heels in the flat until it was dark enough for the late edition, then I hurried to the corner store to buy an evening newspaper.

I saw the headline blazing on the shop-counter. What had merited a column inch in *The Times* that morning now paraded across the whole front page, and its title was heart-stopping. *Marylin, Mary or Marian?!* I folded the paper and hurried back to my flat. Such a headline certainly called for a whiskey and a Waterford one at that.

I poured a shot into my cut-glass and unfolded the paper. I read the headline again, and again I sensed that power of one-upmanship. For whatever lottery the press chose to make of those names, I was possibly the only person in the world who knew the prize draw. I was in all ways elated, and this feeling helped to blunt the edge of the disappointment of the abrupt termination of my crusade. What followed, I read aloud, declaring it, even, like an orator, as a celebration, as it were, of poor Marion's rehabilitation.

Police have discovered the identity of a woman whose body was found on Wimbledon Common early this morning. She was a white woman in her early thirties, and was known variously as Marylin, Mary or Marian. She worked as a prostitute in the Shepherd's Market area, where she was known to have an address. The pathologist's report indicate that she died of savage blows to the head. A murder squad has been set up in Wimbledon Police Station, and reports suggest a number of leads for investigation. Anyone who knew of Marylin, Mary or Marian is asked to contact the Murder Squad on 789 1212. All information will be treated as confidential.

I laughed out loud. Not in celebration of Marion's untimely end, but because of the return of my erstwhile sympathy and affection for Sebastian. It was not just for fat that he had killed; it was for infidelity of the foulest kind. To lose one's wife to the streets is as monstrous an insult as losing her to another woman. In fact it is one and the same thing, for both are aimed at man's castration. I toasted Sebastian's courage. I should have done the same to Connie. I read the report once more, quietly to myself. There were patent gaps in the reporting. For instance, the body had not been identified. The police had *discovered the identity* of the victim. That clearly meant that no relative or friend had come forward to recognise Marion, and the police identity discovery must have been through their 'Missing Persons' file. I could not let the matter rest there. Let the police get on with finding Marion's murderer, whom I knew they now could never find, and I would get on with the search for poor Marion's family. The thought crossed my mind that I would, in confidence, reveal to them the murderer's name.

I took a piece of paper from my chiffonier, and on it I formulated a plan. I knew I must cover my tracks, so I took the lift down to the street, and walked across the park to a public telephone booth. It stood in a rarely frequented area of the park's inner circle. I ascertained that no-one was about, and I slunk into the kiosk with my faintly criminal intent. I dialled the number that was given in the paper. I expected the Murder Squad to answer immediately, but there was no urgency in their response. In fact, I waited in the 'phone booth a good five minutes before someone replied. During which time my hackles rose, and I resolved to spin them a story that included many false trails, just in order to punish them.

Finally an indifferent voice asked if she could help me.

'Help *me*?' I shouted at her. 'You've got a bloody nerve.' All the politeness I had intended, the civilised tone, was lost in my irritation. 'I'm ringing up to help *you*, if you're in the least bit interested.' I cooled a little. 'It's about the Wimbledon murder,' I said.

'Hold on,' she drawled, unruffled. 'I'll connect you.'

Well, believe it or not, I hung on for another five minutes waiting for my connection, during which time I was obliged to feed the meter, and feared that I might be detected. At last a man's voice came on the line, far more reliable this time, and asked if he could be of service. I let that one pass, and slowly I read from my prepared sheet of paper. 'I have some information on the Wimbledon murder,' I said.

'Could I have your name?'

I saw the pen poised on the other end of the line. 'I'm afraid I can't give you my name. I'm a married man. I'm sure you understand.'

'Tell me what you know.' The voice was weary as if it had been respecting confidences all day in return for a shoal of red herrings. Well he was going to get another one from me.

'I knew Marylin,' I said, deliberately using the misnomer. 'I saw her a few times in Shepherd's Market. I went to her place. Number 35, I think it was.'

'55,' he corrected me as automatic response to my mistake. Thick as a brush, I thought, but I blessed him for the information, given in such innocence and stupidity and, in gratitude, I gave him a little titbit for his file.

'She told me she was married. She said her husband lived in Wimbledon. Richard something or other.' I put the phone down quickly, looked furtively out of the glass panels and took my leave of the booth. I scurried into the park and stopped at the rose-garden, taking an inordinate interest in the genus of the plants about which I knew nothing and cared less. But in that moment I could have passed for a respectable horticulturist, and no policeman, popping hot-foot from his Panda, could have thought otherwise. 55 Shepherd's Market, I muttered to myself. It had a mellifluous sound. My feet itched for Mayfair, but I knew I could not go there until at least a week had passed, when the heat was off a little and my phone-call shelved and forgotten. I was pleased with my Richard tit-bit. It was a small punishment for his elusiveness. If the police delved deep enough, they would find him, and he would be there on a plate for my own private investigation. I sniffed at the roses and thought myself very clever. Then I made my way home.

My deviousness merited a drink, I thought. I poured myself a whiskey and was a little disconcerted to discover that the bottle was almost empty. I knew it had been full only the day before. I did not like such thoughts, so I emptied the bottle into my glass in order to dismiss them. I wandered out to the terrace and looked down over the park. I saw a police-car driving slowly along the perimeter. It reached the edge of my apartment block and slowed down further. When it came to the entrance, it stopped, and my heart plunged for a moment into free-fall. I stood there transfixed. Nobody came out of the car, and I was torn between running to find somewhere to hide, and awaiting my arrest and execution. I almost shouted at them that I was waiting. They had followed me at a distance from the park. Of that I was sure. They had seen my exit from the telephone kiosk, having been alerted from headquarters; they had watched my flight to the rose-garden, and benignly observed my feigned horticultural interest. Then they had simply followed me home. But of what was I guilty? I had merely fed them misinformation, a small tit-bit to add to the pile of misleading clues that lunatics phone in from all over the country. No, I was innocent, I told myself, puffing out my chest and, when I next looked below, the car had disappeared. I looked down the road, but there was no trace of it, nor on the perimeter of the park. I wondered whether I had imagined it all, another thought that I did not harbour with relish, and, to dismiss it, I opened another bottle of whiskey.

After a while I was feeling quite mellow, and well-disposed enough to look once more at the Firbank correspondence. I felt sure that I would find a reference to the Shepherd Market days, and it would give me pleasure to read Sebastian's wrath and to sniff out his murderous intent. There would be a certain interest, too, in reading Marion's reply, and to discover what alibi Sebastian had fashioned for her. But first, for the sake of chronology, I had to read her reply to Sebastian's Mirabelle extravagance.

Her letter was as I expected. It was long and repetitive and an absolute echo of Sebastian's view of the evening. She, too, described in detail what she was wearing, and likewise in detail what they had ordered from the menu. She was painstakingly descriptive of the friends they had met, but she was no more forthcoming on their particulars that was her murderer. The salient feature of the letter was its repetition, a style that did not necessarily indicate a lack of words or synonym. On the contrary, the repetition was a very purposeful ploy. It was like an erotic form of verbal lovemaking, and as such was embarrassing to be privy to, and I was forced to hold the letter at a distance, and at a slightly sideways angle. I was beginning to find the whole correspondence tedious in the extreme. But I would plough on.

I picked up the next pair of letters and I noticed to my dismay that there was only one pair of letters that remained to be read. I hesitated. I did not want to exhaust this possible mine of clues too quickly. But Marion's body had been well and truly found. It was now only a matter of picking up the pieces. I could not be far from my quarry. So I took the last pair of letters and secreted them in my chiffonier drawer, hoping to forget where I had put them, and I returned to the terrace with the penultimate pair.

I had a premonition of a great discovery, and I say it not in hindsight. For I remember being absolutely aware, at the time, that this pair of letters that I was about to read would be a key to a number of doors. And because of this premonition, I decided to tease myself a little, and I read the last sentence of Sebastian's letter, before reading the first.

Marion, my dear, he had written, *that was the most significant moment of my life, and I wish to share it with you once more.*

It was clear to me then that this pair of letters did not concern the whoring episode, and I could only conclude that that was contained in the last. Nevertheless, the tone of that last sentence proved that my premonition was not without cause, and I turned to the beginning of the letter in a state of great excitement.

Dearest Marion, I read. I noted the growing affection in his appelation. Indeed, as he moved towards the final plea to be forgiven, I think Sebastian must have loved Marion as he had never loved her before.

I want to recall a particularly happy time, the letter went on. *I remember it in its every detail. I had come back from the office rather early that day, with the intention of taking you to a concert. Rostropovitch was playing at the Festival Hall. You were sitting at the kitchen table, surrounded by kilner jars and all your jam-preserving kit, and as you stoned the plums, your face wore a particular glow that spoke of a profound inner happiness. I suspected its cause, but I dared not ask the question that would verify it. So I kissed you lightly on the forehead and set the kilner jars in line. You always made fun of my need for symmetry. How angry you would make me at times when you did not fold the towels and table-cloths exact, how that small area of overlap would drive me to despair. But that day you smiled as I aligned the jars, and even stroked my hand as I did so. The question was on the tip of my tongue, and it was as if you read it there, for all you did was nod your head. The baby will be born in the Summer, you said.*

I put the letter down, and fairly whooped with joy. I finally had a relative, the victim's child. It was now only a question of ascertaining the date, then taking myself off to Somerset House and its Registry of Births department, and thenceforth to hand over the onerous burden of Marion's decent burial. And I had to work quickly, or else she would be shipped out of the Wimbledon police morgue and buried in a pauper's grave. I looked at the date of the letter. November 2nd. We were now in June. The terrible truth was evident. The baby had never been born. I quickly checked on the date of Sebastian's first letter to his dead wife in which he had announced her burial. January 2nd. I was despondent. Sebastian had a double murder on his hands, for he had killed his progeny as well. Now I understood the nature of the fat he had killed for, and I felt sickened by the deed. Why, even I would have resisted Connie's liquidation, whoring as she was, had she been carrying my seed. *After* the birth of the child, perhaps. I do think Sebastian might have waited. Moreover he had robbed me of a very positive piece of evidence.

I returned to the letter, but now, in the light of what I knew he had done, each loving word of his disgusted me. *Sweetest Marion*, he had written. *How I long to be head of a family*. And on and on in the same vein. Marion's reply, which I felt obliged to read, out of my natural need for order in things, was much the same. A simple echo of her murderer's sentiments, which was not surprising from such a one-sided correspondence. The thought suddenly struck me that there had been no mention in the evening paper of Marion's pregnant state. And upright citizen as I was, that was something I felt I had to remedy. For now I had a double crusade. I had to campaign for the poor foetus as well. I looked over my terrace to ascertain that there were no police cars in the area, and I hurried down into the street, and made for a 'phone-box, a different one this time, that stood in a cul-de-sac of a nearby mews. I dialled the Wimbledon number. I had no intention this time of hanging on until I could be put through to the proper department, and when, after some minutes of waiting, the telephonist answered, I gave it to her loud, quickly and clear.

'The woman found on Wimbledon Common,' I shouted. 'She was pregnant.' I put the 'phone down and ran for my life, only pausing to take breath when I re-entered the foyer of my apartment building.

'Good day, Mr Wakefield,' the porter called from his little box, and his voice startled me. I turned and acknowledged his greeting. But I did not like his look. It was riddled with suspicion. Had the police told him to keep an eye on me, to check the timings of my comings and goings?

'I keep forgetting things,' I said to him. I felt I owed him some explanation for my frequent sorties. Then I regretted what I had said. If the police really suspected me, and the porter was in their confidence, then I was certainly behaving like a hunted creature. I had confessed to the porter my forgetfulness, and he had been witness to my restless day. All such symptoms were marks of a frightened man, one whose terrible crime had only yesterday been discovered.

I took the lift to my flat, and resolved not to leave it again for some time, though I knew that the porter would report my withdrawal as well. I took some whiskey to steady my nerves. I was now convinced that it had been folly to make those two 'phone-calls. I sat there shivering in my chair, fully expecting the Law's knock on my door. I tried to fashion some kind of defence for my behaviour. How did I know that the victim was married and that her husband lived in Wimbledon? How did I know that he was called Richard? And above all, how did I know that the victim was pregnant? In the light of all this leading information, it would surely seem, that I knew the victim very well, well enough perhaps to have quarrelled with her. Well enough to have . . . maybe . . . I shivered. I had read stories of murderers who make back-handed confessions to the police, leaving themselves enough loophole to withdraw. Teasing the Law, as it were, to expose the Law's inefficiency. Such men had often been brought to trial and found guilty. I didn't know what to do. If my suspicions were well-founded, it would be more politic to stay indoors for a while. But I needed an evening paper to follow the developments in the Wimbledon case. *The Times* would more than likely ignore it, especially as it was a case that looked as if it would ultimately be shelved. Whereas the evening paper would cover every lurid detail. Although I was convinced that it was my poor Marion who lay buried there, I still needed the confirmation in black and white newsprint. The thought crossed my mind to feign illness for a week, and ring down and ask the porter to fetch me the evening paper. But that would have been folly, and would only have confirmed the suspicions I knew he harboured of me. I would take a nightly risk, I thought, explaining that I was off for an evening's constitutional. But why the hell should I account for my movements to anybody? I began to hate the porter with a passion. He could go to hell, and to show that I cared nothing for his curiosity, I went out again, and reached the newsagent in time for the early edition of the evening paper. But there was no mention of the Wimbledon case.

★

For the rest of the week, apart from my nocturnal paper-crawl, I stayed indoors and, in my restlessness, consumed a considerable amount of whiskey. This gave me false courage on my nightly sorties for a paper. I did little to disguise my insobriety, and often I would roll past the porter with a hiccup, and care not a damn how his evidence was building up against me.

It was not till the end of the week, that the evening paper carried news that I had waited for. It commanded little space, and was insignificantly reported on the bottom of an inner page. Its headline simply stated, *Body on Wimbledon Common*. Poor Marion had ceased to be a woman. I read the short paragraph below.

The full identity of the woman found on Wimbledon Common last Friday is now known to the police. Following investigations, a man tonight accompanied them to the Wimbledon headquarters, where he is helping police with their enquiries. That old fuzz euphemism. In other words, they were beating the shit out of him.

Though the paragraph was short, it was heavy with information. Marion's full identity had been discovered, and a suspect had been accompanied. The latter item was of less interest to me. It was unsurprising that the police would make some show of arrest, even though they knew, as well as I knew, that it would turn out to be a false lead. Some poor bugger, feeding falsehoods down the blower, had been nabbed when coming out of a telephone-kiosk and 'accompanied'. But it was the former item of news that intrigued me. If the police were so sure of Marion's true identity, why were they withholding it from public knowledge? There was nothing to be ashamed of in being Marion Firbank, nothing left, that is, her whoredom having already hit the headlines. Perhaps, it was her pregnancy, that condition they had seen fit to investigate, following my telephone lead. But I couldn't understand why such a condition should be kept secret. And then the simple solution struck me. I recalled that in television reportage of air and road accidents names are not released until the next of kin have been informed. I was very pleased with this deduction, until I realised that I was sharing my crusade with the police. They too were looking for Marion's next-of-kin. I suddenly felt very uncomfortable to be in their company. But I was cheered by the thought that things were certainly moving. Once investigation was under way, daily developments could be expected. While they were busy in Wimbledon, I felt that I could once again show myself abroad. And bugger the porter. I realised I had been indoors for almost a week, that is, apart from my nightly sorties. I had lain low long enough. It was time to pay a visit to 55 Shepherd's Market.

CHAPTER SIX

Try as I would, I could not shake off this feeling of being followed, and as I passed through the foyer of my building I noticed how the porter stared at me, and how quickly he picked up the telephone in the porter's lodge. I was convinced he was informing headquarters of my sortie. And brazenly at that. I was so unnerved that I returned to the lift and pressed the penthouse button. I noticed the porter's raised eyebrow, and I felt it incumbent on myself to again offer explanation.

'I forgot something,' I said and, as I entered the lift, I realised that I had only refuelled his suspicions of my instability. I was furious with myself. I was desperate to go out. I had an instinctive feeling that in Shepherd's Market I would find the answer to the many questions that troubled me. But no way could I pass that porter again. I toyed with the idea of the fire-escape exit, no mean descent from the penthouse floor. But to lessen the risk of whatever threatened me, I was prepared to make the descent and even to scale it on my return home. I felt slightly cheered by that avenue of escape, but I was still convinced that, despite all the precautions I would take, I would still be tailed. It was a feeling in my back that I had, a tingling as it were, a lingering handprint that I could not shake off. There was only one solution, I decided. That of disguise. Connie's box.

I have not mentioned Connie's box before, and for good reason. I keep it hidden, hoping that it will thus erase itself from my mind. For it is not a pleasant memory. The fact that it is Connie's is unpleasant enough. But more than that. Its contents are painful to recall. It was the single relic she left me and, apart from her ghost which haunts each nook and cranny of my life, it is the only tangible trace of her, her sickening spoor.

Every Christmas, the office where she worked would give a party. A fancy dress party. And the theme was always the same. One's alter ego. As if that were going to change from year to year. For myself, I had no difficulty with my choice. I was a knight in shining armour – the roots of my crusading passion – and to this end I would hire a suit of arms from a theatrical costumier. Connie, for her part too, was in no dilemma as to her other self. A man. Pure and simple. I should have seen the red light then, but one sees only what one can afford to see, that which one is prepared to accommodate or outrightly reject. I was prepared for neither, and preferred to view Connie's choice as her little bit of fun. Moreover, Connie didn't hire. She bought. And buying is serious. It has undertones of permanency. That was a red light, too. And not just one suit. Every year, for the three years that we were married, it was the latest suit in season. And with it, too, went the moustache, the beard and the occasional cane. Connie's box housed all her dreams, and it was an act of utmost logic that she should leave it behind, once those dreams promised fulfilment. I had hidden it in the store-room of my apartment, a large walk-in cupboard affair. Not a particularly inspired place for concealment for I used it for cellarage, and, as must be evident by now, I visit it frequently. So I had little chance of erasing it from my mind. But now, I was more than happy to remember it and the props it offered me for disguise. For the only time in her life, it turned out that Connie had done me a favour and I opened her box with a touch of malice. I tried to ignore the smell that wafted from the wooden chest. For, though it was man's domain, it gave off a distinct female odour. I turned my face away, and rummaged for the cellophane bag which held the beard and moustache and their means of application. I felt around for a hat and cane, and quickly closed the chest on its evocative aroma.

I hurried out of the cellar with my spoils, and went into my dressing-room to create the transformation. I hate to confess that it was fun. The moustache was rather becoming, and the thought crossed my mind that I would grow one, for it gave me the look of a man who had to be reckoned with. I tried the beard but discarded it, for it looked too much like disguise.

The hat, a trilby, gave a neat finishing touch to my air of respectability and the cane completed the picture. I looked at myself in the full-length mirror and I was well pleased. I twiddled my cane, and doffed my hat, both gestures eminently suitable for a tour of Shepherd's Market. I even executed a little tap-dance, and fancied that I was Fred Astaire.

Then I crept out of my back-door and onto the service area, from where I took the first iron step of my descent. Fortunately it was not spiral, else I would have succumbed to vertigo. In any case, I did not dare to look down, and I kept my gaze ahead, negotiating each landing with my cane, which occasionally lodged itself in the slats of wrought-iron. After an interminable series of blind turnings and descents, I found myself on ground level, at the back of my apartment building and well out of the porter's eye. I twirled my moustache and twiddled my cane and went in search of a taxi. Despite my disguise, I could not restrain the occasional look over my shoulder, and I was happy when a taxi appeared. The cabbie was clearly impressed by my get-up, because he called me 'Sir,' and even opened the passenger-door to let me inside. I decided to give him a generous tip, for I was not above rewarding polite service. He dropped me off, as I had instructed, on the edge of Mayfair, so that to a passer-by, even if he were a plain-clothes copper, I would appear to be on my way to my club, or one of the numerous casinos in that area. Whereas to be dropped in Shepherd's Market itself is a brazen indication of what one is after, for the street offers little else after dark.

I was not familiar with the area, so I was surprised to come upon a corner restaurant called Mirabelle, a name that rang a slightly cracked bell from the Firbank letters. Was it possible, I wondered that it was at that very Mirabelle dinner that poor Marion had had her first thought of prostitution? That, being shepherded from taxi to restaurant foyer, she had caught sight and smell of a way of life that had touched some secret and forbidden longing in her heart. Poor Marion. And poor Sebastian too. He who had set such store by the Mirabelle, ignorant of the sewer which skirted it. For sewer it is. Let there be no doubt about that. All women are whores, but most have the decency to operate without fee. It is the introduction of money into the transaction which renders it immoral. I twiddled my cane with self-righteous indignation and turned my steps towards the sewer.

Number 55 stood on the corner, and I passed it a number of times on the opposite side of the street, to case it a little for form's sake. Then, without any preparation, I crossed the road and lifted the shining brass knocker on the door. Only when I dropped it, did I realise that I had no idea of what I would say, and I was relieved that there was no sound from inside. It gave me time to prepare my introduction, should someone eventually open the door. I heard the sound of footsteps, and the door was opened while my pathetic weather-forecast was waiting in the wings. A woman stood there. She was elderly but well-preserved. A thick choker of white pearls camouflaged her wrinkled neck, and a long black lace gown indicated that she dressed for dinner.

'Can I see Marylin?' I said, and I had a sense of déja vu. Not that this woman looked in the least like Sebastian's Irish treasure, but I seemed once before to have asked for a rendezvous with one I knew to be good and dead.

She hesitated. 'She does not work here any more,' she said. 'But there are others. Won't you come in?'

'Where's Marylin gone?' I asked, awaiting her Wimbledon reply.

'She died, I'm afraid.' The woman was no gossip-monger. She did not even pronounce Marion murdered. As far as she was concerned, the girl had died from natural causes endemic to her trade.

'Her poor mother,' I said with sudden inspiration.

'I didn't know she had a mother,' the woman said. 'She told me she was an orphan. She seemed to have no family at all.'

'Where did she come from?' I asked. The loss of a family connection displeased me, and I was no longer concerned with masking my questions in any subtlety.

'That I don't know either,' the woman said. 'We don't ask questions here. She was a lovely girl, but we have others,' she insisted, and she urged me into the parlour.

A group of women were draped over armchairs like satin covers that had been removed.

'Take your pick,' the woman was saying.

I did not look at them. 'I'd like a friend of Marylin's,' I said. I would not so readily abandon my investigation.

'We're all her friends,' one of them said.

'I'll take you,' I answered the woman who had spoken. And then I looked at her. She bore an unnerving resemblance to Connie. I fingered my moustache, and felt, to my horror, that it was slipping.

The woman of my choice took my arm and led me out of the parlour. I dared not take my hand from my moustache, but with the other I held my cane. But even with that support my legs trembled, for the situation that I had landed myself in now terrified me. For I had no idea what I was supposed to do. I had never been inside a brothel before. Such a place had not played a role even in my fantasies. Moreover, I had no appetite for whatever the woman would offer me. And apart from all that, I suspected that I had lost the skill for it, for it had been many years since I had put it into practice. All these thoughts brought on my Connie-anger, and now my body trembled with rage as well as fear.

She led me into a small cell of a bedroom in which there was a double-bed and nothing more. She had to inch herself sideways and sit on it while I hovered at the door, my one hand still grasping my unreliable moustache, while the other twiddled the cane.

'Why don't you take it off?' she smiled.

'Take what off?' I, for my part was not prepared to take anything off, but I was curious as to what she had in mind.

'The moustache,' she said.

'But I can't,' I protested. 'It's my own.'

'Then why are you hanging on to it for dear life?'

I took my hand away and I felt a hairy curtain over one side of my lip. She laughed again, and I felt it politic to join her.

'Lots of them come with beards and moustaches,' she said. 'Wigs too. Don't worry. I've got some adhesive. I'll stick it back on for you.'

I let it droop. 'Look, I haven't come for the usual business,' I said. 'I've come to talk about Marylin.'

'We can do that in bed. Some people like to talk about death,' she said. 'It's a turn-on.'

I shivered.

'Come on, dear,' she said, and suddenly with that phrase, she aged considerably. She leaned over and unfastened my

77

jacket button and swiftly I rapped her over the knuckles with my cane.

'Oh, is that what you want?' she said. 'Why didn't you say so? Nothing to be ashamed of.'

I didn't know what she was talking about. She took the cane from my hand and I felt unarmed, helpless. Then she did the most extraordinary thing. She took off all her clothes, not that there were many of them and the act was completed in a second. She lay on the bed, her legs spread, and I boggled at the sight of her. For in truth, I must confess, it was the first time in all my years of life, that I had seen a naked woman. I was a bottle-fed baby, so I was spared the sight of my mother's flesh, which she kept strictly to herself, and certainly from my father. As to my own married years, those occasions which called for nakedness, were behind locked bathroom doors and nowhere else. It never occurred to me that things should be otherwise. Perhaps it did to Connie, but her whole attitude to these things was salubrious in the extreme, as is evidenced by the way she turned out. But I could do without thoughts of Connie at that moment, and I turned my head.

'Dress yourself at once,' I said to the bedroom wall.

'What the hell's the matter with you?' the woman said. 'If you come to this place, it's only for one thing.' She was plainly angry.

'I don't want that,' I said. 'That's not what I came for. I came to talk about Marylin.' Then I turned to look at her but I kept my eyes on her face. 'I'll pay you for it,' I said. 'As much as you would charge for the other thing.'

She shrugged and put her arms through the sleeve of her dress. I noticed then that it was the only garment she wore. Dressing was thus achieved as swiftly as the stripping.

When it was done, I sat by her side and picked up the cane which lay on the bedspread.

'She was murdered,' she said. 'Did you know that?'

I feigned shock and surprise.

'Don't you read the papers?' she said. 'Wimbledon Common. They found her. Buried.'

'Who did it?' I spluttered.

She laughed. 'It's a risk you run in the trade. Could have been one of hundreds.'

'When I last saw her, she was pregnant,' I ventured.

'That's another risk,' the woman said. 'But that's something you can deal with. She went to our doctor. He sees to those things.'

'Those things?' I asked.

'Gets rid of them.' She paused and looked at me. 'You really are an innocent, aren't you.'

I let that pass. 'Are you married?' I asked her, as an oblique way of getting round to Sebastian.

'Of course,' she said. 'Most of us are.'

'What happened to Marylin's husband?' I said, picking up the cue.

She shrugged her bony shoulders. 'I don't know,' she said. 'I'm sorry for him. They were happy together, I think. On her days off, she always went home.'

'Whereabouts did she live?' I asked. I had nothing to lose by that question so I made it direct.

'Somewhere in Hampstead,' she said.

I asked my final question. 'Did she have any family? Brothers, sisters?'

'I don't think so. She would have told me. We were friends. I miss her.' She put her head on my arm. 'Come on,' she said. 'I'll give you a bit for nothing. For Marylin's sake.'

'No,' I said quickly. I was anxious to get away. She had happily confirmed everything that I already knew. The body on Wimbledon Common was indeed poor Marion's, who had whored in Mayfair, whose husband lived in Hampstead, and whose trade doctor had got rid of their baby. 'How much do I owe you?' I said. She smiled. 'No charge for conversation. Come again,' she said, 'and ask for Sandra. That's me. I'll do for you, like Marylin. I'll give you one of her specials.'

I was curious to discover the nature of Marylin's specials, but I forebore to ask, for I sensed a strange stirring in my groin, an excitement that never in my life had I felt before, but, pleasurable as it was, I knew instinctively that it would lead to trouble. Nevertheless I resolved that as soon as my Marion crusade was over, I would return to visit Sandra. I might even ask her to marry me. And as a token of this sudden affection, I pecked her on the cheek, and quickly took my leave, remembering in time to hold on to my moustache.

★

In the cab on the way home, I wondered how that poor suspect was faring in Wimbledon as he helped the police with their enquiries, and how often he had to plead his innocence before anyone would believe him. I did not want to think of the possibility that he would be charged with murder, much less of the likelihood of his being found guilty. I had no idea what I should do in such an eventuality, so I put all such thoughts from my mind. I did not find that difficult because that small throb in my groin still persisted and continued to give me a sinful pleasure. I thought fondly of Sandra and, though I couldn't remember what she looked like, my affection for her increased.

I wondered about the next step in my crusade. There were only two letters left of the Firbank correspondence and I was loathe to unearth them in case they revealed no clues. All I could hope for was Sebastian's view of Marion's profession. But that would only be a confirmation of what Sandra had told me. That he connived at it, and still found her pleasurable. Had Sandra not mentioned the risks of their trade, I would have questioned whether that aborted baby had indeed been Sebastian's. But in his last letter he was so delighted at his putative fatherhood, and Marion so happy to announce it to him, that I could not help but think that he would baulk at its loss, so I imagined that his last letter would be full of his mourning and his anger and perhaps the very last straw that drove him to murder. But none of this would give me clues as to Marion's kin, and to whom I could release her body for decent burial. I had some hopes that police investigations would uncover some leads pertinent to my search. I could only wait for those clues to be forthcoming. Meanwhile, I was not discontent. I felt I had done a good day's work, and with my fire-escape exits and entrances I could avoid police surveillance, for I was still convinced that they had their eye on me. Then I thought of the climb that lay ahead, and I braced myself.

I instructed the cab-driver to drop me at the back of my building and, when he was out of sight, I began the climb. It was dark, so I did not fear any witness and, as long as I refrained from looking below, my equilibrium was secure. I paused to take off my moustache, for I needed both hands for my balance. I had to stop a number of times during the ascent, and the going was slow, and even slower as I neared the top. By the ninth floor, with five more to go, I told myself that such exercise was good for my health, but my heart beat with such rapidity I feared I might be overdoing it. I rested on every fifth stair, and it was some time before I reached the top and let myself in through my back door. I lay down immediately on my bed. The climb had giddied me, and I dared not close my eyes for the room would spin. So I lay there staring at the ceiling until my tremblings ceased. Then I walked slowly into my living-room and rewarded my day's labours with a shot of whiskey and I noted with some gratitude that Sandra's parting-shot still lingered in my groin.

I must have fallen asleep soon afterwards, and slept deeply and with infinite satisfaction, for when I woke it was morning, and *The Times* rattled to the hall floor. I showered, and breakfasted on my terrace. There was nothing to report on the Wimbledon case. I peered over the terrace expecting to see a police-car parked outside my building. But there was nothing there. Instead I saw the top of the porter's head as it turned up and down the street as if looking for someone. I had no doubt in my mind who he was scouting for. Any minute the police would arrive and collect his latest information as to my comings and goings. I slunk back onto the terrace. I knew I could not venture out and I checked on my fridge and freezer to see if I had enough food for a long siege. Fortunately I had stocked up about a week before my fateful post-office day, a day which now seemed years ago. I would keep myself indoors, I decided, permitting myself a nightly fire-escape sortie in my disguise. For I had to keep abreast with the evening paper. I could show my true face abroad only when an arrest had been made. I refused to think of how I would deal with that miscarriage of justice for I could only think of my freedom.

Thus it was that I stayed indoors for ten days. I took what fresh air I could on my balcony, and the nightly air of my fire-escape climb. I consumed a great deal of whiskey in that period. It was the only way I could still my spiral heart. In the ten evening newspapers I collected during my seige, there was not a slither of news, and I began to despair that I could ever go out in broad daylight again. I noticed that I had begun to tremble a lot, and to think frequently of Sandra whose face I still could not recall.

Then on the eleventh morning, I heard *The Times* rattle to my floor, and something thereafter. I went into the hall. A letter. Face downwards. Not from Australia. That was clear from the colour, and there was some relief in that. I decided to shower and prepare my breakfast first, and then to read the letter at leisure on my terrace. When all was done I put the paper and the letter, still face downwards, on my balcony table, and did what I was now wont to do every morning before settling down. I inched to the edge of my terrace and I looked below. And there, as I somehow expected, but nevertheless viewed with fearful and utter astonishment, a police-car stood, and, as far as I could see, unoccupied. I retreated to my table, trembling. Again I wondered where to hide. I rushed to my bedroom and collected my nocturnal disguise and stuffed it back into Connie's box. Then I returned to the terrace, but I dared not overlook it again. I was convinced that the police had at last given up on the poor devil who had tried so hard to help them with their enquiries, and in view of the porter's daily reports, and my sundry witnessed sorties to telephone-boxes and newsagents, they had come to force my help in their enquiries. I trembled again, but now out of another fear, for the Sandra-throb had gone and left no trace. I poured myself some coffee to steady my nerves. Then I stretched out my hand to turn the letter over. Its contents, I thought, might help to take my mind off things. But one sight of the postmark shattered that hope. Merthyr Tydfil. That strain again. Mad Marion's plea from Merthyr.

I opened the letter. Once again it was written on ruled paper, with many capitals and much underlining, and I knew, without reading it, that it was full of threat. This time there was no appelation. Her anger seethed and could do without courtesies.

Look now Mister, the letter began. *It's been over two weeks since I wrote and you haven't replied. So to tell you the truth, I've got my* suspicions. *I think I'm the Marion Firbank you're looking for. In actual fact, I know I am. And I'll tell you for why I'm suspicious. I know see, that I come from a good family. At least on my father's side. 'Cos my mother who was in service, used to tell me that my father was a Duke or something, and he got her into trouble. If you know what I mean like. Well I know for a fact that the Duke died, and not very long ago, and that he left me a lot of money. I think you are the solicitor that deals with the WILL, and you had to put in an advertisement like you did. That's the LAW, isn't it. I know because I've made enquiries. Well of course, you didn't expect any reply, and I wrote to you and it must have been a bit of a SHOCK. I think you're not replying because you want to keep the money for yourself. Well I'm not having it see, so you'd better reply* straight away. *OR ELSE. Yours faithfully, the* real *MARION FIRBANK. P.S. Straight away mind. I'll give you a week for to do it.*

I put the letter down. The world was a sea of madmen, I thought, and I the only sane island upon it. I had no intention of course of replying to Merthyr Marion's letter and, to confirm my lack of intent, I tore it into pieces, and without moving from my chair I tossed them over my terrace. Then I realised what I had done, and I rushed to the balustrade and watched all that incriminating evidence flutter on its downward trail. I could not ignore the police-car that still stood there, nor the few pieces of paper that had landed on its roof. And I convinced myself that those pieces were the shreds of the name of Marion Firbank, and, pieced together, they were enough to send me to the gallows. I left the balcony, and closetted myself in the living-room. Now I felt a virtual prisoner. Whereas before, I had voluntarily confined myself to my apartment, now it seemed to me that another kept me there. I didn't know what to do. I was convinced the porter was behind that devious investigation that was clearly taking place on the ground floor. As far as the porter was concerned, I had not been seen for ten days or so. Had things been normal, he surely in that time would have enquired as to my welfare. A simple 'phone-call from downstairs would ascertain the reason for my prolonged absence and whether or not I needed a doctor or help of any kind. He had done me such a service once before, when I had perforce to remain indoors due to a long bout of influenza. Yet this time there had been no enquiry. No doubt the police had instructed him to have no contact with me. With that thought I grew very frightened indeed, for with it came another: that he had sent a policeman or indeed, two, for they usually worked in pairs, to keep watch outside my door and to eavesdrop on my doings. I was now terrified to move from my chair, so convinced was I that they were lurking outside my door. Neither was there any way that I could ascertain that they were there. My letter-box gateway for *The Times* and the occasional post opened from the outside. There was no spy- or key-hole of any sort. Even the base of the door was fully wedded to the carpet in the hall. There was no tell-tale gap between. Then my eye caught sight of the telephone, and suddenly I had an idea. I could put that telephone to some use at last. I don't know why I had it installed, for it never rings except for a wrong number, or a promotion now and then for double-glazing or the like. I remembered that there was a certain combination of numbers that, if dialled, would activate the telephone to ring. On picking up the receiver, the response is a simple purring, but those vigilantes outside my door were not to know that. I would use that device, I thought, and thus clear my name. Their presence outside my door was a god-given opportunity to convince them of my innocence.

I crossed to the 'phone and dialled the combination. Then I put the receiver back in its cradle. Almost immediately it rang. I let it sound for a while, then I picked it up and spoke, as is my wont, without any preparation.

'Hullo, Sandra,' I shouted. I didn't want them to strain their ears. 'Lovely to hear from you. No, I haven't been away. I've been in bed for over a week. Bout of 'flu.' I allowed a pause for the invisible Sandra's response. 'Yes. I heard it ring, but I was half asleep.' Another pause. 'No, not all the time. Bed is so boring. I've been out for a walk sometimes to get the evening paper.' I smiled to myself. 'I've been looking every night for a notice of your play, darling.' This last I added for I had heard it was the language of show-business. 'But I've seen nothing yet.' I paused yet again for Sandra's explanation of her non-notices. 'Well they'll come eventually, I suppose,' I comforted her. 'They take time to get round to the fringe. When shall I see you?' I asked. Another pause. Suddenly I had a vision of Sandra lying spread-eagled on her bed on the other end of the line, and the throbbing returned to my groin. As a result my voice wavered, a tone of fear that would bode no good in my eavesdroppers' ears. So I coughed to cover myself. 'Sorry, darling,' I said. 'Frog in my throat.' I allowed another pause. 'Well, maybe we could meet on Sunday,' I said. 'We could go to a symphony concert.' I wanted to assure those outside my door that my pursuits were not only pure but intellectual. 'Then we could have dinner afterwards.' This last tit-bit to impress them with my gentlemanly behaviour. I paused. I did not wish to make a positive time or place of meeting. I would only have found them there before me. 'Then ring me early Monday morning,' I cooed, 'and we'll arrange it then.' The continuous purring in my ear was beginning to deafen me, and it would be a relief to put down the 'phone. But before doing so, 'Goodbye, Sandra,' I said. 'Thanks for ringing.'

I put down the receiver and felt mightily pleased with myself. On two accounts. One, that I had cleverly hood-winked those outside my door, and two, that without any doubt whatever, I was deeply in love with Sandra. I just wished I could remember what she looked like.

I recapped on my conversation. I had explained my confine-ment to the flat. I had given reasons for my nightly sorties. And then I realised that I had not explained my need for the telephone kiosks. Nothing daunted, I picked up the receiver once again, and dialled the combination. I decided on a man this time. I did not want to give the impression of a philan-derer. I let the 'phone ring for a while, and savoured its sound. I thought I might play my little telephone game more often, especially with Sandra who had turned out to be so responsive. How nice of her to 'phone, I thought. I picked up the receiver.

'Hullo, Alistair,' I said off the top of my head. An upper-class name and one to be reckoned with. I waited for him to give me a reason for his call. 'Yes, I know,' I said. 'My 'phone's been out of order on and off. It's all right now though. But I did try to call you. A couple of times,' I added in the direction of the door. 'I went out to a 'phone-box. But there was no reply.' Another pause here. I was rather pleased with my pauses, though the purring was stunning me. They were rather well-timed, I thought. 'Yes, we must get together next week. How's your new book coming along?' I asked. I was intent on making a good impression. I wanted them to know I was a man of many parts. I had the right friends. 'I just got your last book out of the library,' I said. 'The Antarctic one. I'm enjoying it enormously.' I waited again, but it was not Alistair whom I saw on the other end of the line, but Sandra, spread-eagled once more, and ever so slightly finger-ing my cane. I viewed her with infinite joy. Then I remem-bered that Alistair was still on the line. 'Yes, we must meet,' I said, thinking what a bore he was. 'I'll ring you at the week-end.' I paused for his farewell, and hung up and returned my Sandra vision to the armchair. I strained my ear to hear departing footsteps outside my door, but I knew the carpet-pile was thick enough to smother them. I was sorely tempted after a while to open the front door and make sure that they were gone. But I refrained. The police, however satisfied, are never quite satisfied enough.

CHAPTER SEVEN

Listen. Listen carefully. I am not crazy. I am inefficient and unsuccessful. I have owned to that. I am a failure. But I am not a lunatic. There's a big difference.

Without doubt there were police at my door. And they followed me at every sortie. I knew by the pins and needles in my back. They were after me, and for good reason. I was under suspicion and, until some gross miscarriage of justice occurred in Wimbledon, I was confined to my flat and my nocturnal disguise. It was not a happy prospect. For another week I remained indoors, leaving my flat only after dark, on my moustachioed quest for an evening paper. On the eighth day I overslept. I had come in quite late the night before, having taken longer than usual to climb the fire-escape to my flat. I had dropped straight onto my bed, and when the bell rang and woke me, I thought I had dozed off for a while for I was still wearing my moustache. Yet it was light. I looked at my watch. It was mid-day. It took me a little while to reorientate myself, during which time I forgot the bell that had woken me. And then it sounded again, like a summons, and it was clearly no dream. They had come for me. Of that I was certain, and in all my innocence, I felt a measure of relief. I found myself rehearsing some kind of defence, and to that end I decided to retain the moustache. I dusted down the creases in my suit, while the bell rang once more with an irritated staccato rhythm. Let them wait, I thought, while I twiddled my moustache and reached for my cane for the short walk from my bedroom to the answer-'phone in the kitchen.

I have a small television screen attached to the 'phone, but I

87

did not expect to see a picture in it. Cunning callers, and the police would fit into that category, would dodge the screen, so that I could have no inkling of the face or the volume of the opposition. So I was surprised on lifting the 'phone to find a face filling the frame, an angry unknown face which I presumed belonged to a plain-clothes policewoman.

'Hullo. Who is that?' I asked which, from where I stood was, after all, my territorial prerogative.

'Marion Firbank.' The capital letters stuttered down the wire. Mad Marion from Merthyr, daughter of a Stately Home of England, come to claim her due.

'Who d'you want?' I said, playing for time.

'Mr Wakefield.'

'Which Mr Wakefield?' I parried. Prolonged conversation on an inter-com can really wear one down. I had the vantage-point and, from the dismal look on her silly face, I had hopes she would give up and go away.

'Mr Luke Wakefield,' she said, her voice faltering. The capital letters had gone.

'Mr Luke Wakefield?' I repeated. I saw her nod, but she was not supposed to know she was on camera. I paused, then, 'I can't hear you,' I shouted. I looked at her. She was almost in tears.

'Yes,' she whispered.

'He's out,' I said loud and clear, and watched her face fall. I was about to amend it and say that Mr Luke Wakefield was dead, and thus get shot of her forever. But I am not one to tempt providence. A long-established failure like myself knows better than that.

'When will he be back?'

I think she must have been short and was standing on tip-toe, for occasionally she slipped out of shot altogether. I waited for her to come back into frame.

'Pardon?' I said. I was really giving her the business and I was rather enjoying it.

'When will he be back?' she whimpered.

'A few months,' I said. 'Any message?' I asked cheerily.

She slipped out of frame again, and I thought I'd seen the last of her. I hung on a bit, but she never came back. I put down the 'phone and thought myself well rid of her. Until, that is, five minutes later, when the bell rang again. I picked up the 'phone and saw her once again, fully framed this time with an unnerving look of victory on her face.

'I've had a talk with the porter,' she said, her valley accent singing, and the capitals well back in harness. 'He says you're in. Not abroad at all.' Then, laughing, she went off stage.

There and then, I made the decision that on my first day of freedom I would take the lift to the foyer and I would kill the porter. I had just about had enough of his meddling in my affairs, what with his co-operation with the police and leading them up to my front-door to keep vigil there. I twiddled my moustache and mused on the manner of his liquidation, and I was thus employed when the bell rang again. But this time it was another bell and much more ominous. It was the bell of my very own front door, and there was no doubt in my mind that Mad Marion fumed before it. I was flummoxed and did not know which way to turn. I was glad I was still wearing my moustache. It made me feel safer because, while wearing it, I was not the Luke Wakefield Mad Marion sought. But then she had no notion of what the real Luke Wakefield looked like, and would have accepted him, whiskered or otherwise. I dithered. I could not very well *not* answer the door, for a presence of some sort in the flat had been declared through the inter-com. I thought I would pretend that I was Mr Wakefield's valet. I considered that a brilliant solution and, with this in mind, I gladly opened my front door. But I was not prepared for the possibility that Merthyr Marion had an escort. And not just any escort, but my arch-enemy from the lodge downstairs. I sweated with fear when I saw him, so much so that my moustache lost its rigging and drooped down over my chin, robbing me of any possible claim that I had spent the last week in its cultivation. Moreover the role of valet was now unsaleable.

'Mr Wakefield,' the porter said, trying to ignore my wilting plumage. 'This lady insisted on seeing you.' He nudged her forward as he himself withdrew, anxious, no doubt, to avoid the consequences of his presumption. And before I could twiddle my cane, Mad Marion from Merthyr was cooling her sensible heels on my hall floor. She looked around, nosed out the living-room and led me towards it as if I were her guest. She appraised its opulence in one greedy glance and immediately guessed at its provenance.

'There's posh it is,' she said. 'And I'm not a bit surprised, knowing as I do, where all the money comes from.'

I was very hungry and realised that I had not breakfasted. A man can deal with nothing on an empty stomach, and Mad Marion was certainly some adversary. I felt my moustache touching my lower lip, and I almost ate it as I invited her to have coffee with me.

'I haven't come all the way from Merthyr Tydfil for a cup of coffee,' she said. 'I've come for a lot more, I have.' She turned to face me, her eyes ablaze. 'I've come for my due, I have. I've come for my rights.'

'You are mistaken,' I said, and very firmly. I thought I'd better make that clear from the start. Then I realised that, with my drooping moustache, I must have made a poor impression of reliability. So, angrily, I ripped it off, and repeated that she was mistaken.

'Now look,' she said, her patience sorely tried. 'I don't think, to be quite frank with you, Mr Wakefield, that you're what we in the valleys call an honest man. A reliable man. First you say you are not in when you are, then you put on a disguise. Why are you hiding from me? Because you've got something to hide, isn't it?' She took a step forward and looked me squarely in the eye. 'My legacy,' she said. 'My due.'

She was right of course, except for her deductions. I was indeed behaving like a con-man. I tried to think of some defence, but I was desperate for a cup of coffee.

'Let me make some coffee first,' I almost begged her.

'Suit yourself then,' she said, sitting down and clearly well satisfied. My absence of any denial of her story confirmed her in her solid opinion that she had been swindled. She was prepared to wait for my apology and recompence. 'Since you're making, I'll have a cup too, like,' she said.

I felt I was being completely taken over, and I slunk into my kitchen and plugged in the kettle. I thought I ought to prepare some cock and bull story, but I knew that nothing short of a patrician Last Will and Testament, signed in her favour, would satisfy her. So I didn't bother. I set out two cups on a tray and opened my tin of assorted biscuits. I picked out the plain digestive, because that struck me as Mad Marion's exact taste, and I felt like being accommodating. Then I took the tray into the living-room and poured the coffee. I was not prepared to utter one syllable until I'd fortified myself. This I did, and then I passed her a cup and the plate of biscuits. I hoped it would shut her up for a while. And indeed, Mad Marion predictably had the sort of manners that didn't speak with its mouth full. I watched her as the crumbs spattered her chin, and she wiped the corners of her mouth with a very thin screwed-up edge of a small white handkerchief, totally off-target, and I suddenly felt sorry for her. She finished her coffee, wiped her lips once more, then folded her hands in her lap.

'Well where is it, then?' she said.

'What?' I asked.

'My due,' she almost shouted. 'I've come all the way from Merthyr Tydfil, on the bus mind, for to collect my dues. I'll say nothing of what's happened, and I'll forget about the moustache, but I want my money, whatever it is. I've told my Mam about it, and the whole of Merthyr knows, and I'm going to give some of it to the Chapel – I already told the vicar – and with the rest I shall go with my Mam on a cruise. So I've got to be getting back.' She paused for breath, then decided she had said all she had come to say. She crossed her legs at the ankle and waited.

It was clearly my move. I nibbled at a digestive without appetite. I decided to repeat what I had told her in my first letter. I tried hard to remember it, and slowly recalled that India was its key-word.

'Look,' I said, and I leaned towards her with as much sympathy as I could muster. 'I am not a solicitor as you seem to think. I do not work. My mother left me a large legacy.' It was a loaded word, and it was only after I said it that I realised how highly charged it was.

She sneered but said nothing.

'A friend of mine,' I invented, 'who lives in Africa' – from now on I spoke off the top of my head – 'he wanted to trace an old girlfriend of his whom he met while he was a student in Wales. Her name was Marion Firbank and all he knew about her was that she went to India.' My fabrication was world-wide. 'He's black, this friend of mine,' I added, with sudden inspiration, hoping that his colour would sever any connection between herself and the Marion Firbank I was seeking. 'He was her boyfriend,' I said again.

'Let's see his letter then,' she said, unwilling to give up the struggle.

'He didn't write,' I said quickly. 'He telephoned.' I was amazed by my sudden talent for invention.

'From Africa?' she gasped. It was clearly all out of her league.

'He's very rich,' I said, and then it seemed to me that everybody in the world was very rich except poor Merthyr Marion. I felt deeply sorry for her, so sorry indeed, that I leaned forward and put my hand on her knee. I should have known better. For she screamed and with a piercing yell that, to a neighbour's ear, would herald rape.

'I don't believe a word you say,' she said, standing up, and dusting my hand-print from her skirt. 'Africa indeed, I don't believe a word of it.'

But she clearly did, for she started to cry. 'All this way from Merthyr Tydfil,' she whimpered. 'And for nothing. Oh my God,' she sobbed. 'What shall I tell my Mam? And the vicar?' she recalled with horror.

I wanted to lead her back to her chair and sit her down, but I dared not lay a finger on her.

'Look,' I said, as gently as I could. 'How much is a cruise?'

She looked at me with even greater horror.

'I've put you to a lot of trouble,' I said. 'But it was no-one's fault. I'd like to make it up to you in some way.'

'I've got my pride,' she said. The digestive crumbs still spattered her chin, and were at sad odds with her poor claim to dignity.

'How much?' I insisted.

'I don't know,' she said with utter honesty. 'I never enquired, see. It was just something I dreamt about like. For me and my Mam.'

'Look,' I said, 'If I give you a thousand pounds . . .'

She looked at me and quivered. I thought she was going to have a fit of apoplexy.

'Just my fare will be acceptable,' she said quietly and, despite her crumbed chin, she suddenly assumed the stature of nobility.

I was defeated. 'How much was that?' I asked.

'Seven pound, there and back,' she said.

I took £50 from my wallet and stuffed it in her hand, taking care not to touch her flesh in the gesture. 'You can take the train back,' I said. 'It's more comfortable.'

She shook her head.

'Please,' I said. 'For my sake, I feel very bad about the inconvenience.' I would have liked to have taken her out for lunch, but I was house-bound from the Law's eye. I remembered the smoked salmon in the fridge. 'Let me give you lunch before you go,' I pleaded.

She shook her head. 'I'm full up,' she said. 'Full up to here.' She pointed to her throat and started to sob again.

'Would you like a drink?' I said. I could have done with one myself. 'A little whiskey would pep you up a bit.'

She didn't answer and I took it for acceptance. I took two Waterford cut-glasses – the woman was worthy of nothing less – and I poured a generous portion into each one. 'Let's have a toast,' I said, scrambling in my mind for something appropriate. I put the glass in her hand. 'To you, Miss Firbank,' I said.

She did not correct me and I realised, for the first time, that, unlike my own poor Marion, she wasn't married. Now I clearly saw the role of her Mam, the vicar and the Chapel, and her predictable fantasy of the cruise. I had to down some whiskey to clear the lump in my throat.

She raised her glass humbly to her poor self, and sipped a little, then a little more.

'It's like Christmas,' she said, suddenly cheered. Then she sipped again, and colour flushed her cheek. I hoped she was not going to get drunk and reel out of the lift into the foyer below as further evidence to the porter of my wickedness.

'Sip it slowly,' I managed to say to her, 'or it will go to your head.'

But it had gone, all of it, in one final gulp. The glass trembled in her hand, and I quickly reached for it, for Waterford is not to be trifled with. I risked taking her arm and leading her to a chair.

'Sit down a while, Miss Firbank,' I said.

'I'll be all right, Mister,' she said, steadying herself. 'I'll sit down for a bit, then I'll go back home to Merthyr.' I heard a sobbing break in her voice. I knew that the whiskey was a mistake. Visions of Christmas vanish very quickly, as swiftly as dreams of a cruise. She put her head back and closed her eyes. I watched her, and shortly heard a light snore. But quickly she woke again with a snort as if she didn't trust herself to sleep in a stranger's house.

'I must go,' she said, crumbling with embarrassment.

'Wait there,' I said. 'I'll make you some strong coffee,' and I went quickly to the kitchen. As I passed through the hall, I thought I heard a creak behind the front door. The Law had obviously returned. The thought crossed my mind that I should persuade Miss Firbank to stay. She was company of a sort. In time I would tell her about the policemen outside my door. And she would walk me up and down the fire-escape at night, so that there would be a touchable shadow fore and aft. I wondered how old she was, and whether her years could bear the strain of the climb. I had noticed when she had risen first from her chair, that her dress had settled in the cleft of her buttocks. There is a certain age in that, and I doubted whether she was up to the climb.

I made the coffee quickly, and brought it back to the living-room. She was composed by now, and full of apologies for her little lapse.

'I'm not used to it,' she said. 'I've never been to London before, see.' She seemed to think that whiskey and the metropolis were aligned. She drank her coffee and announced that she was perfectly fit to go. Once again I asked her to stay for lunch, but she was anxious to get back to her Mam.

'Thank you, Mister,' she said, 'and I'm sorry for all the trouble. And thank you for the money. You shouldn't have, you know. I'll be going on the bus in any case.'

'Then use it for Christmas,' I said.

'That was true what I wrote about the Duke,' she said. 'And he died, he did. Recent it was. My Mam saw it in the paper.'

'D'you really think he was your father?' I said.

'That's what my Mam thinks. But mind you, she's got a bit of an imagination.' She laughed. 'That's where I get it from. Oh that was nice, that drop of whiskey. London's nice, isn't it. Sooner have Merthyr though. Quiet it is. You know where you are see.'

I thanked her for coming and saw her to the door. I eased it open, and stood behind it, unwilling to face the posse. I did not care what Miss Firbank made of them. She would probably assume they were as endemic a part of London as whiskey. I

94

shut the door after her and listened as I heard the lift door open, but no words were exchanged. She had ignored the police and my heart went out to her. I gave her time to reach the foyer, then I went and stood on my terrace. I looked over the balustrade to view her departure.

The police car was in its usual place. I was getting so used to its presence that I ceased to tremble at the sight of it. Then I saw Miss Firbank emerge, and I swear she was on the arm of the porter. They paused on the steps for a while and seemed to be engaged in animated conversation. And then the terrible truth struck me and so did Miss Firbank's treachery. She and the porter had been in cahoots all the time. She had told him what had happened in my apartment. She had told him that I had confessed to the Wimbledon murder, and that I had given her £50 to hold her tongue. I think I even saw her showing the porter my bribe. I watched her as she took her leave of him, and I could have sworn he kissed her hand.

I returned to my living-room in a mood of deep despondency. Nobody was to be trusted. I seethed with that thought, which led inexorably to that ubiquitous object of my hate. For trust, or rather the lack of it, was embodied by none other than Connie, the great betrayer of all time. I sat in my chair and seethed with Connie-hate till I felt a fever grow upon me. I reached out for my whiskey, and the sight of Merthyr Marion's glass did nothing to improve my temper. I must have drunk myself into a stupor, for when I awoke, it was already dark, and I was too exhausted to make my sortie for an evening paper. I was hungry so I made myself a tasty supper and felt better for it. An early night would do me no harm, I thought and I retired with the fatuous thought that things would be better in the morning. As indeed they turned out to be.

There was news. It had probably broken in the evening paper the night before, that one night of all nights that I did not venture abroad. So I had to make do with its coverage in *The Times*, which, given the nature of that paper and the salubrious story, was generous enough. It had even made the front page, and my eye caught the headline as it lay on the hall floor. *Man charged with Wimbledon Common murder*.

My heart quickened. My feelings were mixed. I was free at last, to go out when and where I pleased, and whiskerless to boot. But some poor bugger was going to pay a terrible price for my freedom. Or, more to the point, my silence. For whoever he was, and whatever evidence they had accrued against him, there was no way he could have murdered my poor Marion. I had to think of a way of saving him, without declaring myself an interferer in Her Majesty's Postal Service. But I delayed such thoughts. As was my wont, I would make a production of every new development in my crusade. I showered and prepared my breakfast, then I took my tray onto the terrace and returned to the hall to pick up the paper. I was sorely tempted to open my front door and there to find proof of my liberation, but I did not as yet wholly believe in it. Instead I peered over my terrace balustrade and, to extraordinary relief, the police car was not there. I sat down, poured my coffee, cracked my eggs and buttered my toast. Then partly fortifying myself with food, I turned to my morning paper. I read the headline again, and then I read it aloud, as if my voice would open the door of my prison and sing of my freedom.

Man charged with Wimbledon Common murder. Then I turned to the matter of the report, whispering it to myself, lest its magic disappear.

Robert Dawkins, a labourer of no fixed address was last night held in Wimbledon Police station, and charged with murder. Police had hitherto concealed details of the victim's identity, known severally as Mary, Marylin and Marian. They have now released final identification.

I put my hand over the paper. I hesitated to read further. I was loathe to share that object of my crusade with others; that name that was known only to me through my illegal perusal of Sebastian's letters. Like any thief, I was unwilling to share my spoils. But despite all my self-assurances, I still harboured a small niggling doubt. Was the body really my poor Marion's? I lowered my hand from the page.

The victim was Mary Shuttleworth, aged 36. Wife of Guy Shuttleworth who lives in South Hampstead. Dawkins is expected to appear in court today.

I started to giggle. I gave a passing thought to poor old Dawkins, but I could not help but acknowledge my relief and pleasure. For I had been liberated on two accounts. My silence was sending no man down for life, and my poor-Marion crusade could continue unimpeded. I could once more get my show on the road. I was so elated that I rushed to my front door and opened it wide. I even looked outside in the many corridors, but the beat was spotlessly clear. I was overcome by a rare feeling of well-being and I felt the need to share my elation. So I went to the telephone and dialled the number combination. I put the 'phone down and, when it began to ring, I let it sound for a while, for the bell was a peal of joy.

'Hullo?' I picked up the receiver at last. 'Who is that? Sandra?' (Pause for spread-eagled focussing.) 'How nice of you to call.' (Another pause.) 'Yes, I'd love to see you. Where?' (Time to choose meeting place.) 'Selfridges. Under the clock. At one. Good. I'll take you for lunch.'

I put the 'phone down and quickly cleared away my break-fast. I would change into a summer suit, I thought. So I took another shower. I am a firm believer in cleanliness. And of all one's parts. That includes cuticles, toe- and finger-nails and eyebrows. Especially eyebrows. For they are a handy vehicle for expression, and can be rendered inarticulate if in poor condition. So I scrubbed and powdered myself and set off in good time for my rendezvous. I was as excited as a boy as I pressed the lift button and, when I reached the foyer and saw the porter in his lodge, my heart welled with forgiveness. I bade him a cheery 'Good morning,' more cheery than he deserved in view of his station, but I felt I owed him an apology. A small one at least.

'Good morning, Mr Wakefield,' he said. 'You haven't been about for a while.'

As I made for the door, I noticed the police car at its usual stand. I hesitated.

'What's that car doing out there?' I asked, with the non-chalance that indicated I had never seen its like before.

'They're setting up speed traps in the park,' he said. 'That one's for communications.'

I smiled and set out into the air with confidence, even acknowledging the two uniformed men who sat waiting in the car for a call to duty.

I had time on my hands, and I decided to walk into town, for it was a fine day and there was spring in my step. I looked forward to renewing my Marion crusade, though I did not care to think of my next move. Unless what was left of the Firbank letters could shed some light on Marion's family, I had no other source of clue. But that day I did not want to think of failure. I was meeting Sandra for lunch, and even a passing thought of Connie could not upset my good temper. I took a short cut through the rose garden, but this time I felt no need to pause and examine the blooms. I was free, I kept telling myself. I was most positively in the clear. Then why did I still feel that lingering hand-print on my back? I was determined to ignore it and, to that end, I hailed a passing cab, and leaned against the back seat and felt safe once more.

I reached Selfridges a good half hour before the appointed time. I avoided the stand beneath the clock and intended only to approach it at the appointed hour. So I whiled away the time in window-gazing on the outer edges of Selfridges and around the square where the shop continued. I found myself staring in a window that was in the process of being dressed. Three or four naked female models stood there patiently awaiting their clothing. I distinctly saw one of them wink at me. And then a window-dresser covered her face with a dress-opening, and when she was clothed she turned her head away. Behind her I saw a man staring at me. I was affronted by his rudeness and I stared back. I willed him to turn away, but he stood his ground, his expression as resolute as my own. I did not think it worthwhile doing battle with him, so I turned away and caught him doing likewise. I smiled at him in token of our truce, and he, at the same time, smiled at me. Then we waved at each other in synchronistic movement. I saw him again and again in all the windows that I stared at, and I wondered who he was.

I half circled the square a number of times, back and forth, until the Selfridges clock struck one. Then I made my way to our point of rendezvous. She had not yet arrived, as I expected. A woman is entitled to be late for an appointment. She has a right to keep a man waiting. This I was pleased to do and the passing minutes fed my excited anticipation. The site of the Selfridges clock is a popular meeting-place. I myself had often met Connie there. I resented being reminded of her, and that resentment stretched to Sandra herself for having suggested the site in the first place. Indeed, as the minutes ticked by, I thought more of Connie than of Sandra, and when I did give Sandra a thought it was with growing animosity. Indeed, by the time the clock struck the half-hour, I thought she had stretched her woman's prerogative a little too far, and the thought crossed my mind to jilt her. But I dallied. She could have had an accident, or there was a hold-up of some kind. It was not like Sandra to be so remiss. She was always so dependable, not like Connie who couldn't be relied upon at all. More and more, my thoughts were Connie-crammed, and I felt I had to move from that spot that so provoked them. I shifted a few windows along, but my anger did not abate. Yet I forced myself to bear it. Suddenly every woman who approached the clock looked like Sandra, though I had entirely forgotten what she looked like. Two o'clock struck, and I still stood there, trusting that Sandra would turn up. Then I thought I saw Merthyr Marion approach, and I ducked into a doorway to avoid her. The time passed and I no longer listened to the chimes. Neither did I know what I was doing there. I noticed it was beginning to grow dark, and I began to fear for myself. I moved slowly out into the street. A car approached and I recognised it as a cab. I gave the driver my address though I was unsure whether I remembered it correctly. I don't recall going up in my lift or opening the door of my flat. The only sure memory I have of that evening is the sound of the telephone as I wandered around the living-room. I let it ring for a while, and then I picked it up. It was Sandra. She had been trying to get me all afternoon, she said. She apologised profusely, but on her way out to meet me she had fallen and broken her leg. She had spent the afternoon in hospital. Poor Luke, she said, would I ever in a lifetime forgive her? I soothed her gently and promised to visit her with flowers.

Listen. Listen carefully. I am not crazy. It's just that when people are mad, they acquire means of defending their lunacy. It's the same with failure. Nothing crazy about that.

CHAPTER EIGHT

Make no mistake about it. I was aware that all was not well. I decided to give my Marion crusade a rest for a while. And London, too. I would take a holiday and restore myself.

There are certain establishments on the south coast of England which cater in all ways for my occasional needs. One can go to these places in a voluntary manner, or be taken in a less than dignified fashion. Either way, it costs the same, a fact which I have never understood. These establishments are well enough known to me, having tasted them quite frequently in my post-Connie life. Before my marriage, I have to say, I had never heard of them.

It was to one of these retreats that I now betook myself, bag and baggage, for a prolonged stay. I bade farewell to the porter in his lodge.

'Going on holiday,' I said, to give him this time a valid reason for my absence.

'Just what you need, Mr Wakefield,' he said. His tone was that of a father talking to his son. He was almost patting my head. 'It'll do you good,' he said. 'You'll come back all better.'

'Better than what?' I had to ask him.

He smiled benignly, unwilling to commit himself further. Had he not at that moment picked up my suitcases, I would have struck him.

★

The train took a couple of hours to get to the coast and, when I arrived at the establishment, I was greeted like a long-lost friend. There is always a tendency to excessive kindness in these sorts of places, and a kind of irritating understanding that passeth all peace. And with good reason, for such places are battlegrounds.

I settled in my room and I flopped onto the bed. I was excessively tired, and I think I had a fever. My intention was to sleep, for a week perhaps, with occasional wakings for the intake of food. All this, I must emphasise, was *my* idea, and I appraised the staff of my purpose. They were happy to serve me. Thus it was that I sank into a twilight. It is a state that I recommend to all insomniacs who fear to sleep because they do not trust those who are watching them. For in a twilight state you can go to sleep and at the same time keep your eye on things. You derive all the remedial benefits of sleep, and, at the same time, you are *aware* of thus profiting. Even dreams are manageable in such a state, because you can view them and switch them off if they threaten disturbance. For my part, I would happily spend the rest of my life in such limbo, but I am told that prolonged twilight can disturb your equilibrium. Whatever that means. But I surmised that, for my needs at the time, one week was enough. Besides, on waking, there are other pleasures for your diversion. For apart from the twilight sleep that such establishments oblige you with, there is company and conversation of a sort. Not that I needed it, or ever sought it out. But such places seem to attract a small body of people who are in desperate need of conversation. Lonely people, whose own lives are so singularly monotonous and uneventful that they have to batten off the lives of others. They will engage you in discussion, pump you on all manner of your private affairs, bleeding you dry for their own vicarious living. But I am sorry for them, and when, on the eighth and last morning of my twilight sleep, one of them approached my bedside, I invited him to take a seat, an act that he would clearly have performed without my invitation, but I wished him to feel at home. I sensed, too, that I had seen him before, and in this very place, and I felt a slight disgust that he should so openly parade his loneliness by choosing the same promenade over and over again.

'How are you?' he began, in a tone of solicitousness with which, from past experience in these establishments, I was very familiar. They always start off by asking after your welfare, as if you, and not they, were in need of solicitous enquiry. But I understand that, too. It is called pre-emptive attack, and I play along with it. So I told him I was well and truly rested, and I asked the same of him, more out of politeness than sincerity. But he shrugged the question aside, as these people always do, for they believe that they are in an eternally perfect condition, and such an enquiry in their direction is totally invalid. You might as well ask after the health of a god. You have to be very tolerant to put up with such nonsense, but I was in a benign mood, having slept and rested well.

'Why did you come here this time?' he asked.

I rather resented his tone. As if he had some kind of lien on the place. He should have known that, were it not for people like me, his life would be a sorry one indeed. I felt he should have been a little more grateful. But greedy and desperate men know no gratitude, so I decided not to expect it. Moreover, I obliged him with the exact details of the cause of my present visit, though I knew perfectly well that during my twilight state he'd already nosed around about my business.

'I'm on a crusade,' I told him, 'and it was all getting a bit too much for me. So I decided to take a break and come down here for a rest.'

Those were my salad days. I know better now. But at that time, I had no idea of how loaded was the word 'crusade'. I had a first hint of its burden by my visitor's raised eyebrow, and I wondered why he'd questioned it, by what right indeed he doubted it at all. So I repeated it, 'I'm on a crusade,' I said, and I relished it by giving him chapter and verse, as that same eyebrow levitated until it vanished into his thinning hair-line and I thought I should never see it again.

'There's a body of a woman on Wimbledon Common,' I told him, 'and I have to find it. I know it's there, but I cannot tell you how I know. For I came by the information through illegal means. But whatever happens, I have to find it. I have to have it exhumed and given a decent burial. So I shall be going home shortly.'

Then his eyebrow fell and I was happy to see it once more, as it assumed its proper place alongside its partner. Indeed so relieved was I, that I laughed, a sound which only served to send it once more into take-off. I decided not to look at him any more. I cannot bear restless eyebrows, for they are token of an unquiet spirit.

He started to talk to me, but I didn't listen. That is after all, your right with parasites. Your only right as a host. You cannot repel their invasion, but there is no need for encouragement. Then suddenly he mentioned Connie and he was clearly waiting for a reaction. Inside I bristled, but I affected nonchalance. I didn't think Connie was any of his business, and whatever he thought of the word 'crusade' it was, in my opinion, a far far more normal term that 'Connie'.

'What terrible thing did she rob you of when she left?'

'My cock,' I said without thinking. I thought that would be enough to send him on his way. And it was, for after a little while, out of the corner of my eye, I saw him move from the bed, no doubt to batten off another poor and generous suckee like myself, and as he left I heard him say, 'You'd better stay a little longer, I think. Get yourself truly fit.'

I smiled to myself as I listened to his vanishing footsteps. Then, when I could hear them no more, I rose from my bed and dressed myself, intent on taking a stroll around the grounds. That is another common factor about these establishments. They all have grounds. Not just your ordinary common-or-garden, but manicured parks with plants of every genus and hue. And as I strolled around the herbaceous borders, I was reminded very much of home, and a certain nostalgia crept up upon me, and grew with such strength that I even longed for a sight of my old and trusting porter.

I made my way back to my room to pack my bag. I think I must have been followed – my dorsal pins and needles warned me – for once in my room, I was soon surrounded by a group of parasites who seemed to be vying with each other for the sauces of my life. One of them actually had the temerity to touch me, nay, seize me even, and another to prick my arm with his pathetic offer of friendship. And thus I was twilighted once more and, I must confess, with little resistance, for anything was preferable to their constant and inept wooing for my confidence.

*

But too soon my main and most persistent wooer was at my bedside once more. I opened a weary eye. 'I have to go home,' I said. 'You know I have important things to do.'

'Still with your crusade?' he said.

I was angry now, for I resented his belittling of my task. It was a noble philanthropic pursuit that I was engaged upon and he sullied it with his contempt. I stuck my feet out of the bed, and I feared a weakness in my knees.

'I have to go home,' I said again.

He laid a hand on my thigh and I felt too weak to shrink from him.

'You should go home and do normal things,' he said, and I hated the gentleness in his voice.

'I will,' I said weakly.

'The crusade?'

That wretched eyebrow again. 'No,' I said. I knew by then that 'crusade' was not normal.

'What then?' the man asked me.

I scratched in my mind for 'normal' things that people do. I have no wife to batter, or I would have offered that. I have no children to cripple with my expectations. No normal things. 'I have to weed and water the plants on my terrace,' I said with sudden and, I thought, divine inspiration. I averted my face, fearful of the eyebrow, but I heard the sweeping syllables that plunged like parachutes from its flight.

'People who cannot weed and water themselves will gratefully turn their attention to other targets. It's a common means of avoiding self-confrontation.'

I looked him squarely in his single-eyebrowed face. 'You're full of shit,' I said. Insult requires little strength, and that was all I could muster.

I must have fallen asleep shortly afterwards, for I don't remember him leaving the room. But in that third twilight of mine, I grew in wiliness, and when I awoke from it, some three weeks after my arrival at the place, my mind was not clear at all, but clouded with ineffable cunning. During my sleep, I had had a total recall of my previous escape from this establishment and, on waking, it was my mind's sole clarity. Gratitude was the key.

My visitor came shortly after I woke.

'How are you?' he said.

I hesitated. You must never be too sure of your well-being. 'I'm feeling a little better, I think. Thank you very much.' I even managed a smile.

'Ready to go home?' he baited me.

'I'm not sure,' I said. 'I think perhaps in a few days. If you agree.'

I had never seen his eyebrow so still, and I had a distinct feeling he would miss me profoundly.

'What will you do when you go home?' he asked.

'There'll be a lot to catch up with,' I said. 'Bills to pay. Letters to answer.' All 'normal' things, however one construed them.

'Another few days then?'

I smiled at him. 'Thank you, Doctor,' I said. That word is the breakthrough. It opens a million doors, and if you couple it with gratitude, as I was careful to do, the world is your oyster.

So I hung around for a few more days, eating well and strolling in the grounds. From time to time my wooer paid suit, and I responded to all his advances, chastising myself for my earlier rejection. At the end of that week, I left with his blessing.

I was not so certain of myself that I thought that I would never set eyes on him again. There are certain people who enter your life, and who never, despite all your efforts, depart from it. Like Connie, for instance. I bristled at that thought. I had gone to that establishment for the express purpose of putting her out of my mind and, though she had been more or less out of it for three weeks, she was my first conscious thought as I passed out of its gates. But I would not let it disturb me. I was now able to sieve my mind of the cunning that had engineered my escape and now it was clear and full of awareness. I was conscious that my 'episode' was over. That is an establishment term for turnings such as mine. Once complete you are able to return to what they call normal life and even water and weed your plants without threatening undertones. The dorsal pins and needles are buried in your memory and totally denied. The 'episode' was over and, by the time I returned to my apartment in London, I had begun to wonder why and where I had been.

I was overjoyed to see my porter who was waiting to carry my bags to the lift. He told me that the radar trap had been removed. The police had found a better vantage-point for ambush. But such information did not interest me, for I myself did not drive a car. When I reached my penthouse I put my key in the door with a contented sense of homecoming.

The key turned easily enough in the lock, but the door itself resisted, and as I pushed I heard much rustling of paper. An inordinate amount of post, I thought, and then I recollected that I had omitted to stop the newspaper, and all the newsprint, heavy with useless import, finally gave way. I stood in my hall and found it *Times*-lined, together with the Sundays and their supplements that were nudging the walls. I regretted my lack of thrift, but the thought quickly passed, because I saw the bonus in such waste. Three weeks worth of obituaries to savour and, in my acute sense of return and survival, this was relish indeed. I stooped to pile them up, intending to put them into some kind of order for, though obituaries bear little repetition, one must scrutinise them with a certain respect to chronology. For if Mrs X or Mr Y dies on a Tuesday, the world is a different place on the Wednesday that follows it. There must be order in all things. Cause must follow effect, but in the particular as well as the general. Otherwise, all is confusion.

So I scanned the dates on each front page and piled the papers accordingly. It was during this filing procedure that I discovered my scattered post that had accumulated during my absence. I tried to concentrate on the familiar buff-windowed envelopes of bills and notices. I concentrated on all this mindless pile of communication for a very simple reason. I had to, for out of the corner of my eye, I had spotted that dreaded Australian blue, with its reliable promise of disturbance in all things. I got on with my filing task and, when it was done, I took the pile of papers into my living-room. I left the post scattered on the hall floor, but in my disturbance of it the blue smear now flowered in its full rectangle, and around it there was a decent space, as if the other communications had given it a wide berth. I left it lying there, and picked up the rest of the post. These too I put on my living-room table, and went quickly to my terrace to view those plants that I had so sincerely promised to water. But that square patch of blue lay imprinted on my mind's eye. I would have felt less disturbed had it been an open postcard with a message fit for anyone's eye. But even Connie had a small sense of decorum, and that folded envelope spelt private, and therefore injurious. I picked up the top copy of *The Times*, in an attempt to put it out of my mind.

I turned to the Deaths Column and read every single announcement. Very slowly. I had been so long deprived of death, I was like a man coming off a long fast. I had to digest my relief very slowly. I mostly savoured the end lines of each announcement, those occasional instructions as to where to send donations, for such addresses give an indication of the cause of death. Though I could never understand why one should wish to benefit a disease which had caused one's own destruction. It being the holiday season, a number of deaths had occurred abroad, by drowning in one instance, or in a crash in one of those unreliable foreign coaches in another. Both deaths from unnatural causes, an uncommon enough incident in *The Times*. A man named Zaks was the last to die in that edition, at the age of ninety-six and in his sleep, and he rounded off the column nicely. I turned to the next *Times* in line, and the time passed swiftly as I engrossed myself in my own survival, and all thought of the blue rectangle vanished from my mind.

I was coming to the end of the accumulated pile. I was pretty well saturated with death by this time, but I plodded on, and half-way down the column I spotted a familiar name. And it came as a shock, for that name too, like Connie's, had faded from my mind. Firbank. My mouth fell open. How death-prone that family was. I read the notice aloud.

On July 30th, in Florida, Marion Firbank, aged 86. Widow of Sir Alistair Firbank of the Kings' Rifles. Mother of Sebastian (deceased March). Deeply mourned by Christine and Edward (Times trans-lation of Chrissie and Ted) and a host of friends. Burial in Tampa, Florida. Memorial service to be announced later.

I put the paper down. There was much to relish from the announcement, not least of all, her name. Marion Firbank. How Sebastian must have loved his mother, I thought, that he should actually seek out a wife with her very name. For a moment I forgot what Sebastian had actually done to that wife of his; it was enough that he had translated his filial affection into matrimonial terms. He had come of good stock, too. The Kings' Rifles is not to be trifled with, and a knight, to boot. But most relishable of all in the announcement was the promise of a memorial service. I would read that *Times* column from day to day. I would note its date, time and place of venue, and there I would present myself in the sure knowledge that I would meet the elusive Richard, that key to my crusade. I decided to do nothing more in my search for Marion's body, until that meeting. I felt a vast surge of relief, and I gave a fond thought to that doctor of mine, who would have applauded my resistance to crusade.

I was suddenly hungry and I went to my kitchen to prepare lunch. As I crossed the hall, I noticed that sky-blue menace and kicked it with contempt into the kitchen. I knew I would have to read it, but I intended to give it no production. I would open it and scan its contents while I was in the process of making a mushroom omelette and a salad, the menu I intended for my light lunch. I held the envelope between my teeth as I cracked the eggs into a bowl. Then I took a kitchen knife and slit the edges. With one hand I beat the eggs, while with the other I unfolded the missive and began to read.

Now I pride myself on my culinary skill with omelettes. The secret lies in knowing exactly the right moment when to stop beating. There is a precise second, for instance, when sugar will caramelise; to overstep that sublime instant leads to ruination. It is the same with omelettes. To overbeat is to destroy, and if I would blame Connie for nothing more, it would be that she certainly spoiled my lunch that day. For the contents of her letter were so infuriating, that I translated my spleen onto the spinning fork in my hand, with the result that the mixture had to be abandoned. I would never forgive her.

Dear Luke, she had written. *Stephanie and I are coming back to England to have our baby. I hope you will be happy to see me again.*

I think that it was at this point that I overstepped the omelette moment of truth. Thereafter all was lost. My hand was a whirling dervish as I read on.

Mrs Martin, my gynaecologist, has to be in London when the baby is due, and since she has looked after me from inception, I would like her to attend my delivery. We shall be arriving, all three of us (ha ha), in a couple of weeks. We don't know yet where we are staying, but I shall ring you when we are settled. I hope your name is in the book. I hope too that you are well, Yours, Connie.

I threw the eggs down the sink and abandoned all hope and appetite for lunch. I put the letter aside. I dared not read it again, for in truth, I was fearful of Connie's visit. I dreaded seeing her again. I had hoped that in her continual absence my anger would abate, but now her appearance could only refuel my rage. I could, of course, refuse to see her, but I have to confess there was small part of me that hankered after Connie-hate. If ever I were to overcome it, I would have no alternative target for my energy. Yes, I needed Connie around, but I could do without Stephanie and the 'ha ha' Connie referred to. I did not want Connie's happiness. I wanted her pain as token of my punishment of her. There was a measure of relief in the thought that my telephone number was ex-directory. When I had come into my inheritance, I thought that that would be an expedient move. But I knew that Connie was not past showing up on my doorstep, and happily presenting herself on camera, and if she should position herself at the right distance, her wretched 'ha ha' as well.

My future was bleak. The impending memorial service for Sebastian's mother was the only bright light on the horizon. That, and the possible clues that the last of the Firbank letters might offer. 'Every cloud had a silver lining,' I said to myself, for a man in crisis can only resort to cliché. 'There is light at the end of the tunnel,' I said, as I broke more eggs into the bowl. And 'After winter comes the spring,' accompanied my beating. And so, platitude by platitude, I prepared my lunch, and hoped that appetite would follow.

I took my tray onto the terrace together with the packet of Firbank letters. I muttered to myself that everything was part of life's rich tapestry. Having thus sunk to the very nadir of banality, I reached, full of hope, for the last Firbank package. I was surprised and a little disconcerted to find that there was only one letter left. Not a pair as I had expected. The single missive was from Sebastian, the penultimate to his plea for forgiveness, that strange letter that had, on that fateful post-office Tuesday, first sent me on my crusade. And to this penultimate message, Marion had not even bothered to reply. Perhaps it was her indifference that had finally prompted Sebastian's belated apology. I poured my coffee, sampled my omelette, which was up to my normally high culinary standard, and unfolded the letter.

Dear Marion, I read. *Things are changing between us. I don't think we can go on much longer. Your behaviour last Saturday at Wimbledon, spelt for me the end of our marriage.*

I put the letter down. That magic word. That holy graveyard where Marion lay. Surely in this letter I would find the reason for this choice of site and, with it, some clue that would pin-point her grave. I took a gulp of coffee to stem my excitement, and I read on.

Your behaviour at Richard's parents' home was insulting in the extreme. You knew that Richard was my closest friend, and that his parents had extended their hospitality to you with no stint. It was, after all, his mother's 80th birthday, and I do think you might have put yourself out to be civil. Instead you behaved like the nagging wife you have grown to be. You resented every moment when attention from your fat person was withdrawn. Yes, fat, Marion. I knew you were carrying our child, or so you told me. But now I was confused. You had enough cunning to cover your obesity with a claim of pregancy. During the course of that terrible afternoon, I came to believe that you had conned me, and not only into fatherhood, but into marriage too. Still, I do not hold that against you. You are a woman after all. Yet I could not envisage any prolongation of our partnership, and I decided there and then, that it must come to an end. Yours, Sebastian Firbank.

I noticed how my hand trembled as I read the letter. It was no wonder that Marion hadn't replied. Had he really expected her to connive in her own destruction? To echo his thoughts and feelings as she had done in previous letters? I was, to say the least, deeply disappointed in that man whose profile had once so enticed me. Disappointed, too, in the letter itself, for it did not wholly explain Sebastian's choice of site for Marion's interment. The fact that Richard's parents lived in Wimbledon did not seem to me sufficient reason for its location as Marion's burial-ground. Then I recalled Sebastian's phrase, 'there and then', and I surmised that it was probably in that house that Sebastian had decided to kill her. Then suddenly, in a flash of clarity, I divined that he had killed her *on* that very day, and possibly on their way home from Richard's parents' house. Moreover Richard was with them, and there was no doubt in my mind that Richard was an accomplice in the crime. I would meet him at the memorial service. Of that I was sure. I realised that I would have to play my cards very carefully. Murderers are not to be dallied with. It would be up to me to approach him, for he would have no reason to engage me in conversation. I might possibly use that old stand-by of mine, that weather opening gambit, and hope in time to elicit from him an enquiry as to what I was doing in that place. I wondered in what capacity I would be acceptable to him. I would be chary of claiming myself as a friend of Sebastian, or even of his late departed mother. So I chose, rather cleverly, I thought, to claim a friendship with Marion in a pre-Sebastian time and place. In other words, I was a childhood friend of Marion in her Merthyr days. We went to school together. Her parents and mine were active in Chapel affairs. Oh, I could spin a tale when called upon. No, I hadn't seen too much of her since her marriage, though I'd met her with Sebastian once. I'd read in the papers that Sebastian had died. I was sorry. How is Marion? (Careful of the tense there.) I rather expected to see her here. This last with that old nonchalance of mine, at which I am a past master. At this point I would watch Richard's face very closely for his reaction.

I was rather pleased with my fabrication, and I looked forward to the memorial service to give it an airing. Meanwhile, I decided, I would practise it, and over the next few days I gave it to an imagined Richard in my living-room. His face and his person was still acutely clear in my mind, and had been since the day of Sebastian's funeral, so I had no difficulty in recalling them. He was a good few inches taller than I and, in rehearsal, I found myself looking up at him in my declaration. Later on that week, I caused my telephone to ring, and I delivered my speech to a Richard even more invisible than in my drawing-room, a far greater test of credibility. After a couple of weeks, I was fluent and full of confidence, and it was, as if in reward for my diligence, that the announcement eventually appeared in my paper. *A memorial service to celebrate the life of the late Lady Firbank will take place on Friday, November 16th, at 11 o'clock at St Mary's, Westminster.*

I had been given almost a fortnight's notice. I would spend that time in peace, fortifying myself for the renewal of my crusade. But that peace was denied me.

*

A few days after the announcement, early one morning, while I was setting myself to breakfast on the terrace, my buzzer sounded with a tone of alarm. I had not had a Connie-thought for some days, so engrossed was I in my anticipation of a Richard-encounter. Even when the inter-com sounded, I did not think of Connie. I recalled that the window-cleaner was well overdue for his monthly visit, and I went into my kitchen

and happily lifted the receiver, with no thought of ill consequence, confident of viewing a step-ladder on my screen, with
a hint of the cleaner in the background.

But, instead, I was almost slapped in the face by a belly,
which, in its clearly enceinte condition, overlapped the frame,
and I knew that somewhere above or behind it, loomed down
under.

'It's Connie,' the belly said.

I swallowed. I knew there was no way of avoiding her.
That, at some time or another, I would have to confront her.
But mostly it was Stephanie whom I feared. How was I to
know whether or not she was hiding out of frame?

I temporised. 'Pardon?' I said, hoping perhaps to give the
picture time to change, that Connie's belly would shift with
impatience and, in so doing, would perhaps reveal her travelling companion. But the belly was fixed.

'It's Connie,' it shouted, piercing my ear-drum.

I threw in the sponge. 'Come up,' I said. 'It's the penthouse,'
and I pressed the release button on the door.

I was trembling. I went through my living-room door and I
viewed the luxurious appointments of my flat, hoping to find
some compensatory comfort therein. I heard the lift ascend,
and, desperate for some defence, I had a flash of divine
inspiration. I ran to my 'phone and dialled the number that
would activate the bell. I had timed it beautifully, for as I put
the 'phone down Connie pressed the buzzer. Then the 'phone
began to ring and she could hear it loud and clear. I let it ring a
few times, then I opened the door. 'Come in,' I said, not
looking at her, but noting with relief that she was alone. 'Just
let me get this call,' I said, and I left her standing in the hall,
well in sight of my luxurious life-style, as well as in ear-shot of
my conversation.

And this is what she heard.

'Hullo? Sandra? Darling, how lovely to hear from you.
(Pause.) Yes, I got your invitation. Of course I'll be there.
(Pause.) No, sweetheart, I won't have time, I'm pretty booked
up till then. Marion's in from Wales, and I'm spending most of
my time with her. (Pause.) Of course I do. (Flirtatiously.)
Why d'you have to ask? (Pause.) Well I'll see you on Saturday.
Bye. (Pause.) But I've told you a hundred times. (Pause.) OK.
(Softly.) I love you.'

I put the 'phone down, giggling, glad to be relieved of the purring drone in my ear. 'Come in,' I said to her.

Then I looked at her properly for the first time, and the tingling hangover from the spread-eagled Sandra gave me the courage to smile at her.

CHAPTER NINE

Procreation is something we have to learn to live with, but I confess that I don't go overboard for it. It's a dirty business; its results so open to the public eye. But I could detect no shame in Connie. She had done nothing to camouflage her swelling; indeed she seemed to parade it with pride. Moreover, she wore a look of innocence that would have fooled nobody. I presumed she wanted to present a virgin-like appearance, which I suppose was fitting, since her condition was occasioned, not by human contact, but by a mere needle. Her Madonna-expression gave off a whiff of immaculate conception.

I asked her to sit down, hoping that, sedentary, her state would be less offensive on the eye. I refrained from touching her, for I knew where she had been. She beached like a whale onto the armchair, and I wondered how on earth she would rise again. Connie had never been a pretty woman. I had met her first by candlelight, and therefore presumed that all her subsequent appearances were on her off-days, though those days ran into years. Her present condition did nothing to improve her looks, for the swelling had seemed to affect the face as well. I found her quite repulsive. Moreover the Sandra-image was fast fading from my mind, a fact which did not improve my disposition towards Connie. I felt that her presence in my quarters had a touch of invasion, and I was not pleased.

'What do you want?' I said.

She looked at me, astonished. 'Nothing,' she said. 'What should I want? I simply came to see you.'

'You must have a reason,' I insisted. Apart from the 'ha ha', she had visited without her appendage. That surely indicated an overture to reconciliation. I envisaged her return, yet I had no idea where in my apartment I could put her. The 'ha ha' was out of the question of course. She could go away somewhere and have it straightway adopted, or that Stephanie of hers, if she were so inclined, could take it back down under. I would give Connie the small spare room, I decided. There was no wardrobe, but she could live out of a suitcase. That would impress on her the impermanence of her status. She could take her meals in the kitchen, and occasionally, if I were not using it, I would allow her my terrace, in return for weeding and planting, which would save on the gardener. I would avoid her person as much as possible, and allow confrontation only for the purpose of punishment. As these thoughts trailed through my mind, I grew excited, and I was about to tell her that I would consider her application to return, when she said, 'No reason at all. I simply wanted to see you. I know I caused you pain when I left, and I imagine you're over it now. I wanted to see that you were happy. Like I am.'

It took me a little time to re-focus on her blurred and swollen person as it tenanted my Parker-Knoll armchair, since I had last seen her weeding and digging on my terrace.

'I would like to bring Stephanie here. There's no reason why we shouldn't all be friends.'

Then I heard what she had said. And I blew. I suppose there resides a small area of tenderness in me so, although I wanted to throw her bodily out of my flat, I refrained. In any case, I didn't wish to touch her. So I moved to the back of the armchair and, with all my strength, I simply tipped it over. She landed on her 'ha ha' on the floor.

'Get out,' I said quietly. I was pleased with my low decibel tone. It was impressive, for it robbed Connie of words. Or perhaps she was merely winded. I watched her gather her plurality together, and move towards the door. I noticed her attempt at dignity, and her failure, too. For she stumbled. Hardly a gait of glory. She said not a word, but she flung me a look of militant vulnerability, and I had to confess that her eloquent silence approached the dignity she sought. And then she was gone, as if she had never been, with no trace behind her, but for the horrifying evidence of the upturned chair. I felt suddenly sick with remorse, and I rushed out of my flat in time to hear the lift doors closing. 'I'm sorry,' I screamed into the closed well. My knees were trembling and a terrible sense of loss and defeat overtook me, for Connie had taken away my manhood, but, much worse, I had proved to her that it was gone. I stumbled back into the living-room and tried to avoid the upturned chair. I grasped at the notion that it had all been a dream and, to support it, I shut my eyes, groped for the chair and upturned it to its proper position. Then I sat on it, embedded myself in it, as if I had not moved from there the whole morning. But even I, master of self-delusion, could not deny the violent vibrations that lingered in the room, that something had happened in that space that, by any standards, was shameful and unpardonable.

It taught me a lesson: I must never see Connie again. My Connie-anger was permanent, and perhaps I was rightly entitled to it, yet I could contain it only in the absence of physical target. Else I was doomed yet again to visit those south coast establishments whose proprietors would be offensively unsurprised by my return. No. I must not see her again. But somehow I had to make amends. I had no trace of her. No address. No registration at a hospital. But I remembered the Doctor Martin Connie had mentioned in her letter. A gynaecologist from Melbourne. That was enough data with which to start an investigation. Such a search held out the promise of a mini-crusade, and I rose light-hearted from my chair. I reached for the yellow pages directory. I would phone every hospital in London and track Dr Martin down. No mean assignment, I can tell you. Yet I had much appetite for it. It had been many weeks since I had followed a clue in my Marion crusade, but I had lost nothing in diligence or enthusiasm. I underlined the dozen or so large training hospitals that operate in the city, and I made a start on the Royal Free. I know it well. It is my local, and sited a mere stone's throw from Sebastian's house in the crescent. I was suddenly wary. Simply because I had temporarily transferred my diligence from the Marion to the Martin crusade did not mean that they were in any way similar. No. I must beware of any assumption of parallelism. There are crusades and there are campaigns, and that was the difference between Marion and Martin.

I dialled the number and asked for obstetrics. I was told to hold on, which I did, and for some time, and it was a good five minutes before I solicited the information that no Dr Martin worked in that department or ever had done. It was the same story from the next three hospitals and the duration of time of connection lengthened with each call. My temper began to fray. On my eighth call I was well nigh into a frenzy. My voice had reached a feverish female pitch and I decided to exploit it.

'Obstetrics,' I screamed into the receiver. 'And quick, for God's sake, I'm in labour.'

'Hold on,' came the same indifferent voice that must have operated each and every one of the hospital switchboards in London.

I spluttered with rage and was obliged to wait another five minutes for connection. But as it turned out, the wait was worth while. Yes, a Dr Brenda Martin from Melbourne, Australia, was on secondment to the Middlesex Hospital for six months. I put down the 'phone. I had traced Connie's connection. From such information, Connie's whereabouts were a walkover.

My spirits were high and I decided to take a stroll to the Middlesex, and there make discreet enquiries. In view of the possibility that Connie could eventually be recompensed for my shoddy behaviour, all my erstwhile shame evaporated. Indeed, I had almost forgotten the deed that merited compensation of any kind. Such compensation, whatever it might turn out to be, would be a simple act, on my part, of unprovoked generosity. I am not a nice man.

If I stand on the left-hand side of my terrace, I can see the Middlesex Hospital even though the post-office tower does its best to impede my view. As the crow flies, it is no more than a mile or so, and I reckoned that in my high spirits and unwebbed feet I could cover it in much less than an hour. I set out on my campaign trail.

I do not like hospitals. I have been fortunate enough to avoid them most of my life. My single hospital experience was not as a patient but as a visitor. Being ill is one thing; viewing illness is quite another, and I consider the visitor's role the more arduous, for ill people are tedious and disturb one's equilibrium. I had not thought of that visit for some time, for its recall was painful. But now on my way to the disinfected wards, the shrieking silence of illness and the eternally disturbed peace of recovery, I was bound to think of it once more.

The patient was my father, that noble ineffectual man from

whom I inherited my talent for failure. Indeed, my father went so far as to die of it. And precisely in this manner. His life, like mine, had been a catalogue of failures, but his list was much longer, even though he was little more than my present age when he died. I myself was sixteen at the time and, what with my irregular schooling, I was already well-embarked on my career of vain labour. My father had just failed in his most recent business venture, and my mother chose that very time to abscond with another man who I now knew answered to the generous name of Mr Curtis. My father turned on the gas-tap – in those days, domestic gas was still toxic – and he simply placed his head in the gas-oven. But as happened regularly in our house, through want of the right change, or sheer neglect, the meter ran out and there was not enough gas to send him off good and proper. But enough to choke him a little, and render him very short of good breath. It was I who found him, his chin cupped on the lowest iron rung where my mother was wont to heat the Sunday dinner plates. I ran into the street and to the telephone kiosk and dialled 999. In those days one was connected immediately after the last digit had run its course, and within minutes the ambulance was at our door, and my father inside it, covered with a red blanket and with a mask over his face. I sat by his side and listened to the bell ringing and would have been happy were it not for the sound of my father's desperate breathing. 'Made a right buggers' muddle of that one,' he gasped.

They bundled him into a bed and they told me that he would recover, and I didn't know whether or not that was good news. And he *did* recover, at least from his suicide attempt, that ultimate bungling of his life. But a day before he was due to be discharged, his temperature rose and he was feverish to the point of delirium. He died mysteriously a week later, along with two other convalescent patients in his ward. Legionnaires' disease was what they put on the certificate. To my young ears it had a noble ring. It gave his death some dignity, as if he had died in the call of duty, up there in the front line, in the service of his country. I thought he should have been awarded a posthumous medal. But instead, his body hung around for an indecent space of time while the hospital authorities held an enquiry. Then he was buried with little ceremony, while I stood dry-eyed at the graveside, and my mother pretended to cry. And that was the last I saw of either of them.

I was in sight of the hospital. I was surprised that I had covered the ground so quickly. It was possibly because of that memory that I had recalled. I had been anxious to get it over and done with, and I had transferred my need of haste to my legs.

I intended to go straight to the maternity wing, because I would not waste my enquiries in fruitless quarters. I strode with confidence into the reception-area, which looked unnervingly like that very hell where I had awaited news of my father. My step had lost its spring, and I lumbered towards the lift, the doors of which were about to open. There was a sudden rush of air behind me, and I was bodily pushed to one side. Then a large figure, intent on removing all impediment to her passage, burst into the lift and pressed the close button before anyone else could enter. Her face was suffused with worry and desperation, so much so, that those of us who were left stranded, were obliged to forgive her for her gross behaviour. But not I. For though she had been blind to mine, I had seen the woman's face. Stephanie from down under, but now very much on my doorstep. I was confused. First, I had to deal with the feeling of sickening disgust on seeing her again. I had met her but once, and by accident, though I knew in hindsight, that Connie had engineered our meeting. Then I had to deal with the question of what she was doing here at this time, and so obviously in a state of acute distress. And then the answer struck me like a thunderbolt. Connie was already in hospital, an emergency no doubt, in premature labour brought on by that fall when she had so stupidly tripped in my apartment, and Florence Stephanie Nightingale was on her desperate way to deliverance. I refused the lift when the doors opened, and I stood aside and wondered what I should do. I refused to feel guilty and it was a full-time job to shift those feelings aside. I went back to the reception area and picked up the house-phone. I asked to be connected with the maternity department. Another long wait, while I prepared what I imagined was a paternal voice.

'D'you have Mrs Connie Wakefield there?' I asked.

I was told to hold the line, which I did, but not for long. 'No,' came the swift reply.

I put the 'phone down, relieved. Then that accidental fall in my flat had had no dire consequences. I decided to wait in the lobby for Stephanie's re-appearance, and then, unseen, follow her home. I did not have to wait long. After a short while, she re-appeared. I hid behind a pillar, and from this vantage-point I saw her emerge from the lift, or rather, erupt from it, for she was still in desperate haste, and make her way with bulldog determination to the flower shop at the end of the reception corridor. I was puzzled. I waited and, through the distant plate-glass window of the shop, I watched her being served. Then she emerged, bearing roses, and made straight for the lift once more, and shortly disappeared inside.

The sickening truth hit me. I scratched in my mind to recall Connie's maiden name, then I made for the 'phone once more.

'D'you have a Miss Connie Andrews there?' I asked. There was nothing paternal in my voice. To my ear, it sounded offended and resigned.

'Yes,' the nurse said, 'she was admitted this afternoon.'

I put the 'phone down quickly. I did not ask how she was. I suppose I was afraid to know. That enormous bunch of roses, to say nothing of its enormous bearer, had unnerved me considerably. But more than anything else, I was angry. I was trembling with my rage. Miss Connie Andrews. Or Miz, as their kind call themselves. Miz Connie had well and truly buried me. The notion of Wakefield was no longer viable in her life. I was a nothing, without even an indication of a has-been. I would have accepted a hyphenated Wakefield-Andrews, or, at a push, even an Andrews-Wakefield, if her priorities had been so inclined. But to be so unmentioned, and therefore so unmentionable. I forswore all thought of Connie-compensation. I had meant to send her flowers once I had tracked her down. No. I had meant to send her a complete layette for the new baby. No. I had intended to make an endowment in the baby's name that would look after its education. Indeed, I had meant to support it for life. But bugger the baby. And bugger her.

I was too depressed to walk home. Walking induces contemplation, and I could not risk that. So I hailed a cab, and tried to take my mind off my mind. It was rush-hour, and the traffic was painfully slow. My fists were clenched. I thought I had never hated so much. But there was something more. I had to admit to a certain anxiety as to Miz Andrews' condition. The cab was idling at green traffic lights, with no passage to continue on its way. I shoved the fare into the cabbie's hand and alighted quickly, and dodging the cars I made my way into the park, and from there ran all the way home. For my need for movement was obsessional. I did not stop until I entered the lift and, even inside, I jogged, and came to rest only when I entered my flat and settled myself into that terrible armchair, so that I could obliterate it from my sight. I looked at my watch. It had been two hours since Miz Andrews had visited. I knew nothing about babies or how long these things took. I have to confess that, much as I hated her, I needed desperately to know how she was. I went to the telephone and dialled the hospital number. I wondered about my voice. Was I a father, a husband, a brother, a friend? Or simply a rejected suitor. Each role commanded a different voice, and I was at a loss to choose that which suited me best. And yet, in the very core of my heart, I knew. And I knew it with absolute certainty.

'Maternity,' I requested. And was connected swiftly. 'How is Miz Connie Andrews?' I asked. I heard the break in my voice.

'One moment,' someone said, and went away. Then she returned. 'Who are you?' she said.

I did not hesitate. I was conscious of my rights. 'I'm the father,' I said.

'Well your wife's in the labour ward. There's no news yet. She's comfortable.'

'When should I ring again?'

'In an hour perhaps. Or two. You could, of course, wait here.'

'I'm not in London,' I said quickly, and I was sorely tempted to return to the hospital. But I could not face an encounter with Stephanie. 'I'll ring back,' I said, and I replaced the receiver.

For the next hour I paced my living-room, avoiding that chair on each turn. Somewhere down under, a nameless Australian stud was swilling his beer without a thought of what he had engendered, and on his behalf I paced. I paced, too, on behalf of all those men who had been robbed, like me, of fatherhood. It was some way of atoning to my gender. As the hour struck, I rang again. No, there was still no news. It could be quite a time. The morning perhaps. But I did not believe her, and on each hour I dialled again. At sometime around midnight, the nursing-shift changed, and I was obliged to give my credentials once more. On my declaration of paternity, I thought I detected a slight suspicion in her voice, as if she indeed knew the non-provenance of the child, that the sire could have been one in a million or more, and therefore there was no sire at all. She was probably a Miz too. But I was not daunted by her doubts and I continued to ring as the hours passed by. Between 'phone calls, I paced my room and as the dawn broke I became so excited that I set out my drinks on the coffee-table, in preparation for a toast. I took one of my large Waterford glasses and set it beside my cut-glass decanter. And I went further. I actually unwrapped a cigar from my box of havanas, clipped its end with a Georgian silver clipper, and laid a box of matches on the side. Now all I needed was a baby. I was in labour along with Connie, and I stifled any thought that the large Stephanie was in our company.

At five in the morning I rang again, and then at six. There was still no news, but the nurse volunteered that they were expecting some shortly. In view of that piece of information, I could barely pace out the hour, and at 6.30 I rang again. The nurse ascertained my status once more and, though her voice still harboured doubts, I supposed she reckoned that good news need not be filtered.

'You have a son,' she said. 'He weighed 7½ pounds. Your wife is well and she's sleeping.'

I thanked her, though no sound came from my mouth, so filled was I with the grandeur of my new status. I lit my cigar, poured myself a large whiskey, and raised my glass in a toast.

'To my son,' I said to the four stark walls, and I drank quickly to shield my ears from the echo of my own hollow voice. For I felt a depression creep upon me. For whom could I tell, and with whom could I share my dubious joy? So I drank and I drank, toasting with every sip, but wordlessly and without name. I drank until sleep was heavy enough on my eye, so that no thought of Stephanie could threaten it. Then I lay on my bed and slept till noon.

★

My first waking thought was that of fatherhood, and I rose quickly and showered before it could sour. I needed desperately to see my son. The thought of seeing Connie disturbed me enough and I would deal with it with flowers. But the whole of Kew Gardens could not ease my passage with Stephanie. I would find out the visiting times in Maternity, then make some excuse to call off-season, as it were, in the hope of avoiding my usurper. On enquiry I discovered that afternoon and evenings were free for visitors.

I breakfasted on my terrace. I had to lower the awning because it was a little cold. Autumn was approaching. I thought I would take my son ski-ing. I put on my grey worsted, a fitting apparel, I thought, for my new status, and I took a cab to the best florist in London. There I ordered a bouquet of flowers more for its size than its quality, though I did not stint on the latter. But I needed some shield for my entry, one large enough to hide my face, and with luck most of my body, too. For I counted on Connie's astonishment, that she would be too overwhelmed by the gift to take immediate account of its bearer. And thus armed, I made my way to the hospital.

The nurse in charge questioned my visiting at such an early hour, but she could not help but be impressed by my offering. It was too large and too opulent to deny. Its size shrieked urgency. She told me that Miz Andrews was in the end bed on the left-hand side. I was glad that Connie was in a corner, a position which afforded privacy of a sort, yet I had to negotiate the length of the ward almost blinded by my offering. The going was slow. I found a convenient peep-hole between a full-blooded chrysanthemum and a spindly stem of fern, and it was enough to light my passage to port. Half-way down the ward, I spotted Connie, my son in her arms. I watched her catch sight of me, or rather the propulsion of an approaching missile. I caught the hint of a puzzled smile between the ferns and, thus encouraged, I reached the end of the ward and stopped beside her bed. I dared not shift the flowers from my face, but from behind them I murmured my apologies. I waited for some reaction.

'They're lovely,' she said.

I was not yet confident that she was fully aware of the person who bore them. So I said once again through the ferns, 'I'm sorry about yesterday.' That specific, I thought, would narrow the field a little.

'I know you are,' she said.

Then I thought it safe to lower my shield. I laid the flowers on the bed. She raised her face for a kiss, turning her cheek for my target. I pecked her, and in so doing had the first sight of my son. I looked at him for a long time, and in his puckered face I saw a distinct resemblance to my own father. He was a Wakefield all right, but I forebore to say so.

'He's beautiful,' I said. 'May I hold him?'

She handed the parcel over, a little reluctantly, I thought, for she could see I was nervous. I had never held a baby in my arms before. I was frightened, not so much of its fragility, but of the extraordinary thrust of power it seemed to give off. I wondered whether I had threatened my father in the same way. But it was not an unpleasant feeling. I would happily have subjected myself to the baby's every need, and would have felt enriched by it. I had never considered myself in relation to children before, but now it struck me that my erstwhile lack of parenthood was the sole cause of my overall failure in life, and that that, now remedied, would clear the path to a promising future. I gave a passing thought to my Marion-crusade, that pursuit that had occupied my every moment since that Tuesday visit to the post-office. Now for the first time, its priority was overtaken. In my new role I would have little time for campaign. But I must not let my thoughts run away with me.

I looked closely at the baby which seemed to be staring back at me with some glimmer of recognition. 'What will you call him?' I said, having a string of names on my tongue. But I felt that Connie should have a share in the choice. I am not what they call a chauvinistic man.

'I was thinking of calling him Luke,' she said. 'It's what I would have called a baby of yours.' She was smiling and stretched out her arms to relieve me of our son. My heart fluttered. That christening was Connie's way of asking me to take her back. Of that I was sure. In my mind I began to arrange their accommodation. Luke would have a room of his own. That small room adjacent to our bedroom with a communicating door between. The spare room would accommodate the nanny who could use the second bathroom. Every morning I would take Luke for a walk across the park, and on holidays I would teach him to swim, to sail and to ski. I grew so excited it must have shown on my face, for she said, 'Are you happy with that name?'

I drew up a chair and sat by the bed. 'Not only the name,' I said. 'I'm glad you're coming home. This time the marriage will work. Luke will make it so.'

I saw her shrink a little. She leaned over the other side of the bed and placed the baby in the cot. Then she folded her hands on her lap and looked me straight in the eye.

'Luke,' she said gently, and it was that tone of kindness that unnerved me. No good news would come of it. She kept her eyes on my face. 'I'm not coming back,' she said. 'Ever. In a couple of weeks, Stephanie and I are taking the baby back to Melbourne. We have a life there. I'm happy there. We're happy together.'

I looked down at my hands and saw that my fists were clenched and reckless. I knew I had to get out of that place; I had to rein in my mind. I knew, too, that I had to hold my tongue, for the loosening of the one would unhinge the other. There was a new sensation, too, something I had not felt for many years. Indeed I do not remember ever having felt it before. Simply, and in short, I wanted very much to cry. I felt the tears pricking behind my eyes and I was ashamed. I looked at my shield of flowers on the bed, and the thought crossed my mind to take them back. But in my tormented spirit, there was a desperate need for movement, and I could do without impediment.

In any case, I was going into a battle that needed no arms, for it was going to be a very simple struggle with myself. I did not trust myself to look at Connie, and certainly I would not risk the baby. I staggered out of my chair, my body sweating. I don't remember leaving the ward or the hospital, and certainly there was no recollection of a lift. I must have broken into a run from the side of Connie's bed, and the first time I took stock of myself, I was pausing for breath on a bench in the park. I remember that the last number that had panted from my mouth was one thousand and forty-four, the saying of which was enough to cover four strides. I had thus not allowed a single extraneous thought to ruffle my already ruffled mind. I had numbed it with numbers, and as I sat on that bench, my grey worsted clinging to the sweat of my skin, I knew that I could not move a step further. That I must seek no privacy for my pain, but there and then, and on that very spot, I must, unarmed, do battle with myself. And there and then, I gave myself up to weeping. My tears were for loss, for memorial, for the blinding nightmare of my shattered miserable life. A woman passed me by, a dog in tow. It was a puppy, and it dragged on its chain to muzzle my trouser-leg. The woman looked at the grown-up worsted crying like a child, and I saw that she was frightened and she dragged the dog away. Her fear frightened me, too, and I felt pins and needles in my back. 'God help me,' I cried aloud, 'but save me from another dose of south coasts.'

I had to get back to my crusade. Marion was now my sole link with sanity. I rose from the bench, dusted myself down, and made my way back to my apartment. As I passed through the foyer, the porter was coming out of his lodge. He noted my distressed and dishevelled state.

'Are you all right, Mr Wakefield?' he said.

'I just had some bad news,' I told him. 'My wife died.'

'Oh, I am sorry,' he said, opening the lift door. He looked puzzled, as well he might, for he had no idea that I had ever been married. 'We'd been separated a long time,' I enlightened him, 'but it's still upsetting.'

'Of course,' he said, shutting the door, and no doubt glad to be shot of me for another's bereavement can be inconvenient in the extreme.

By the time I reached my penthouse, I was sobbing once more. I leaned against the doors of my terrace and gave myself up to my own misery. And after a while, I felt strangely relieved. I had come to tears late in life, and I marvelled at their purging power.

CHAPTER TEN

No, I did not go back to a south coast establishment. I was firmly rooted in my tear-stained penthouse apartment, and I was well and truly back on the Marion trail. For shortly after my days of mourning, a clue landed in my lap. I came across it by sheer accident, and from my usual source. *The Times* Death Column. It was a pretty short Column that day, not enough to satisfy any survivor's appetite, and to supplement it I turned to what I call the posh deaths, those that merit a character assessment of a kind and, moreover, are entitled to a special obituary page. A Who's Who's in death, as it were. On the whole it makes for dull reading, because the notices are invariably complimentary, and give off an air of total incredibility. That morning a major-general had died, whose long life had been tedious in the extreme. He had moved from duty to duty, from service to service, and from one piece of moral rectitude to another. He had left a wife and three children, and I bet they were jolly glad to be shot of him.

The next posh death was that of a missionary, a member of that vocation that requires a total lack of self-esteem, and I just could not be bothered to examine it. I glanced at the opposite page which advertised London and Country properties for sale. It is a page I rarely read, for I have no intention of moving from my apartment, so it holds little interest for me. But one notice caught my eye. It stood out from the others because it was framed in a black rectangle. It announced a sale by auction and, as is usual in such sales, the full address of the property was given. I read it with infinite pleasure. 64 Hampstead Crescent. The house of Sebastian's neighbour, and no doubt a mine of information as to the goings-on next door. A description of the house followed and, though I had no interest in its square footage or sanitary arrangements, I read all the particulars very carefully, because I had to feign the very real interest of a possible buyer.

I rang the agent immediately and asked for an appointment to view. I gave my name as Andrews. I don't know why. It was just that I felt safer with an alias. I told him I was in London for a few days only, and thus required a prompt appointment. After asking me to hold the line for a while, while he contacted the vendor, he came back with the information that I could view that very afternoon.

'The name is Pearson,' he said.

I decided to spend the morning in preparation, itemising all those Sebastian-questions I wished to ask, and finding some way of making them pertinent to my interest in the purchase of the house.

But as was my wont, I made no preparations at all. But at least, as I stood outside number 64, I knew I would not have to rely on a weather-forecast to gain entry, nor ask after the health of one whom I knew to be dead. I was about to make a legitimate call, one for which I had an appointment, and I rang the bell with confidence.

A little round lady opened the door. 'Mr Andrews?' she asked.

I'd forgotten about my alias and I hesitated. And shivered, too, for that surname rang a cracked bell. I nodded because I did not trust my voice, and she asked me into the hall.

Once inside the house, I felt more at ease, for it recalled Sebastian's entrance next door. Structurally it was exactly the same, though there was a great difference in its décor. Whereas Sebastian's foyer was white and hung with pictures, this one was flocked with red wallpaper, without a picture in sight.

'Mrs Pearson?' I said.

'That's right. Shall we start at the top of the house?'

She led the way up the stairs, while I marshalled thoughts relevant to house-purchase. I had had some previous experience in property-surveying, for before I had settled on my penthouse apartment I had viewed a number of possibilities, and had learned to look for the drawbacks in structure, and to ask the right questions. I was not in the least interested in the former, but I intended to pose a few of the latter in order to authenticate my presence in the house. I weighed in as we climbed the stairs.

'How old is this house?' I asked, with an historian's interest.

'1830,' she replied promptly. 'But the side wing was added at the turn of the century. You'll notice the structural difference.'

I was heartened. The woman knew all the answers and could, without doubt, satisfy the oblique queries I would make regarding the goings-on over the garden wall. But I would leave all that till last, when the ground floor would be inspected, and the garden along with it. By that time we should have struck up a relationship that would even allow for a little gossip. Why, she might even offer me tea and, in return, who knows? I might even enlist her in my crusade. I grew very excited, so much so that I tripped on the stairs to the top landing. I steadied myself quickly and she did not remark on it. She was clearly a woman of good breeding.

The top floor was quickly dealt with. Four small attic rooms in all, unfurnished and unused. She explained that they had once been used by her children, 'who have now fled the nest'.

'You have children, Mr Andrews?' she asked.

'Yes,' I said chattily. 'We've just had a son. My first. My wife's still in hospital.'

'Oh, how exciting,' she said, unexcited, and she turned to lead me down to the first floor. I was sorry that she did not pump me for more details as, for example, the baby's weight and its name. She gave the impression that she hadn't believed a word I'd said, and I had to fight down a feeling of resentment.

She showed me into the master bedroom. 'Oh, that's beautiful,' I said, because I felt it was expected of me. It was an expensive room, of impeccable taste and order, that led one to believe that very little went on in the bed. I followed her into the ensuite bathroom, with its piles of neatly-folded towels and bars of guest soaps, an arrangement clearly for the benefit of prospective viewers. I sighed my satisfaction.

'We like this room,' Mrs Pearson said. 'It has a lovely view of the garden.'

My heart quickened at the word. She led me to the window to admire it. At a quick glance I could see that the garden was beautifully landscaped, with not a blade of grass out of true. But what caught my eye, for the first floor was a good vantage-point, was the wilderness of Sebastian's garden next door. I looked along the gardens of the whole street, and all were as immaculate as Mrs Pearson's. Sebastian's stood out like a refreshing eyesore.

'It's beautiful, your garden,' I said, 'but what a pity about next door.'

'Yes,' she said. 'The owner died. He loved that garden. Now they've let it go to rack and ruin.'

'But isn't there anyone to look after it?' I hoped she couldn't hear the thumping of my heart. 'His wife? Children?'

'He wasn't married,' she said. 'At least, I never saw a woman about the place. But I didn't know too much about him.' She turned to face me. 'D'you know, Mr Andrews,' she said, as if offering a confidence, 'we lived next door to each other for ten years, and I don't think we exchanged one word in that time. That's London for you.'

'Wouldn't happen in the country,' I said, for I had to say something if only for the noise of it, to cover my heart's knocking. For what Mrs Pearson had told me confirmed a certain suspicion I'd harboured ever since reading Sebastian's first letter. That he had intended to murder Marion from the very beginning. So of course he would not care to display her as part of the household, as a frequenter, for instance of his garden, available for all the neighbours to see. Of course, he could take her out to the Mirabelle with the Webbs and the Martins and to Richard's house in Wimbledon, where he put her about simply as his current girlfriend. It was no wonder Mrs Pearson had not seen a woman about the house. What she had told me in no way helped further my crusade, but it had given me a further insight into Sebastian's character, which I was finding more and more unlikeable.

I turned away from the window. There was now no point in further enquiries. If, in Mrs Pearson's mind, Sebastian had no wife, then it was futile to raise the subject of that wife's relatives. I was ready to leave, but I had perforce, out of courtesy, to finish the round of the property, and there were four more bedrooms to go, to say nothing of the reception areas on the ground floor. Mrs Pearson was droning on about corniced ceilings, original fireplaces, and the quality of the fitted wardrobes, and I feigned interest and appreciation. I think I might have overdone the latter, for by the time we had done with the study and drawing-rooms I was fairly drooling with flattery, and she took it as a sure sign that a sale was in the bag. And I did nothing to disillusion her. Indeed, I asked her how soon she could move out, and would she have any objection to my sending someone to measure up for curtains. I was rather enjoying myself. Finally I managed to take my leave, with promises of seeing my bank manager that very day, and being in touch with the agent very soon. I did not fear that she would ask for a deposit. She was too much of a lady for that. But she offered to hold the sale until I was in touch with her. I thanked her and felt like a heel, but I am used to such feelings and have learned to live with them.

As I walked down the drive, I cast a glance at number 62. The brass knocker and the single bell, those signs of one-family residence, had been removed, and, in their place, there was a panel of intercoms, with loudspeakers for identification. It was no wonder Mrs Pearson was selling. She was no likely neighbour to a rooming-house.

I returned to my penthouse with a slight feeling of let-down, and with no more leads to follow in my crusade until the memorial service for Sebastian's mother. I tried to restrain my expectations of that event, because I knew that, if Richard were not in attendance, I would have come to an impasse, and poor Marion's name would remain on the missing persons' file. But more distressing than that was the thought of how I would, crusaderless, pass my time, and such thoughts brought Connie to my mind and all the anger and frustration of their wake. I imagined that she was still in hospital, and would shortly be on her way down under, and I could look forward to spasmodic postcards. I doubted whether she would mention the baby. I had frightened her with my presumption. Indeed there was the possibility that she would never write to me again, and that I should lose contact with her for ever, and that thought drove me close to despair. I poured myself some whiskey to calm myself, and then another. But instead of calming me, it brought on a feeling of deep self-disgust. It wasn't that I had done ill in life, but that I had done nothing good, and the urge came upon me to do just one decent thing. I had no difficulty in my choice, for my contacts in life are very few indeed. So I looked up Mrs Pearson's number in the directory, and I dialled.

'Mrs Pearson?' I asked when she answered. 'This is Mr Andrews. I'm sorry, but something has happened and I'm not able to buy your house. I thought I would let you know because I didn't want you to refuse another offer.'

'That's very civil of you, Mr Andrews. I do hope nothing untoward has happened.'

'My wife has just died,' I said, and I put the 'phone down.

★

For the next week, the waiting week until the service, I cooled my heels in my flat, and drank far more than was good for me. I sobered up the day before the service and, for the first time in a week, I left my apartment and went for a walk in the park to clear my head. On my way, I passed the newsagent and I noticed the headline of the evening paper. *Dawkins sentenced to Life.* The name rang a distant bell, and slowly I connected it with a long-ago abortive clue. I felt faintly ashamed that I had set so much store by it. I didn't even bother to buy a paper. If Dawkins was guilty, then he would get his just deserts. I am not in favour of murder. One can wish people dead, and with all one's heart. Nothing wrong with that. One can pray for an enemy's demise, and with luck, one day, God might be listening. And if not God, then someone else, who does not acknowledge the thin and jagged line between wish and fulfillment. Dawkins was one of those. So was Sebastian. So perhaps was the enigmatic Richard. But that, I would soon discover. A memorial service can jog many memories, other than those related particularly to the deceased. I would catch Richard on the hop. I did not dare allow a thought that he might not be there.

But he was. And in exactly the same attitude as I had last seen him. Walking with a slight melancholy stoop, and I suspected in the same dark brown suit that he had worn at Sebastian's funeral. I was standing to one side outside the church porch, and I stared at him unashamedly, and with great joy. I knew him so well, and so much about him, that I half expected him to acknowledge me with equal familiarity. But I had to remind myself that he knew me not at all, so I took advantage of this one-sided condition, and I stared at him, viewing him from all angles. There was little to be read in his appearance, little more, that is, than I already knew. He was clearly a man of taste with an interest in the arts. I knew that that art was painting, but it could well have been poetry and literature. He had that faintly unreliable look, but I must confess I found it attractive in the extreme. I had great hopes of him.

There was a goodly crowd of people gathering in the forecourt and, in my role of gatecrasher, I was glad of it. From where I stood, I followed Richard as he made his way to a group of people at the far end of the court. And, in amongst them, I spotted Auntie Chrissie and Uncle Ted. Chrissie let out a scream of excitement on seeing Richard, and rushed to him, arms outstretched, a manner of behaviour I found most ill-fitting to the occasion. I noticed how Richard shrunk in her embrace. Aunt Chrissie struck me as being an art-lover rather than a connoisseur but then, on second thoughts, I considered she was more likely to be an artist lover, which term would include all those who busied themselves with creative pursuits. As she released Richard from her grasp, and introduced him to those around her, I sensed that she was a name-dropper too, and I saw how Uncle Ted cringed at her exuberance. I decided that as soon as I learned of Richard's second name I would look him up in *Who's Who*, and discover for what reason his name was so clearly droppable. I'd look up Sebastian's, too, and I wondered why I hadn't thought of it before.

More and more people were coming into the forecourt, and most of them had a distinguished air. A number of the men wore uniforms, festooned with medals and ribbons, and all of them were very old. I presumed they were the left-overs from the Kings' Rifles, that regiment of their comrade-in-arms, whose widow they had come to remember. They were stooped and frail and, between them all, I doubted whether they could have loaded and carried a pea-shooter. I felt moved towards them. I am a great admirer of service, but only when it is done. When it is done, and when it is survived. I cannot bear to see it in action.

It seemed that the arrival of the Old Guard sanctioned the service to begin, and I saw Aunt Chrissie and Uncle Ted move towards the church door, followed by Richard and others in their wake. I presumed that the chief mourners would sit in the front row, so I stood aside while they crossed the threshold, then entered myelf, so that I could be close at hand. I had brought with me my mourning face, fitting to a front memorial pew, and this I now put on and made my way down the aisle. I took the seat at the end of the third row, a mere head behind Richard's, and obliquely, for he sat on the aisle seat in the second row on the other side. I was satisfied. I could see him without being seen. I rose from my seat and let others pass. I refused to move along and thus lose my vantage-point, and my stubbornness no doubt irritated the passers-by. I explained to one of them that I had a wooden leg, and she smiled with sympathy. I made a mental note to limp my way out of the church.

Very soon the congregation was seated, and an invisible orchestra played something familiar but to which I could put no name. However it was called, its tone was one of solemnity, and was meant, I suppose, to put us in the mood of remembrance. I looked around the assembly to make sure that they were doing just that. And no doubt they were, though they might have been recalling events that had nothing to do with the present circumstances. Old loves, for example, old triumphs, or simple domestic recollections of having left the oven on. Which I firmly believe one had, a middle-aged lady in the back row, who rose from her seat very quickly, and sped with little decorum out of the church. I, for my part, had nothing to remember of Mrs Marion Firbank senior, so I spent my time mourning her junior counterpart, of whose past life I knew even less. But at least I knew she was dead and, apart possibly from Richard, was the only one who knew, and thus she was legitimate target for mourning.

The music came to an end, and a priest entered stage left and mounted the pulpit.

'We have gathered here to celebrate the life of Marion Firbank,' he said, as if he were giving us hot news. 'In their deaths they shall be remembered.'

I settled myself in for a string of platitudes, and was amply rewarded, and after a while I switched off my ears, and concentrated on my approach to Richard after the service. I rehearsed my little speech, over and over again, until the man by my side nudged me crossly, and I realised I had been talking aloud. 'Yes, I knew Marion very well,' he had heard me say, and I thanked God that that was what he heard, for how was he to know I was referring to a corpse decomposing somewhere in Wimbledon, unplatitudinised from any pulpit? I apologised and clenched my teeth, so that my thoughts would not betray me again.

I continued rehearsing my speech, looking at Richard all the time. I couldn't help thinking that he wasn't listening either. Perhaps he, too, was remembering the younger Marion, of whom he perhaps had helped to dispose. I could not help but read a look of remorse on his face. The priest was uttering his final truism. 'In the midst of life, etc.' Then he stepped down, and his place was taken by one of my crumbling old guard, who took his stand directly in front of the audience. He did not usurp the pulpit, either out of respect for the Cloth, or an inability to climb the steps. I suspect the latter, for the old codger had difficulty enough in standing. He was leaning on a thin elegant cane, which threatened any moment to snap. He, too, gave us the news that we had come for remembrance. Then he set off to remember, not the widow of his comrade-in-arms, but that very comrade himself, and we were treated to a military account of their last campaign. There was a sudden stir of interest in the hall, as if to applaud his irrelevancy, since the subject he was avoiding was not in any case worth pursuing. He took us over the Somme and into the muddy trenches. His blue eyes watered with the joy of recall. He had clearly told the story a hundred times. With it he had bored the knickers off his wife, children and grandchildren. Its telling had swiftly cleared the bars of many clubs, and had emptied sundry drawing-rooms. But I was hearing it for the first time, and I revelled in it. I went with him into the trenches, and I wallowed with him in the mud. If there'd been a war on, I would have left the church and enlisted forthwith. He even told a joke about the stench of the dug-outs, and there was a ripple of laughter in the church, as shocking as speech in a Trappist retreat. He was just about to go over the top, filled with rum like the hundreds of poor buggers in front of him. Marion Firbank's better half was at his side. At least for a moment. And then suddenly, he wasn't. The old soldier had looked down and seen a spike, and somewhere impaled upon it his comrade-in-arms. A shiver went through the congregation, and through the old codger too, and without any more ado, he made his reminiscent way down the aisle. How like Sebastian his father had died, I thought, and with that same suddenness, and with one friend by his side.

There was a short interval then, as there had to be, in order to give the congregation time to recollect the purpose of the gathering. And to confirm this, a gentleman strode firmly onto the platform, and glowered at the mourners, as if to say that the fun was over, and that he was getting back to business. Which he did, in his first sentence, reminding us yet again of poor old Mrs Firbank senior, whose ghost had been so rudely pushed aside.

'Marion Firbank,' he said, 'was a good lady, a woman of good works.'

Well, if anything will turn me off, it's good works, and I started rehearsing my Richard approach once more. Then with half an ear, I caught the name of Sebastian.

'She was much bereaved in her life,' he was saying. 'The death of her husband was a great blow, and the loss of Alistair, her eldest son, in the Second World War. And then her youngest, Sebastian, who died shortly before her.'

I listened still, to give him a chance to elaborate on that final blow to Mrs Firbank's heart, but he left it at that, and went on to enumerate the good lady's good works. I turned off again, and ruminated on that one piece of information of which I had been hitherto unaware. Sebastian had had an elder brother, named for his father Alistair, and he had been killed in the Second World War. This tit-bit did not in any way help my crusade but it did perhaps explain the melancholy of Sebastian's profile. I began to miss him again and, out of respect, I applauded his mother's good works of which her admirer was still spouting from the platform. She had presumably sat on endless committees dispensing charity and good will, and no doubt most of the congregation were committee members too, for occasionally there came a sigh of approval from the body of the hall. I too grunted my appreciation, for I didn't want to feel out of things. But even good things must come to an end and Mrs Firbank's list of charities was no exception. The speaker stepped down and, as he did so, the band struck up again, and once more with a familiar tune that I could not name. But this time it was not mournful. Its tone was of splendour and glory and possibly the signature tune of the

Kings' Rifles. For it was a melody that called for a salute, a march past, and possibly a goat as a mascot. Whatever, it was very catchy, and I noticed how the congregation took on a marching step as they left the church.

I let Richard go before me and, mindful of my peg-leg, I limped after him. Once outside the church, I abandoned my disability, and walked briskly to a spot where he would be directly in my line of vision. I intended to smile at him when he looked in my direction. Which he did, very shortly. I had to be very careful with my smile. It must not be an inviting one. Neither must it be a smile of familiarity for he knew me not at all. Somewhere in between it lay, a smile that was an acknowledgement of having had a shared experience, that of remembrance. So I gave it to him, and it must have been of exact quality, for he responded immediately. Indeed he did more than that. He started to approach me. I had not expected such a response, and I grew nervous. My mouth was dry and I knew I'd forgotten my lines.

'Hullo,' he said, his smile lingering. 'What did you think of the service?'

I was grateful he had not asked me a more personal question.

I looked at him. He had the same compelling air that had first attracted me to Sebastian. 'It was certainly varied,' I said. I was waiting for him to ask me what I was doing there, and suddenly my rehearsed speech sneaked back onto my tongue. But he was content to pursue his first question and, in a way, I was glad of the reprieve.

'I thought that old soldier a welcome relief,' he said, 'especially after all those pulpit God-bits.'

I warmed to him. 'I can't say I went overboard for them. But one expects that sort of thing, I suppose.'

'Are you coming back to the house?' he asked.

My heart fluttered. I was being offered more than I had dared to hope for. 'I haven't been asked,' I said.

'Of course you must come. D'you have a car?'

'No. I came by cab.'

'Then I'll fix you a lift,' he said.

'Where is it?'

'At Chris and Ted's. Champers. That sort of thing. Hang on a bit.'

He left me and sought out a couple who were standing near

by. I watched him exchange words with them, then he called me to his side.

'This is Sir William and Lady Mayford,' he said, 'and I don't know your name?'

I was so shocked by the swiftness of the proceedings, and the wealth of promise that they offered, that I had no time to think of an alias, and it was not a good moment to show hesitation.

'Luke,' I said. 'Luke Wakefield.'

I tried to remember the last time that someone has asked my name, and I recalled Mrs Pearson who had had to be satisfied with Andrews. But to whom had I last given Wakefield, of my own free and willing will? I could not remember such an occasion, and the inference was frightening. But I smiled at my newly acquired escorts, who clearly had class, a fact confirmed by the shining white Rolls to which they lead me and the uniformed chauffeur who opened the door. I allowed Lady Mayford to enter first, and I sat beside her. The back seat of the Rolls was ample enough to have seated Sir William as well, but he chose to sit opposite us in a seat that the chauffeur upheld for that purpose. The whole procedure was performed in absolute silence, and the purring of the engine, as we took off, hardly disturbed the hush inside the car. So quiet it seemed, that Lady Wayford's sudden whisper startled me.

'What did you think of the service, Mr Wakefield?' she said.

Her tone gave no hint as to what she herself thought of it, as to whether it merited applause or criticism, and I regretted it, for I dearly wished to agree with her. So I played safe, taking care not to commit myself. 'I thought it varied,' I said, at which Sir William let out a guffaw, and said, 'That's putting it very mildly.'

Thus encouraged, I ventured an opinion. 'I thought the old soldier's contribution rather out of place,' I said, then regretted it, for I felt I should have known the old codger's name. He was probably a Firbank relative, if not an old and well-known friend.

'Who the hell was he?' Sir William asked, and I could have hugged him for being in the same dark as I.

'One of old Alistair's lot,' Lady Mayfield stated the obvious. 'I thought he was rather a dear. Much more interesting than that bore of a pulpit-man. If I remember rightly, he made exactly the same speech at Sebastian's send-off. I think it's a standard one. He just changes the names.'

My heart fluttered as I heard Sebastian's name, and my mouth watered with questions that I desperately wanted to ask. But much as I liked my escorts, I did not dare nurture a familiarity with them, for fear that they might ask questions of *me* and investigate my right of presence in their car. So I held my quavering tongue. I thought it best to change the subject entirely, and to get away from the dangerous Firbank ground. And once more, I sought refuge in meteorology. Boring but safe, I thought.

'We shall have an early autumn this year,' I said. 'I walked across the park this morning, and it was strewn with leaves.'

'So is my garden,' Lady Mayford said, and that put an end to the subject. But I ploughed on.

'I only have a terrace,' I said, 'but I overlook Regent's Park. Best of both worlds, I suppose.'

'Didn't old Sebastian live round there? Hampstead or something?' Sir William asked.

'Yes,' I said, hoping that that would be enough. In any case, I didn't trust my voice. I had often murmured the name Sebastian to myself, both in irritation and affection, and often enough I had read it. But to hear it dropped from another person's lips was another experience altogether. I felt it as something of an intrusion for, however well this escort of mine knew Sebastian, he could never have come near to the intimacy that I enjoyed. I regarded Sebastian with a certain proprietary right; I knew his heart, I knew his mind. But above all, I knew his terrible secret, and I vaguely resented that someone should drop that wondrous name without being privy to all that knowledge. I waited for some mention of Marion. Now surely was the time to remark on her disappearance. But nothing was forthcoming. It was the other Marion they now saw fit to discuss, that one whom we had lately celebrated.

'I don't think dear old Marion would have approved of that service at all,' Lady Mayford was saying. 'She would have liked someone to mention her paintings, I'm sure. It was the only thing that mattered to her.'

'But what could anybody say, dear?' Sir William asked. 'She was a god-damn awful painter.'

'I've seen worse,' I said, thinking I ought to put my oar in, in order to add a slight authenticity to my presence in their car. I had picked up a small clue. The elder Marion, that one who had died of natural causes, painted, and painted badly, but it led me no further in her namesake's crusade.

I looked out of the window and recognised the environs of Sebastian's former home. I hoped we would soon arrive at our destination, for the confined conditions of our travelling threatened a certain intimacy and questions that I could do without. On the other hand, I hoped we would not stop too soon, for that Hampstead area was also the cleaning-ground of Sebastian's Irish treasure, who, if they lived round about, might also be doing for Chris and Ted, and I could do without running into her again. So I was glad when the car picked up speed and made its way to the old Hampstead Garden suburb, a rich area, and thus ill-served by public transport, and pretty inaccessible, even for a determined Irish treasure.

There was silence in the car and I willed it to continue, even though there remained the threat of it being broken. And shortly it was, and with another intimate name.

'So nice to see old Richard again,' Sir William said. 'I don't think I've seen him since Sebastian died.'

A sentence loaded indeed. My past six months life's history was encapsulated in those two names.

'Seems to have aged a bit, I thought,' Lady Mayford said.

I felt duty-bound to make some contribution, since Richard was presumably, in their eyes, my friend.

'D'you think so?' I said. I had to be non-committal.

'These bachelors,' Lady Mayford laughed.

I don't know why she laughed, but I saw it as a clue of sorts. There would be no Mrs Richard to contend with, and that narrowed the field of investigation a little. I laughed a little too, without knowing the reason, but in order not to feel out of things.

'Are you married, Mr Wakefield?' Lady Mayford asked.

'Yes,' I said, almost too quickly perhaps, but I sensed her view that not to be married was unrespectable, and I wanted to please and to prove worthy of a lift in their Rolls. 'My wife's in hospital actually,' I said. 'She's just had a baby. Our first.'

'Congratulations old boy.' Sir William patted my knee. 'A son and heir?'

I nodded.

'Has he a name?' Lady Wayford asked.

'Luke. Like me,' I said.

'That's as it should be,' Sir William said, and he sighed with satisfaction.

The car was slowing down and I was glad of it. I had voluntarily entered very deep waters indeed, and it was a relief to have sight of shore. We had pulled into a cul-de-sac, one of the many that skirt the heath extension. It was already filled with cars, but miraculously a space appeared, as I suspect it always does for a Rolls, as if by divine right, and we beached smoothly into the kerb. I knew how to behave myself, so I made no attempt to open the door. But Sir William leaned over and lowered the handle, and as the door opened, the chauffeur held it on the other side. I allowed Lady Mayford to alight, and then, at Sir William's insistence, I followed myself.

We walked singly up the drive of the house, myself keeping to the rear to hide my trembling. For indeed, I was sick with apprehension and excitement. With sideways glances I cased the drive, planning the most strategic getaway, should escape prove necessary. I noted the many bushes that would do for concealment and the vast open lawn that lay behind. We were nearing the door of the house and I prayed that old Irish was well out of the way. So it was with a measure of relief that I viewed a tall butler in short white coat and trousers, who was doing for door-man. He ushered us inside. The drawing-room was already crowded with people in a mood of post-memorial hilarity. I caught sight of Richard straightway, and he of me, and he made his way towards me. Then my mouth fell open. Not at the thought of his so eager approach but that I had seen something on the drawing-room wall. A portrait of a very beautiful woman. I stared at her. I knew that I knew her, as intimately as Sebastian. Richard reached my side, and he followed my gaze.

'Beautiful, isn't she?' he said.

I nodded, swallowing. Was it Marion? In view of the story I intended to give Richard, I could hardly fail to recognise a so-called childhood friend. So I dared not ask who was the sitter. But Richard obliged.

'Marion,' he said, almost to himself. 'Just after she and Sebastian were married.'

I turned from the picture and faced him. I needed to see his face, to view in infinite detail his reaction to what I was about to say. He must have felt me looking at him, for he turned too, and looked me in the eye. I felt like a photographer whose sitter had suddenly achieved perfection. And I clicked the shutter.

'I know,' I said, measuring every syllable. 'I knew her in her Merthyr days. We were children together.'

I watched him pale, and so closely did I watch, that the colouring seemed to wash over his face in slow motion, beginning on his cheek, and spreading upwards and down, with such menace in its motion that I expected his face to spurt with white blood. I refrained from putting out an arm to support him. In that moment, I knew with absolute certainty that his hands, too, were smeared with Marion's blood. I noticed how he pulled himself together. It was a particularly visual performance. He straightened his shoulders, tossed back his hair, and took my arm.

'Did you really?' he said. 'We must talk about her. What was she like when she was a child? She never introduced Sebastian to her friends. That's why we haven't met, I suppose. Still, it's never too late. Come, let's get some champers.'

He had obviously regained his composure, and his grip on my arm was firm but friendly. He paused by a moving tray to collect two glasses of champagne.

'Let's go into the garden,' he said. 'There are not so many people out there.'

Then fear struck me. He meant to take me to a quiet place, and there, with little scruple, do me in. I was a deeply inconvenient piece of evidence.

'It's a bit chilly,' I said, my voice quivering with fear, which I hoped he'd take for cold. 'Let's stay here.'

'As you wish,' he said, then he guided me to the corner of the room and two small armchairs.

'Is this all right?' he asked, with utmost concern.

I nodded and he relinquished my arm. But I felt no freedom in it for, as we sat down together, facing one another, I felt that I was his prisoner, and a target for an affectionate but ruthless grilling.

CHAPTER ELEVEN

It must be abundantly clear by now that I am a man incessantly dogged by feelings of guilt, though pure and utter innocence trails in my wake. And it was such feelings that flooded me as I sat there with Richard, my glass raised in a trembling hand.

'Let's drink to Marion,' Richard was saying.

'To Marion,' I echoed. Then, 'Where is she?' I asked. 'I rather expected she might be here.'

'Oh, didn't you know?' he said, and I watched his face very carefully. 'She left. Went off about a year ago. Sebastian was broken. No-one knows where she is.'

His natural colour had returned to his face, and I noticed that he held his glass in a firm and steady hand. What a crass and consummate nerve the man had, I thought. Now that Sebastian was dead, he was the only person in the world who knew exactly where poor Marion was, while I had only a general idea of the location.

'Gone?' I said. 'But where? Did she go back to Merthyr?'

Richard shrugged. 'Maybe,' he said. 'When she first went, Sebastian made enquiries in all the likely places. He even employed a private detective. Then gradually he lost heart for it, and he let her be.'

They were a pair of hardened criminals, I thought, who had actually had the gall to employ a detective to look for one whom they had killed and buried.

'What about her mother?' I asked, shooting into the dark. 'Is she still alive?'

'Excuse me, Richard.' A man made his way towards us through the crowd. 'But Ted is desperate for your help. He's trying to shake off that old codger.'

Richard rose. 'I'll be back,' he said, and he left me with the fate of Marion's mother hanging in the air. I was very confused. There were so many questions that I needed to ask, but I had to fashion them very carefully in case I betrayed my ignorance of Marion and whatever family she possessed. It's true I had been but once to Merthyr, but what little I knew about that one-eyed town was at least first-hand, unlike my knowledge of Marion that had been sieved through more than one agency. I watched Richard as he prised the old codger away from Ted, and guided him to a crowd of people near the door. He kept looking back in my direction, and very soon he made his way towards me, hiding his haste, I thought, as if he were loathe to leave me alone and prey to others' questionings. And well he might be, I thought, for I had many beans to spill.

He took my arm again. 'I have to leave,' he said. 'I have an appointment in town. Can I give you a lift?' he asked. 'We can talk on the way.'

Perhaps I only imagined a slight pressure on my arm. 'I live in Regent's Park,' I said.

'I'll drop you.' He finished his champagne in a gulp and I followed him. On the way to the door, I paused to look at Marion's portrait once more. I needed to memorise every detail, her face, her colouring, the texture of her hair and skin. Richard could well grill me on those details at any time. He dawdled at my side.

'When did you last see her?' he said.

'I ran into her about eighteen months ago. In an art gallery. Sebastian was with her. I'd not met him before. I read in *The Times* that he died. But I haven't seen Marion since that time.'

I felt him staring at me, and I wondered whether it was advisable to drive with him. I waited until we reached the carriage-way.

'I think I'll walk,' I said, as we approached his car. 'I've a friend not far from here. I'll drop in on my way home.'

'As you wish,' Richard said. 'But we should meet again. Come to dinner next week.'

I hesitated. I would have felt safer on home ground. 'Why don't you come to me?' I said. I recalled my living-room bell that rang direct to the porter's lodge. If there were trouble, the porter would be at my door in a trice. Besides, I was proud of my penthouse, and I wished this Richard to know that poor Marion had had substantial friends.

'Thursday,' I said. I handed him my card. He looked at it with undisguised curiosity.

'I'll be glad to,' he said.

'Eight o'clock. Don't dress,' I added. 'Informal. Just the two of us.' Was I asking for trouble, I wondered. Yet there was no discovery without risk, and I made a mental note to check that the porter's bell was in working order.

He got into his car, and waited until I'd started to walk down the drive. I knew that he was going to make sure that I was leaving. He did not want me scattering my Marion tit-bits about Uncle Ted's drawing-rooms. So I assured him of my leave-taking by walking down the drive at a swift pace, and turning determinedly into the main road. After a while, I was able to wave to him as he drove by in his car. When he was out of sight, I sat on the wall of one of the houses and considered what I had done. It did not take me long. It seemed to me that each event of that day had led me with utmost logic into the lion's den. Not only had I followed Richard to that place but, in the latter stages, I had actually led him there. I had even chosen the location. He was to dine with me on Thursday.

I would have almost a week to make my preparations. I was willing enough, but I was ill-equipped. I was very short on clues. I needed to know a lot more about Marion, or I would fail Richard's inevitable cross-examination. And to pass that, I needed another source of information. Once again I recalled the portrait as an exercise in memory and, as I did so, I realised where my next clue lay. It was without doubt in the artistic hands of the man, or possibly the woman, who had painted her. It was an obvious deduction, and I turned my delighted steps back to the house. I had no difficulty in re-entry. The front door was open wide. The butler had obviously given up on his porter duties, and was fully employed in re-filling glasses for endless Marion-toasts, not my poor Marion, but theirs.

I took a glass from a passing tray, and stole over to the portrait. Then furtively I lifted my glass to the woman who was the object of my crusade. While doing so, I peered closely round the inner edges of the frame, seeking a signature. There was nothing. But on the lower half of the gilt frame I did notice the scratched remains of a red sticker that had not been wholly removed. A sign that indicated that, at some time, the picture had hung in an exhibition, and had been sold from a gallery. It was a clue of sorts though I did not know what I could make of it. I deeply regretted the lack of signature. I suspected that it was inscribed somewhere on the back of the canvas, but it would have been inappropriate, in this gathering and with the status of gate-crasher at that, to unhook it from the wall. I lowered my glass and, as I did so, I heard a voice beside me.

'A beautiful painting, isn't it?'

The voice was familiar and pleasantly so, and I turned to find that old be-ribboned codger, who had clearly run out of listeners and was now bent on bending my ear.

'Yes,' I said. 'It is beautiful. Who painted it, d'you know?'

'Richard, of course,' he said. 'Doesn't do much of it now. Too busy with his collections. Pity.'

I digested the information, and I saw another clue come to grief. For Richard was an untappable source for Marion information, since he probably expected exactly that from me. I was about to ask the old codger if he knew the sitter, but he was well on his way into a story of a leave he had spent in Paris with old Alistair, his comrade-in-arms. I think the story must have been triggered by our talk of painters, for his tale took place on the Left Bank, and involved an artist's model. I was listening with only half an ear, but I watched as his pale blue eyes moistened with memory and loving.

'Oh, we had a great time together, Alistair and I,' he was saying. How he must have hated the elder Mrs Marion Firbank, I thought, that she had so come between himself and his friend. It was no wonder he gave her such short shrift at her memorial. For him, she had died many many years too late. He was staring right past me into the far distance, no doubt viewing L'Eglise de Sacré Coeur across the Seine, so he did not notice me slipping from his side and making my way out of the house.

As I walked down the drive, I pondered over my latest tit-bit. Richard had painted Marion's portrait. My earlier suspicions that he and Marion had had an affair, were now confirmed. According to the letters, Marion had been hurtful to Richard, but possibly that was only a ruse to put Sebastian off the scent. In time Sebastian had discovered the treachery and she had paid for it with her life. In the light of this reasoning, I had to accept that Richard had had nothing to do with the murder, that he genuinely thought she had upped and gone, and that, apart from adultery, he was as innocent as I, and with this thought I warmed to him and I began to look forward to our dinner engagement. If what I surmised was the truth, then Marion's absence must hurt him deeply. He had loved her. Of that I was sure. The trust between sitter and painter was clearly evident on the canvas. And therefore the love, too. Perhaps I would confide in him, I thought. I would break the news very gently. I would tell him that she whom he loved was dead, and by his friend's hand. Then I would have to tell him how I knew, by what illicit manner I had come by my information. And he would understand, and I would enlist him under my Wimbledon banner, and together we would crusade. Richard would be my friend as once he had been Sebastian's. I could hardly contain my excitement. I walked to the main street and I found a cab, and on my way home I pondered on the menu for our dinner à deux. By the time I reached my apartment, I had decided on three courses together with the wines that would accompany them. I intended to make it a simple affair, for ostentation is a pit-fall of the nouveau riche, and I was at pains to avoid it. I had decided on a salmon mousse as an hors d'oeuvre, with a chilled Chablis to escort it. I would follow that with a boeuf-en-croute, one of my specialities, helped on its path by one of my finer clarets. To round off the meal, I had a perfect Chateau Yquem, and the dessert had to be fashioned in its favour. Raspberries, expensively out of season, but obtainable, and whipped cream. Coffee and armagnac would follow, by which time our friendship and conspiracy would be secure.

*

Apart from shopping and preparation, I spent much of the week in rehearsal. I collected the Firbank correspondence, and leaned the package of letters against a drawer of my open chiffonier, rather in the same position as I had originally found and purloined them from Sebastian's desk. Then I paced the room or sat at my dining-room table, fashioning my speeches according to my judgement of Richard's part in the affair. To this end, I had to rehearse two approaches, one for the assumption of his guilt, and the other of his innocence. I found the latter far more pleasant for I knew it would lead to friendship and crusade, so I tended to give it a greater rehearsal. I did not want to think of Richard as an accomplice in crime, but nonetheless I had to prepare myself for such an eventuality. And it was on this that I now concentrated. I anticipated his grilling. He would ask me to describe Marion as a child, and to this end I would reduce the portrait to childish proportions. I would invent our school escapades, and draw on my scanty knowledge of Merthyr to place them in an acceptable setting. I had met Sebastian only once, and then fleetingly, so I was entitled to know him not at all. But what happened, I would ask him, to Marion's mother, brother, younger sister? I would throw this random kin into the kitty and see what Richard would make of it. If he were to plead ignorance of all this, as far I was concerned he was guilty, for it would certainly not be in his interest to lead me to those who might question Marion's disappearance. If, on the other hand, he would give me names, then together we could set out on a voyage of discovery.

It was a happy week and contained not one Connie-thought, and would have continued to do so, had I not received a postcard on the very morning of my dinner-date with Richard. It fell on top of my *Times*, and could have been read from where I stood, for it had no envelope or fold of any kind. My eye had caught the name of Connie, which had at first seemed strange to me, so remote had she become since my Richard-encounter. But at that moment I felt the old frenzy come upon me. I picked up the card, intending to give it no production, and read it straightway.

Connie Andrews and Stephanie Millar announce the arrival of their son, Luke Adrian. Born October 12th, 1982.

My name and address were written on the back of the card. Connie's sense of timing never failed. I tried not to feel despondent, but once again I was close to tears. Not for Connie or Stephanie or Adrian, which latter was probably the name of Stephanie's cock-robbed husband, but for that Luke who belonged to me and would never be mine. I looked at the postmark. Hounslow. The franking for London Airport. And I sat there and then on the floor of my hall, and I wept. I knew that I would have to pull myself together. There was much to

148

be done before Richard's arrival. I would not even have time for my daily dose of Death in *The Times*. But despite all the chores to be done, I could not resist it, for, as is already known, I am an addict in that quarter. I remained sitting on the floor, and I turned to the appropriate page. The Birth Column, with indisputable logic, preceded that of Death, and one can hardly miss scanning it until the beginning of the wanted list comes into view. And as if my card were not enough, I saw its reprint, bold as brass in the columns of *The Times*. It was the first of the list, and thus unmissable. *Andrews Millar*, with not even a hyphen for singularity. The name 'Luke' screamed off the page, and I was reduced to tears once more. But soon the tears turned to anger, and I rose from the floor and rampaged about my kitchen, venting my spleen on the bleeding piece of fillet that lay on the marble slab. To my raving eye it looked unnervingly like Connie. I picked it up, taking care first to wrap it in a tea-towel, and I beat it with all my strength on the tiled kitchen floor. After a while of beating, it struck me forcibly that I was in the process of ruining my dinner, and I swore that, if the fillet were damaged in any way, I would fly to Melbourne and kill Connie. I unwrapped the meat carefully from its cloth, and I held it at arm's length and I viewed it. Almost any cut of beef, with the exception of fillet, could do with a little bit of tenderising. But this *was* fillet, and I had gilded the lily. It hung mournfully from my fingers with such an offended look that I had to turn my face away. I laid it on the slab and soothed it as best I could, stroking it along its grain. I willed it to breathe again and to regain its pristine bloom, but it looked as if it would never forgive me. I picked up Connie's card and tore it into little pieces over the marble slab. It was by way of a meek apology. Then I left the kitchen and poured myself a large whiskey to steady my nerves.

I had to pull myself together. That night's dinner might well prove the last station of my crusade, which would lead either to victory or defeat of the most humiliating kind. I dared not think of the latter, for that spelt out a future of Connie-hate and days of idleness to feed it. I downed my whiskey and returned to the kitchen, and, without looking at the fillet, I made a start on the croute. As time passed, I calmed a little – there is nothing like cooking to cast a reasonable perspective on all things – and by the time the croute was prepared, spread with a fine duck paté and a sprinkle of mushrooms, I was ready to take a second glass of whiskey to consolidate my good temper. This I drank in the kitchen, while I prepared the mousse. When all was done, I was forced to take another look at the fillet which I had scrupulously avoided during my preparations. It had that battered-wife look, whose bruising only seemed to highlight the erstwhile beauty. The mien was unforgiving, but with the promise that it would come back for more. But that I could not allow, so I picked it up gently and laid it like a babe on the oven grill. It looked lifeless enough, fit for burial, and I gave it a gentle send-off at number seven sealing heat. I sipped again at my whiskey, for at the sight of the fillet my good temper had slipped a little, and, thus fortified, I set about to lay my table. I made use of all my lavish appointments of napery and silver. I intended, for poor Marion's sake, to make a good impression. Then I returned to the kitchen and, without looking, I took the fillet from the oven. To know that someone is dead is one thing; to insist on seeing the body is quite another. That is an act of masochism that I can do without. I laid it blindly on the croute, and quickly fastened the pastry around it. Shrouded, it was viewable, and even pleasing on the eye. I took the prepared pastry roses and laid them symmetrically along the spine. Then I pierced it in unseen places, and brushed the whole with yolk of egg. I was more than satisfied with its appearance and, to celebrate my small culinary success, I poured myself another whiskey.

Now all was prepared and the long afternoon stretched before me, and threatened to unnerve me entire. For I had not wholly shaken off my fear of Richard's visit, and the possibility that I, with all my inconvenient knowledge, was a suitable case for disposal. Then I remembered my emergency bell, which safety-valve had escaped my mind in the past few days. I knelt down and located it under the carpet. It was well off-range from the dining-table, at which place we would already be seated, I thought, when and if danger threatened. So I moved the table so that the bell would lie almost under my foot where I would be seated at dinner. I had decided to place Richard opposite me with his back to the dining-room door. For I myself do not feel safe with my back to anything, unless it is for the express purpose of erasing the pins and needles.

Otherwise, I like to have an all-round view of things. When I'd moved the table, I settled myself in my chair and, with my foot, I gingerly sought out the bump under the carpet. But still I was not satisfied. I wanted to make sure that it worked. I had used it only once before, and that a long time ago. And by accident as well. I had only recently moved into my apartment. It was early morning, shortly after I'd received one of Connie's glad-you're-not-here postcards. It was a Tuesday, my post-office day, and it cast an early cloud on what promised to be my only adventure of the week. I was so incensed, that, as was my wont in such states, I reached for the bottle, and drank myself into a stupor. I was sitting at the dining-room table at the time, or rather rolling on it, and I must have slumped to the floor and landed on the bell, for a great and awesome ringing suddenly sobered me. Within seconds, the porter was at my door, concerned and questioning. I don't remember what cock and bull story I gave him, but I recall his incredulous look, and I am sure that his suspicions of me dated from that time. It was all Connie's fault, as are most things since she left me. But all that was a long time ago, and it was possible that the bell had rusted and atrophied from want of use. I had to test it and take the consequences.

But first I rehearsed what I would say to my porter. My excuse would be simple, and laced with ample apology. I was moving furniture, I would say, and I had entirely forgotten that the bell was there. But first I went to my bathroom to rinse my mouth with peppermint water. The lingering smell of whiskey on my breath would not impress the porter at this time of day. That done, I settled myself down and imagined that Richard was facing me.

'You know too much for your own good,' I heard him say, 'and I am disposed to get rid of you.'

He spoke politely, sipping his Chablis/claret/Yquem between his words. I nudged my trembling shoe towards the bump, placed it bull's-eye, and pressed for all I was worth. Not a sound. The silence screamed in the room. I pressed again and again, and at all angles, thinking there might be a short wire inside. But there was no sound, only the squeak of my shoe at its abortive fumblings. Then I did hear a noise, and a ringing one at that. But it did not come from underneath the floor, and I stood up and listened as my front door bell pealed through the flat with its insistent ringing.

Then I heard a voice.

'Mr Wakefield. Mr Wakefield.'

And I wondered what on earth was the matter. I went to the door. 'Who is it?' I shouted through the panel.

'The porter.'

'What d'you want?' I shouted.

'What do *I* want,' came the reply. 'It's you who rang.'

I opened the door. 'Rang what?' I said.

'The alarm.' He was panting on the threshold.

'I didn't hear anything,' I said, with utmost honesty.

'It almost blew me out of my lodge.'

I asked him to come in. 'Then you heard it for both of us. I'm sorry, but I was moving the table and I must have stepped on it. But I heard nothing. Could you look at it?'

I lifted the carpet and he got down on his knees. He fiddled with the contraption and very quickly spotted the loose wire. 'Fix that in a jiffy,' he said. He switched off the mains and got to work with my screw-driver. Then he tested it. It screamed through the flat.

'That ought to call the fire-brigade,' he laughed.

But the whole business worried me. If indeed I needed his help, would he not regard it as another false alarm of the cry-wolf kind? Yet how could I tell him I expected trouble that very evening, without risking his advice to take a short break on the south coast?

'You never know when I might need it,' I said airily. 'Why, I might really need it later on today.' I laughed, a little too heartily, I realised, for I saw his eyebrow leap. 'You never know,' I added wearily, but already I saw him that evening sitting in his lodge ignoring my alarm and even switching it off in his irritation.

'I'll have you fired,' I said.

'Pardon, Mr Wakefield?'

'I'm so sorry,' I mumbled. 'I was rehearsing a part in a play. Amateur dramatics,' I explained. 'I play the part of a shop-steward.' My thespian sights were painfully low, but I marvelled at my invention. But the porter seemed unimpressed and his second eyebrow now joined the first in take-off. I knew he was definitely seeing me off to the south coast.

He was making his way tentatively towards the front door, and I knew with certainty that there could be no hope of rescue from his lodge. And now, for the first time since I had mounted my crusade, I began to resent the object of my campaign. I wish that I had never heard of Marion, and that Richard was a new-found friend who was coming to dine, and with whom I could tour London and abroad, and with whose accompanying signature I would send postcards to Melbourne from exotic parts. There were a million other things to talk about besides Marion Firbank, yet I had to acknowledge that talk of her was the sole object of his coming.

I thought I might as well fill in the time with a final rehearsal of my Marion-friendship. But for that I needed a drink. The whiskey bottle was almost empty. I began to wonder who had been at my booze. I suspected the porter. He had certainly been eager to make his getaway. I opened another bottle and resolved to challenge the porter on the following day. But the thought of him only served to remind me of how indifferent he would be to my alarm, and I considered seeking other forms of defending myself should Richard be bent on my destruction.

I thought a heavy object of sorts would fit the bill, and to that end I scanned my living-room for something suitable. I had no fireplace so there was no poker, that convenient weapon for ladies in Hollywood films. The only possibility was the two-foot granite door-stopper which had taken two muscle-removal men to lift. From where I stood I ransacked my bedrooms, my two bathrooms and my study. You may well wonder why I have a study. I have occasionally wondered at it, too, and have come to the conclusion that it is only people who don't study who need a room not to do it in.

In all these rooms, I could see nothing that would suit my purpose. The kitchen was my last resort. I had no doubt that I would find something there, but I was reluctant to avail myself of its resources for, by the very nature of their location, they are bound to be somewhat plebeian, and that is not my style, even though I may be fighting for my life. But I couldn't afford to be choosy. In any case, I could wield an onion-grater with some élan if called upon to do so. I rifled the drawers and cupboards and, in the last cupboard under the sink, I found what I was seeking.

Some years ago, having chanced upon a Chinese restaurant, I grew enamoured of their food, and I had taken myself to an emporium and equipped my kitchen with all manner of bamboo steamers, woks and choppers, and together with a cookery book I besported myself for many weeks in experiment of Chinese cuisine. I soon tired of it, however, for Chinese is an impossible method of cooking for one. It's like going alone to Glyndebourne. Moreover, every time I used the chopper, and in Chinese cooking that is a frequent exercise, I could not help but think of Connie, and you know by now where such thoughts lead. So I had abandoned my oriental adventure, but the wok and the bamboo and the chopper were put aside for a rainy day. And such a day, I thought, was now. I grasped the handle of the chopper and withdrew it from its wooden cradle. It was a rather mighty affair, that could, if held at a certain angle, break your wrist in two. But I was adept at its handling, at least for the chopping of vegetables and meat, and a head is meat of a kind. I shuddered at the thought. I looked at the chopper with a certain nostalgia, for its use in its time had brought me great pleasure. Now it would have to serve some other purpose, a purpose which I am sure its kind had often served, way beyond Chinese kitchens, in the streets and hide-outs of gangster-land anywhere.

But a drawing-room? That was indeed a problem. Where on earth in a penthouse drawing-room could one position a Chinese chopper and hope that it might pass as part of the furnishings? I took it into my living-room, and looked about me. I considered the glass book-shelf. An African vase stood next to an empty silver salver, which reflected the stern glass of a Georgian decanter. Very posh. It struck me that a chopper on that shelf would be so out of place that it might pass as an endearing piece of eccentricity, and I chose that for its setting. But I thought I must camouflage it a little. Not the chopper itself, but its sturdy wooden handle. For the blade shone like a moonbeam, and as innocently too. Indeed the blade might well pass as a mirror, and through that instrument that might shortly dismember it, Richard might well take a fleeting glance at his head. But all this was theory, for I could not imagine lifting the chopper, leave alone wielding it, unless I could totally convince myself that Richard's head was a shallot or a chicken wing. But even for theory one must be prepared. So I took a deep vase and planted the handle inside it. Around it I arranged three or four chrysanthemums. The whole ensemble looked like an off-day Dali. I feared it might become a conversation piece, but I would have to take that risk. I would simply claim that I thought it was art, and to hell with Richard's connoisseurship.

Now everything was ready. The dinner was set for cooking, the table was laid, the drinks were at the ready, the coffee-tray prepared. Yet I had never felt so unarmed, so unrehearsed, so vulnerable. There were still some hours to go before Richard would arrive, and I decided to have a bath, for I can think of no better way of killing time. This I did, but though I dallied and wallowed in foam, when all was done, there were still some hours till evening. I was tired too, so I decided on a nap, another form of tide-over. It would refresh me too, I thought. But day-sleep for me had always been difficult unless I take a little alcohol to help me on my way. I went to the bottle, taking care not to pour too much. But I failed to take into account my heated post-bath state, a condition, I am told, that is very susceptible to alcohol. Well, one cannot win them all, all of the time. I staggered to my bed. I remember laying myself down, and having just about enough strength to lift my feet onto the bed, and, like Alice, I went through the looking-glass, though that mirror reflected only fruit and veg and a hint of poor Marion at the bottom of the pile. I was unconscious of the gathering dark, or how my hall clock trembled on the stroke of eight. But a bell made me stir, and its repetition stirred me again. I awoke suddenly, conscious only of a raging thirst, and then, very slowly, I gathered my wits about me. The bell rang once more, and I ran into the hall as the clock struck eight. Richard, if nothing else, was punctual. I reached for my Chinese silk dressing-gown, and ran to my answer-phone. As I pressed the button, I saw Richard's face superbly framed on the screen.

'Hullo,' I said.

'Richard.'

'Come up. It's the penthouse.'

I put aside all thought of suiting myself. Indeed, had I given my manner of dressing a thought, I might well have decided on my silk dressing-gown, for it was lush and rich, and deeply idle, and could not fail to make an impression. I tidied my hair and knotted the belt of my robe. I was glad he had thus woken me, for it allowed me no time for further nervous anticipation. I heard the lift doors open. I was too excited to wait for his ring so I opened the door wide to welcome him. He looked at me with pleasurable astonishment.

'Already?' he said, laughing.

I was not quite sure what he meant. Or perhaps I was, and I was too raw to accommodate his meaning, so I laughed with him, hoping that it would do.

'Come in,' I said. 'I fell asleep and your bell woke me. I'll go and change.'

'No, please,' he said, taking my arm. I let it lie there as I led him into the sitting-room.

'That's a beautiful robe, and absolutely suits this apartment.'

I led him to my Parker-Knoll, and I wondered when he was going to release my arm. Then the thought crossed my mind that, that evening, Marion would prove the least of my problems. But why did his touch so excite me?

'Scotch?' I asked.

'Lovely,' he said.

He slipped his arm out of mine but its print seared my skin.

I poured him a generous Waterford, then I sidled over towards the shelf, and removed my pathetic arsenal. I knew with some relief that I would not need it. I took it into the kitchen, murmuring some excuse of forgetfulness. Then I lit the oven to get the croute going, set the timer and joined Richard in a Waterford glass.

'What a beautiful apartment,' he said.

'I'm glad you like it,' and indeed I was, and no longer on poor Marion's behalf. It occurred to me that we might well pass the entire evening without mention of her name.

CHAPTER TWELVE

But I was wrong and very quickly proved to be so. For he raised his glass.

'To Marion,' he said, 'and to her good health, wherever she may be.'

I could have told him exactly where she was, more or less, given a tree or two, and added, too, that she was far beyond toasting, either by whiskey or by fire.

'I can't understand that no-one knows where she is. You don't think anything has happened to her, do you?' I asked.

'Like what?'

I noticed that Richard was on his guard, and I began to regret the hasty removal of my weaponry. 'She may be ill,' I said. Then I paused and averted his glance. 'Or worse.'

'We would have heard, I think,' Richard said. 'Bad news has no travel problems.'

In my mind I recapped what he had said, and all of it was equally open to the verdict of guilty or innocent.

'Tell me about her,' he said. 'What was she like as a child?'

Here it was, the first question and, despite all my rehearsal, my tongue dried. I tried to recall that portrait on Auntie Chrissie's wall, but it was blurred beyond definition. I grasped frantically at the memory of that one-horse town in the valley, but nothing suggested to me the Marion whom I knew so intimately and whom I had never known. 'She was full of fun,' I said, off the top of my head. I tried to recall my own schooldays, but there was little fun in them. But I placed Marion in our playground in the midst of all the bullies who were picking on me, and Marion came to my rescue, and loosened my tongue. And opened my eyes, too, to the portrait on Aunt Chrissie's wall. 'She had a shock of red hair,' I said, 'and she was always in trouble. Bit of a tomboy too. Took on all the bullies. She was a fighter. And a protector. Sort of person who'd go on crusades.' I was running away with myself, I thought, and I reined myself in a little to curb my enthusiasm. Richard was smiling all the while. His lip curled slightly, with the edge of suspicion, perhaps, or it could have been delight.

'How come you were living in Wales?' he asked.

A fair enough question. 'That's where I was born,' I said, without hesitation. 'In Merthyr.' I prayed he would not ask me for a Welsh accent. 'My father was a pit-foreman,' I went on. I was pleased with that little invention. It was the first time in my life I'd had the opportunity to give my father a little dignity. 'They loved him down at the pit,' I went on. 'The men were his friends. Like Marion's father. Forgotten his name now. Jenkins, was it?' Another random shot.

Richard shrugged. 'I never knew. I don't think Sebastian knew either.'

'But it must be on the marriage certificate,' I said.

He smiled again. That strange half-suspicious smile. 'I suppose so. But Sebastian never mentioned it. It's not the sort of thing that anyone needs to know.'

Not much, I thought, with Andrews preying on my mind. But I let it pass. I was disappointed. Marion's maiden name was crucial to any search of her family. But I needed a rest from his questions and I rose and topped up his glass. Then I passed him a silver dish of salted almonds, and perhaps I only imagined that he touched my fingers ever so lightly as I drew the dish away.

'Hungry?' I said, and I wondered why my voice was squeaking.

He nodded.

'Excuse me,' I said, 'I must check on the oven.'

'D'you need any help?'

'No. It's all ready. I won't be long.' I needed to be alone, to collect the thoughts I ought to be thinking, and those feelings I ought not to feel.

I leaned over the marble slab in the kitchen. I was glad of the respite. But I didn't want to think, so I busied myself with the salmon mousse, and took the chablis from the fridge. But I couldn't not think, for I knew that something very strange was stirring. I didn't know whether it was dangerous or safe, or even whether it was good or bad, but I knew without doubt that it thrilled me in a way that I had never known before. I thought perhaps it might all be a dream, and that I was still in bed, and that Richard had not yet arrived. And so to confirm its truth, I called out his name, and the very sound of it from my lips made me tremble. He did not answer, but instead appeared at the kitchen door.

'I suspect you're a very good cook,' he said.

'I like cooking,' I said, 'especially for friends.' Then I regretted that word. 'Company' would have done just as well.

'Did you see a lot of Marion when she was married?' I asked.

I don't know why I myself volunteered the Marion subject that I wished to avoid. Perhaps I feared that Richard might broach another subject that I would be even more unqualified to handle than that of Marion.

'Yes. I saw a lot of her,' he was saying. 'Sebastian had been my close friend for many years. But let's not talk about Marion,' he said.

I busied myself with the mousse that had already been amply busied with, and the toast that was amply toasted, and I took it into the dining-room. I asked Richard to bring the wine, and we settled ourselves for the first course. I felt the need for silence and, if not that, then some small chit-chat of absolute trivia, and I found it strange that I, whose life was orchestrated with silences and nothings, should now have appetite for just that style of score.

'I hope it's chilled enough,' I said, as I poured the Chablis, knowing that it was chilled perfectly to a turn.

'I wait on you,' he said, raising his glass.

I hoped he wasn't going to toast Marion again in Pavlovian response to each glass, because I had a number of wines to taste that evening. But instead, he said something else, and I wasn't sure whether I would have preferred Marion.

'To us,' he said, 'and to our friendship.'

I could not bring myself to echo him, because it would have sounded too like commitment, so I simply smiled and sipped, and pronounced the wine chilled enough.

I served the mousse and waited for compliment. But Richard managed to sample it entire without comment. I concluded that he himself was no mean cook, and there is no domaine more riddled with envy than that of haute cuisine. I was confident that this was the only area in my life in which I was no failure; that, and possibly pilfering. And I took his silence as the greatest compliment. But then it came.

'I think that was the greatest mousse I have ever tasted,' he said. 'The acid test of a mousse is its aftertaste, and I needed to finish it before passing judgement.'

Now I myself am a very simple man. I like to cook, eat, and cook again. I see no point in pre- or post-mortems. It is the same with wine. You chambré, chill or decant, and then you drink, and when it is finished, you start all over again, and the less said about the whole process, the better. But I was prepared to allow that sort of talk from Richard because at least it kept us off Marion for a while. But whenever I thought of Marion, it was as if some telepathic communication brought her to Richard's tongue.

'Marion was a wonderful cook,' he said.

'Were they happy together?' I asked.

'Very,' he said. 'As long as it lasted.'

I didn't want to go into its dénouement. Its reasons were already known to me from the letters. Colonisation and obesity, grounds enough for divorce, but hardly enough for murder. And, to steer away from the subject, I collected the hors d'oeuvre plates and took them to the kitchen. It was no surprise that Richard followed me.

'I'm fascinated about you and Marion,' he said.

'Why?' I almost dropped the fillet as I drew it from the oven.

'I've never met anyone who knew Marion. Even while she was with Sebastian.'

I wanted to ask him about the Webbs and the Martins and all that Mirabelle crowd to whom Sebastian was wont to show her off. But I held my tongue, for such information came from my illegal letter-source.

'But they must have had friends,' I said. 'Didn't they go out at all?'

'Rarely,' he said. 'Marion was a home bird.'

Then I remembered Mrs Pearson next door, and how she had never seen a woman about the place.

'She was very fond of gardening, I remember,' I said. 'Did they have a garden?' I, too, could lay traps.

'Yes, but I don't think she ever used it. She must have changed a lot since you knew her.'

I wondered why Richard was insisting on Marion's invisibility. It made no sense to me. He couldn't prove that I had never known Marion. As far as he was concerned, she was my childhood friend.

'I saw very little of her after Merthyr,' I said, 'and then she was with Sebastian.' I hoped he'd let the matter rest there.

'How does that look?' I said, whipping the foil off the croute and slipping the meat onto a platter.

'Most impressive,' he said. 'Do you always cook like this?'

'Only for company,' I said. I wasn't going to let him know that I always dined alone.

'D'you have many friends?' he asked.

I was careful not to exaggerate. 'Not many,' I said, 'but those I have are very close.' I thought of Sandra and Alistair at the end of a tapped telephone line, and the newsagent and the porter and Mad Marion from Merthyr. I could muster no more.

'You're a loner, I think,' he said. 'Were you ever married?'

Another subject I could well do without. 'Once,' I said. 'But I left her. She's in Australia with my son. Went back to her mother.'

'Don't you miss your boy?'

'Yes, but I go there or he comes here. It works well enough.'

I laid some pieces of cress around the croute and gave the platter to Richard. I followed with the vegetables.

'You do live awfully well,' Richard said as he took his seat once more.

'We aim to please,' I said, and I couldn't imagine where such a phrase had come from. I had never used it before, and it smacked of flirtation and theatricality. It was a tone quite alien to me, and dangerously daring. I had availed myself of an idiom that belonged to a society totally different from my own, of a language that hinted of a twilight zone that I had never entered. But Richard must have known it well, for he stretched his arm across the table, and touched my hand with his. It was the gesture that clearly punctuated the phrase, and brought it to a stop.

I poured the claret, and stood to cut the croute. My hands were trembling.

'Come, come,' Richard said. 'Relax.'

'I'm fine,' I practically shouted at him, and I went on cutting the fillet, consoling myself with the thought that I was slicing Connie. When it was done, I said, 'Shall I serve you?' and again the alien phrase startled me. Richard's presence had clearly loosened my tongue on a vernacular which, though so seemingly foreign, managed to fall from my lips as if it were my mother tongue.

'I'd love that,' he said, and again it seemed an exact grammatical response. He looked at me all the while that I was serving, so that I had to look up and acknowledge him with a smile. It was a relief to start eating. This time, Richard took only a mouthful before passing judgement.

'It's exactly right. So difficult with a croute,' he said. 'To synchronise the ripeness of the pastry and the meat. It's a dish I never attempt. Much too precarious.'

I warmed to his admission of fallibility, a trait that has always attracted me.

'This is a beautiful apartment,' he said. 'But it lacks just one thing.'

'Yes?' I asked.

'Paintings. Not a single painting. Why is that?' he asked.

'I don't know much about art,' I said with utmost honesty. 'I wouldn't know what to buy.'

'It's not a question of knowing,' he said. 'You buy what pleases you.'

'I go to art galleries a lot,' I said, glad to put my erstwhile research to some use. I was anxious to prolong the discussion since it did not call into question my Marion acquaintanceship. 'D'you like painting?' I said. He was not supposed to know I knew he was a painter.

'It's my profession,' he said. 'Or used to be. I haven't painted since Sebastian died.'

'I'm sorry,' I said.

'Oh, it's nothing,' he said hurriedly. 'I paint portraits. That one of Marion is mine.'

'Really?' I feigned surprise. 'It's beautiful.'

'I painted all Sebastian's wives,' he said.

My fork was midway between my plate and my mouth, and it stopped of its own accord. I watched the pastry peel from the meat and drop back onto the plate. I swear its fall took a minute or two, and I could not take my eyes off it. When it landed it fell to the echo of Richard's last words.

'*All* his wives?' I said. My fork hovered mid-air.

'Marion was Sebastian's third wife.'

'What happened to them all?' My voice was that of a prosecutor.

'They left.'

'Disappeared?' I could not resist it.

'In a manner of speaking, I suppose.'

I let it lie. In the space of a second, my single crusade had tripled. And of two of them I didn't even know the name. And were they all Wimbledon-buried? Or had Sebastian varied his bone-yards? After all, his theme of murder was powerful enough to sustain abundant variations. And did he write to them too, poor X and poor Y? And did they too respond from the grave? Sebastian's postage bill must have been astronomical. I had by now lost all appetite for my fillet, but I noticed how Richard ate heartily, and his undiminished appetite convinced me once again that he was a criminal and a hardened one at that. Again I regretted the removal of my small arsenal and I thought I might nip into the kitchen on some pretext and retrieve it. But I could not leave the table while Richard was still eating. I worked on my fillet once more, but it was hard to shut my eyes to those three poor wandering ghosts. It was as if they were hovering in my living-room, pleading me for their peace. I recalled that the two unknowns had sat for Richard's portraiture, and I wondered whether one day he would have the gall to show them to me. And then, as if reading my thoughts, he said, 'You must let me cook for you soon, and I'll show you some of my work.'

I shivered inside. 'I'd like that,' I said, keeping my voice steady, but I was relieved, too, since with that invitation, he envisaged a future for me. He would not kill me this night. He would give me one of his cooked dinners first.

He finished his fillet and again complimented me. I rose to clear the plates and, as I expected, he followed me.

'What kind of man was Sebastian?' I asked. I don't know what prompted me to ask that question. Perhaps it was because conversation had seemed to flag a little since his off-hand announcement of Sebastian's philanderings. Or perhaps I thought that any clue to Sebastian's character might lead me to Marion, and to her poor sisters in limbo.

'He was a charmer,' Richard said, 'as you can imagine. He loved paintings. That's how we first met. He came to one of my exhibitions.'

'Where was that?' I asked, wondering whether he had shown in any of the galleries on my crusade round.

'The Waterloo,' he said, and I remembered it well, for it was in that very gallery that I had signed Sebastian's name in the visitors' book. I wondered what Richard's surname was, but now was hardly the time to ask. I hoped before leaving that he would give me his card.

'He was rather beautiful, too, I thought,' Richard was saying. 'Well, you met him. Didn't you think so?'

'I met him only fleetingly,' I said, not wishing to become involved in a discussion of Sebastian's features even though I knew them infinitely better than I knew Marion's. 'Marion merely introduced me,' I said. 'I was just talking to her.'

'What about?' he said. His tone was deliberately casual, as if he wished to mask his urgent need to know the subject of our conversation. He needed to know exactly how much I knew. But I would give him nothing.

'She told me she was happy,' I said, to put him off the scent, 'but we talked mainly about Merthyr and the old days.' I didn't want to talk any more about that fictitious meeting, so I took the bowl of raspberries out of the fridge, and handed it to him. He gave a final gasp at the luxury of it all, and turned towards the dining-room. I followed with the Yquem and the cream, and we resumed our meal.

The last course was eaten in comparative silence. I suppose we both had much to think about. I wondered about his next move as he was probably wondering about mine. I considered I held the trump card, since I had proof of at least one murder and circumstantial evidence of two more.

I suggested coffee and brandy around the fake log-fire and, like a dutiful dog, he followed me once more into the kitchen. We waited in silence, intent on the coffee as it dripped through the filter, both of us, I suspect, grateful for some spectacle, however trivial, that would obviate conversation for a while. But once by the fireside, with coffee, armagnac and cigars, words of a sort had to be exchanged. His eyes were wandering around the room.

'That's a beautiful piece,' he said, pointing to the African vase on the glass shelf, that erstwhile arms repository of mine. He rose and went towards it. 'Where did you get it?' he said.

'In Africa.' The lie had now become the norm for me. During the whole course of the evening, we had exchanged one falsity for another, and I saw no point now in veracity.

'Where about?' he said.

'The Congo,' I hazarded, shooting into the dark continent.

'I would have thought it more Southern Africa,' he said.

'Do have some more coffee,' I said. I wanted to bring him back to the table. I didn't feel safe with my back to him. He returned and I filled his cup. 'I'm so sorry,' I said, 'but did you want milk? I entirely forgot to ask.'

'Well frankly,' he said, 'I think I would prefer it white. Strong coffee keeps me awake.'

I rose to go to the kitchen and, as if from habit, I hovered for his shadow. But this time he did not follow me. I was glad of it, and I took my time in the kitchen while I poured the milk into a jug. I even did a little silent clearing up to prolong the period of what I considered reprieve. Then, in my time, I returned to the living-room. I don't know why, but I was surprised to find him in the same position in which I'd left him and I felt a surge of relief. I poured his coffee and I noticed that he drank it very quickly. I noted, too, that his brandy glass was empty. I had a strange feeling that he was in a hurry to take his leave. And suddenly I didn't want him to go. Those old forbidden feelings stirred in me once again, re-fuelled by his touch on my arm when he refused my offer of a further armagnac.

'No,' he said rising. 'I really must go. I've work tomorrow. It's been a wondrous evening,' he said, and next time it's my turn.'

He was making for the door, with undue haste, I thought, and with no offer of his card, or an arrangement for a further meeting.

'I'll phone you,' he said. 'Very soon,' and he touched my arm again and smiled. He opened the door himself, so anxious he seemed to go without formal leave-taking. Nevertheless, I took him out to the lift, and waited till it arrived at my floor.

Then he did an extraordinary thing. As the lift door opened, he bent forward, and very lightly kissed me on the cheek. My joy was unbounded. I was glad when the door closed, and he was out of sight of my boyish tremblings. I stood outside the lift for a while, unable to move. Then I steadied myself and returned to my apartment. His departure had been so swift that it took me some time to adjust to his absence. Then I sat in his chair, poured myself another brandy into his glass, and leaned back to savour the evening.

And as I did so, my eye caught the top of my chiffonier, and the glaring gap on its surface, and I understood with a certain horror why Richard had made such a swift getaway. The letters were gone. The Firbank correspondence had disappeared, filched in exactly the same way, and with exactly the same skill and nerve that I myself had appropriated them under the nose of Sebastian's Irish treasure.

I needed to go to the desk to confirm the dreadful vacancy, to understand that, once and for all, my crusade was at an end. But I could not rise from my chair. I had to accept that I no longer possessed a single shred of evidence of Marion's murder, leave alone that of Sebastian's other wives. I was left with only my memory which I knew would sooner or later fade in fantasy. In time the name Firbank would ring a distant bell, probably tolling from a south coast resort. I shuddered, and I knew that for the sake of my own sanity, whatever that meant, I could not give up my campaign. I knew that somewhere, there were three unclaimed bodies going begging. I knew, too, that one of their murderers was dead and beyond punishment. But I knew, with the same certainty, that an assassin was loose, and was lately in my drawing-room whence he had quickly stolen with the only evidence I held against him.

I had to see him again. But I had no idea of his address nor even of his second name. I could of course, go back to the Waterloo Gallery, and check on all the Richards who had shown there in its time. But that might be a long-winded route, and could, in view of my past palsied visit, involve me in certain embarrassment. A much shorter, and possibly more profitable route, seemed to me to be via Aunt Chrissie. I knew her address, and I had a tenuous means of access. I was a friend of Marion. I'd seen the portrait. I'd been impressed. Could I possibly look at it again? A fool-proof method of entrée, I thought, which dispensed with the need of a weary weather-forecast. With this resolve, I gathered the strength to rise from my chair. I did not need to ascertain the gap on my desk. A gap is a gap, and in such a state of negativity, there can be no illusion about it. I started to clear the table and, despite my fury with Richard, I could not help but recall him with affection and, as I did so, I felt that same tingling in my veins that his touch had sparked. I knew that he would be in touch with me soon, and that his reasons for doing so would be nothing to do with Marion and her poor sisters. This evening had clearly been an event in my life, a turning-point, I was sure, though into what labyrinth I could not as yet surmise.

★

The following morning, I awoke with renewed appetite for my crusade. I dressed in my memorial suit, checked the directory for Aunt Chrissie's address, and took a cab, my courage, and my unrehearsed entrance to Mrs Ewbank's drawing-room. It was quite a long journey, and I recognised some of the landmarks we had passed on the previous run. When I arrived, I paused at the end of the drive. As with all my hit and miss visits since embarking on my Marion crusade, I tried not to think of the sheer folly of my clue-seeking. For folly it was, and a madman's pursuit, but I was obsessed with my campaign, and now even more so since I had met Richard. So, having paused for I know not what, I practically sprinted up the drive and pressed the bell. After a short wait Aunt Chrissie herself opened the door and I was glad of it, for servants are an impediment to smooth entry. She smiled with polite non-recognition.

'My name is Luke Wakefield,' I said. 'I was here last week after the memorial to Mrs Firbank.'

'Oh yes,' she said, hovering for a further reason for my call.

'I saw a portrait,' I plodded on. 'Of Marion, Sebastian's wife. It's haunted me ever since,' I said, and not without a degree of honesty. 'I wondered if I could look at it again?'

'Of course,' she said, opening the door wide. 'I'm so glad you like it. It's one of the best portraits that Richard's ever done. Of course she was a beautiful subject.'

She led me into the drawing-room. 'There,' she said. 'Stand

there.' She pointed to the forefront of the settee. 'You can see it best from there.'

I did as I was told and I studied the painting with a well-feigned interest that would validate my curiosity for what lay behind the portrait.

'D' you know her?' Aunt Chrissie asked.

I noted her tense. She knew nothing about Wimbledon.

'Yes,' I said. 'We were childhood friends in Wales.'

'Merthyr wasn't it?' Aunt Chrissie said. 'I remember Sebastian said he'd met her in Merthyr.'

'We lost touch,' I said. 'There was a gap of about ten years. Then I met her once with Sebastian.'

'She was a very quiet girl, wasn't she?' Aunt Chrissie said. 'Not easy to get to know. Sebastian brought her here once for dinner. She was very shy.'

'Bit of a tomboy at school,' I said, feeling I ought to put some sort of oar in.

'She changed apparently,' Aunt Chrissie said, 'after her father died. He was a miner you know. She wasn't anywhere near Sebastian's class. But Sebastian was something of a teacher, you know. Bit of a missionary, too, I think. He wanted to mould and to teach.' She paused. 'Would you like some coffee, Mr Wakefield?'

I accepted gladly. Aunt Chrissie was a mine of information, and while she was out in the kitchen I took time to examine her room. A silver-framed photograph of the late Mrs Marion Firbank, she whom we had recently celebrated, stood on a small console. Beside it, likewise framed, was a picture of an older man, whom I took for the late lamented Alistair of the Kings' Rifles. Behind that, and almost hidden by a vase of roses, was a large photograph and, between the rose-leaves, I could discern Marion, in that very same red dress in which she had sat for Richard. I picked up the frame very carefully, and saw that it was a wedding photograph. Sebastian, in a grey morning-suit, with a white carnation in his buttonhole, stood by Marion's side, his arm in hers. I studied the photograph, and it was thus that Aunt Chrissie found me when she returned with the coffee.

'Yes,' she said. 'That was taken at their wedding. I have others. Would you like to see them?'

'Yes. Very much,' I said. I took the tray from her hands and set it on the table while she went to a small secretaire and, from one of the drawers, extracted a small photograph album.

'Pour if you like,' she said, coming back to her seat. I poured, while she leafed through the book for the appropriate pages. For myself, I would have gladly thumbed the pages from cover to cover.

'Here we are,' Aunt Chrissie said. She patted the sofa beside her, and again I did as I was told.

'This was at the reception after the registry.'

It was a large photograph taken in a private drawing-room which I presumed to be Sebastian's. In fact, through the far door, I could see a hint of that study where I had first come across the Firbank correspondence.

'There's Marion, Sebastian's mother,' Aunt Chrissie pointed her red polished nail on the latest late Marion. 'That's me,' she said excitedly, 'in my straw hat.'

'Very becoming,' I said, while all the time I was looking for Richard among the celebrants. But there was no sign of him.

'I don't see Richard,' I said.

'No, he was in New York at the time. He had an exhibition there. He sent a telegram though. I remember it was funny, but I don't recall the exact joke. Some reference, I think, to Sebastian's other wives.'

'Was he married before?' I said, feigning innocence.

'Twice,' Aunt Chrissie said. 'But it was when Seb was living in France. They were both French women, but I never met either of them.'

France, I thought, and probably Paris. Then, narrowing the field, I pin-pointed the Bois de Boulogne as Sebastian's chosen bone-yard. I was relieved. Let the French police deal with that bodies-search, and I could once more singularise my crusade.

'Anyway,' Aunt Chrissie was saying, 'Sebastian told me that Marion was for keeps. I never understood why she left or where she went. And no-one's ever heard from her since.'

And I could tell you exactly why, I thought. Poor innocent Aunt Chrissie who had set such store by Marion. I felt suddenly depressed. Although Aunt Chrissie had poured out such a stream of information, she had only confirmed what Richard had already told me, and I was no nearer that holy grail than I had been when I first started out on my crusade. I did not know which way to turn. It must have shown on my face for Aunt Chrissie said, 'And are you an artist Mr Wakefield? You have that lost look.'

I was sorry to disappoint her. She was clearly so hungry for the artistic temperament. 'No,' I said.

'Then what do you do?' She was hopefully prepared perhaps to accept something on the artistic fringe.

'Nothing,' I said, dashing her hopes completely.

'Then how do you live?' she said. 'Or is that a private matter?'

'Not at all,' I told her. 'I'm simply a very rich man.'

She seemed satisfied. Wealth was next to creativity, though I myself would give it a different priority. I was now anxious to take my leave, for I expected no more information from that quarter.

I rose from my seat. 'You were very kind to let me look at the portrait again,' I said.

'You do admire it, don't you?' she said. 'I have some photographs of it, you know. Would you like one?'

She was offering me gold. I saw myself moving from door to door, though which specific doors I could not imagine, presenting myself as a private detective. 'Do you know this woman?' I would ask, and I wouldn't even need to comment on the weather.

She went to a drawer in the console and rifled through some papers. Then she passed me a black and white reproduction of Richard's work. I thanked her profusely. She would never know how she had once more set me on my crusade. And I resolved that as soon as I should find Marion's body, Aunt Chrissie would be the first whom I would appraise.

As I took my leave, she asked me to come again.

'Feast your eyes on it at any time,' she said. 'Who knows, if enough people think about her often enough, she might one day return.'

'Perhaps,' I said, hating to disillusion her.

As I walked down the drive, I took the photograph out of its envelope and studied it again. And though I was glad to have it in my possession, I did not rightly know what to do with it, how or with whom to put it to some use. And again depression overcame me. As I walked down the avenue to the main road, I heard footsteps behind me. I turned quickly but there was no-one in sight. I retraced my steps. All the houses in the avenue sported driveways that were mostly wooded on either side. I peered into each one of them, hoping to catch my pursuer. I saw and heard nobody. But I took precautions. I simply walked backwards towards the main road but, even in that protected state, I could not ignore the pins and needles in my back. I hailed a cab and leaned against the protective leather of its seat and I took stock of my situation. My pursuer was without doubt Richard, who by now had certainly read the Firbank correspondence and had realised the enormity of the threat that I presented him. It was in his interest to put me down. Fear struck me, and I resolved that, once home, I would keep to my apartment for a while. I might even have to resort to the fire-escape and the moustache once again. I looked upon that prospect with horror.

When I entered the foyer of my building, the porter came out of his lodge to greet me and prepare my lift. I ignored him for I smelt his treachery. Richard had probably already enlisted him in the hunt.

CHAPTER THIRTEEN

Over the next few days a great lethargy crept over me, and I was not even tempted to my moustache and fire-escape. I was satisfied to stay apartment-bound. I was careful now to stick to routine. Each morning I rose, showered and prepared my breakfast. Then, if the weather were clement enough, I would take my tray under the awning on the terrace and collect my *Times* from the hall. In those days, I savoured the Deaths Column with even more relish that I had hitherto. Perhaps it was because I feared that I would not be able to savour it much longer, that I myself might soon be featured in that Column for someone else to survive and relish. And that someone else could only be Richard. The thought of him bred fear in me, and sometimes I thought I heard him loiter outside my door where he lay in wait for me. Often during that time I looked over my balcony to check the whereabouts of my porter and, if he were outside the building, I knew with certainty what business he was about. In short, I was well on the way to the south coast, except that I still had the wit to know where my pins and needles would lead me. The wit, too, to keep myself out of harm's way. So apart from my breakfasts on the balcony, I kept to my bed for most of that week, sleeping most of the time as I would have done on the south coast, but without the irritating interference of all those parasites.

I read *The Times* daily from cover to cover, starting always with that most reliable tool in my survival kit, that friendly Deaths Column of mine. But one morning, I saw my name in print, and, being 'Wakefield', the sign-off of the Column. I actually thought I'd read it. *Wakefield. Luke, aged 38, died of fright, November 14th. Deeply mourned by his wife Connie and son,*

172

Luke. When I came to read it over, it had blurred into a Mrs Waters who, in typical *Times* fashion, had died of natural causes at the ripe old age of 103. And unsurprisingly, she had been survived by nobody. I suppose that to read one's own obituary notice is to have reached the very nadir of self-diminishment, and I covered my head with a blanket and slept the day away. Or would have, had not the telephone bell disturbed me. I shot up in bed and let it ring for a while to make sure I was not dreaming. But it truly was ringing, pealing by my side, and for the first time in many months without my activation. I have an extension at my bed-side, and I reached out for the receiver. My gesture was languid and deliberately slow. I was fostering the illusion that my telephone never stopped ringing, and so real was this fantasy that I took no time off to question who it might be on the other end of the line. My 'Hullo' was languid too, a tone that quickly evaporated when I heard the voice of the caller and felt it on my skin.

Richard.

'Hullo,' he said cheerily. 'How are you old boy?'

I re-capped quickly. This was the voice of a man who knew all that I knew, who had filched the evidence of all my information, who was after my blood for his own survival. As a result, my response was cool. 'I'm well,' I lied. 'And you?'

'Missing you,' he said to my skin. 'My turn to cook. How about Wednesday?'

I had no idea what day it was, or how many post-Chrissie days I had slept away. Nor of the month, the year nor the season. But I still harboured the remnants of that languid fantasy of being so much in demand and I said, 'Could you hold a minute? I have to look at my book. It's in the other room,' I added, to give myself time to absorb the sudden turn my life had taken. I muffled the receiver in the blanket and I looked at the date in the current copy of the *Times*. It was winter, November and a Saturday. I counted on my fingers. I was given four days to make my preparations. But for such an encounter four days was too many, and four thousand not enough. I picked up the receiver. 'Yes, I am free on Wednesday,' I said. 'I'd love to have dinner with you.'

'Fine,' Richard said. 'Let me give you the address.'

I had no pencil handy, and I dared not trust my memory.

'Can you hold again, Richard?' I said, adding his name, so

that he would not lose patience with me. 'I have to get a pen.'

I rushed to the kitchen and took my memo-pad off the wall. I didn't want to keep Richard waiting in case he lost appetite for our rendezvous. I rushed back to the 'phone and tried to still my breath. 'I've got one,' I said.

'Three Castle Mews, SW3. It's off the Kings Road,' he said.

'I know it,' I answered, though having no idea where it was, except that it was Chelsea and marginally short of the river beyond which landmark I gave no serious thought. But Chelsea was an area where a man about town counted many friends, and I was not about to claim ignorance of such a quarter. 'What time?' I said.

'Eightish. Informal.'

I wondered whether he was referring to my silk dressing-gown.

'And I have a surprise for you,' he added.

'Yes?' I said. 'And you're not going to tell me?'

'Of course not,' he said. 'But you'll see. You'll like it. I'll see you Wednesday.'

'Look forward,' I said, and I put the 'phone down. And certainly I was looking forward, but with as much terror as excitement. For I might well be walking into a lion's den.

I got out of bed, showered again and dressed. I felt a sudden need for routine. I made my breakfast, I checked on the terrace which I found too cloudy and I put my tray on the dining-room table. Then I began to collect my thoughts. Richard had evidence that I knew what I oughtn't to know. And that evidence he had stolen, so that even if I were to go to the police and admit my interference with Her Majesty's mail, I had no proof of the fantastic tale I was weaving. The thought of blackmailing Richard crossed my mind, but for even that base pursuit I needed some concrete evidence. I had been totally disarmed and was doomed to carry that terrible proofless knowledge for the rest of my days. Poor Marion.

I tried to imagine our Wednesday conversation. It was possible that Richard would make no mention of the letters, for that would invite his own incrimination. For surely he would be anxious to know how I had come by them, and his curiosity would get the better of him. In which case, I would confess all and, in return for my own honesty, I would be entitled to some from him. I grew excited. The image of Richard at confession, and therefore at my mercy, wired my body with such thrilling shock that I had to grip the sides of the dining-room table. I would be privy to the outpourings of a murderer and I would hold him in thrall for ever. Suddenly I lost all my fear of him, and I could hardly wait for our appointed hour. I wondered what surprise he had in store for me. I guessed that it might be a picture and possibly one of his own. And so certain I became of the nature of his surprise that I looked round my living-room to judge where I could best hang it. I suspected it would be small, as are all gifts of men of good taste, and I decided on the space above the glass shelf. That area which already housed my fake-Congo vase would pass as culture corner. I was well satisfied with all the conclusions I had reached and, suddenly, out of nowhere, out of no anger, out of no frustration, came a Connie-thought. I could not understand it, for I was indeed in a state of almost smug contentment. Yet I did not trust it. I did not trust its alien provenance, and I quickly cleared away the breakfast things in an effort to put it aside. But that Connie-thought dogged me, even as I left my apartment, took the lift, greeted the porter, and made my way into the park. Finally, unable to shake it off, I sat down on a bench and I acknowledged it. But when I examined it, I realised that it was not of Connie that I was thinking, but of Connie and myself and the miserable years we had spent together. The thought that it had been miserable, or, more to the point, that I was acknowledging its misery, was something new too. For in that acknowledgement I myself was accepting part of the blame. We were miserable together because we gave each other nothing, not because we had nothing to give, but because both of us had chosen the wrong targets for donation. The failure of my marriage was a failure of choice, as it had been for Connie. I got up from the bench and walked quickly across the lawn and into the shade of the trees. For some reason I needed darkness; I knew now where my thoughts were perilously guiding me. For without doubt they were leading me into the chasm of forgiveness, and I did not know that I was ready for that journey of no return. For how could I fill the rest of my days without my hate and anger, those great sources of energy that had propelled so many of my years. And why did I think of my mother at that time? And then of my father, with a lump in my mind? I found myself breaking into a run. I needed motion as I have always done when thoughts are uncontainable. I sprinted around the flower-beds with no eye for the blooms except that I noticed that there were few of them, which meant the onset of winter, which same season was spelt out in the leafless grove I was making for, of trees that would offer no darkness or shade. Then suddenly I stood still and faced the prospect of what I could only call my redemption. A big word, and I cringed before it as I would from any enemy. I was not yet willing to be hors de combat, lame, disarmed, unmanned, and I longed for a letter from Connie to feed my hate once more. Or I would write to her myself, and thus nurture that anger that had kept me alive, that had daily fed my fury to survive. I started running again, and did not stop until I reached my apartment block. Even as I waited for the lift, I jogged to hold the rhythm of my failing spleen, and the porter raised his eyebrow and no doubt harboured a south coast thought. I jogged all the way up in the lift, and in front of my penthouse door as I reached for my keys. Then I ran to my chiffonier, took pen and paper, and came to rest only when I sat at the desk and saw how the pen trembled in my hand.

Dear Connie, I wrote. Then I put the pen down and calmed myself. *Dear Connie*, I read, and I could think of nothing more to say. And I knew that, even if I sat there for the whole day, no further words would come. Then it struck me that perhaps *Dear Connie* was enough, and of such adequacy, that there was no need even to send it. I knew then that I was close to forgiveness, but the word jarred my mind with an almost physical pain. It was a foreign word that had landed on alien ground without papers to support its presence. It was awaiting its deportation. But where could I send it? I knew then that I was stuck with it, and that one day I might fathom its meaning.

*

For the next few days I took care to maintain my routine, fragile as it was. As I showered and dressed each morning, I noticed with some small alarm that I was losing considerable weight. It was not that I was eating or drinking less. Indeed, my excited anticipation of my dinner with Richard drove me to the bottle or Waterford with some speed and frequency. And I could only conclude that it was Connie-hate that I was shedding, that anger, that over the years, had accumulated pounds on my flesh. I wondered how long the process would continue and whether, in the course of time, my skeleton would find even my skin a hate-impediment, and would flower alone in pure and innocent glory. Perhaps self-annihilation was the ultimate meaning of forgiveness and that was a thought that I found deeply depressing, for Richard had entered my life, that confessed and penitent murderer, and now was no time to give up the ghost even if its payoff was divine forgiveness.

On the day before my Richard dinner, I tightened two notches on the belt of my trousers, and I set about to make myself a hearty breakfast. It was warm on the terrace that morning, a pale winter warmth, still and without wind, and I was glad to use the balcony, though I knew I would soon have to close it up for the winter. But I found comfort in these seasonal thoughts, for they were new to me. I poured my coffee, and cracked my eggs. Despite my loss of weight, I had not lost one whit of appetite, a fact that pleased me for I wanted to do justice to Richard's catering. I set about imagining the menu which I produced as exotic in the extreme. I fancied quails' eggs as a starter, and possibly a pheasant to follow, for it was the season. I did not rule out a cheeseboard, though I myself did not favour it. But each to his own. I imagined sundry desserts, but could not pin-point one that would suit Richard. He seemed to me to be a savoury man. But I did not wish to think too much about Richard, or to nurture great expectations of our meeting. My Marion crusade had been dogged from its inception by disappointments of all kinds. But it was hard not to think of Richard, and I spent the rest of the day doing just that, yet trying all the time to put him out of my mind.

At six o'clock on the following day I started to make my preparations. I was in a state of high excitement. To calm myself, I forced my ear to listen to the news, which was a catalogue of strikes, coups and calamities. I could evince no interest in any of the items. I could not imagine that there were lives going on outside my own. I gave the news its headline timing, and then I ran myself a hot bath. I am a shower man by nature. For me, a bath is something else and has little to do with ablution. It is a condition conducive to contemplation and it was that of which I was in need, if for no other reason than to calm myself. To facilitate this process, I added a relaxant to the bath-water, and I sank myself into its foam and tried to get my mind off my mind. This latter is a time-consuming occupation, and I don't know how long I lay there, but I was suddenly conscious of a certain chill in my immediate surroundings. I poured my skinny self out of the bath, and consulted my watch. It was a quarter after seven. I fought down a rising panic. The calm that I had acquired while foam-submerged, had vanished as if it had never been. I rushed to my wardrobe and withdrew my favourite grey flannel. Looking down at myself I noticed that I had over-talced, and I shook and shimmied as a shower of powder filmed the brown carpet around my feet. I dressed hurriedly, applied some dabs of cologne, and drew from its plastic wrapper my camel-hair coat, which I wore only on special occasions. In fact, as I put it on, I realised I had never worn it before, and I was obliged to unhook the price-tag from the sleeve button before setting out on my way. I was well pleased with my appearance and my stride was jaunty as I passed through the foyer and acknowledged the porter who clearly could not cope with my ever-changing moods. I looked at my watch. 7.45. I would be a little late, but that would be to my credit, for it would show the nonchalance of one who knew he had the upper hand.

A taxi drew up at my building, and I gave the cabbie the Chelsea address. Then I leaned back in the leather seat and considered that this moment marked the beginning of possibly the most important event in my life. That it would mark the abandonment of my crusade, or equally the beginning of its resolution. The choice depended on Richard's co-operation. I had an overwhelming feeling of power, and it was this feeling that prompted me grossly to over-tip the cabbie as he dropped me off at Richard's door.

The entrance was through a wrought-iron gate which led to a courtyard. An old Victorian lamplight stood at the centre, its gas mantle replaced by neon. There were about four doors skirting the little square. I looked round and spotted numbers 1, 2 and 4. I had to presume that the unmarked door belonged to Richard. Such affectation intrigued me. Richard needed the caché of ex-directory, but he was making bloody sure that he was contactable none the less, simply by a process of elimination. I stepped up to his front door and I looked at my watch. 8.15. It showed a lack of eagerness which stopped just short this side of discourtesy. I was satisfied, and with confidence I rang the bell. I heard it resound loudly through the house, and I waited. I waited some time. I was not prepared to ring again. It would have blunted the studied effect of my late arrival. But no doubt Richard was also playing the nonchalant game, and it was a question of who would hold out the longer. I pinned my hands to my side. I scanned the outside windows of the house, but there was no sign of Richard behind them. Thus, unseen to each other, we were already at war. I suspected that Richard was lurking behind the front door, awaiting my second plea for entry. But he could wait, I thought. I clenched my hands behind my back. And I waited. Then I thought I heard a step behind the door. But still the door did not open. I decided to take a terrible risk. I turned noisily on my heel and walked back into the courtyard, grinding the gravel under my feet with each step. The risk paid off. As I reached the lamp-post I heard the door open. First round to Wakefield, I thought. I turned and saw Richard framed in the doorway. He was smiling, the good loser that he was, and, in response, I felt myself hurrying back to the door.

'Come in,' he said. 'And welcome.'

He was wearing a black silk dressing-gown, I noticed, clearly what he meant by informal. I followed him into his living-room and was astonished by its luxury. But I took care not to over-enthuse, for that would have shown poor taste, so I complimented him politely on his life-style and left it at that.

'What will you drink?' he asked.

'A scotch,' I said. A scotch is what one asks for. A whiskey is what one drinks alone. His Waterford was not lost on me, slightly smaller than mine, I thought, but superbly cut. He took a scotch too, and clinked his glass to mine.

'To our friendship,' he said.

That depends on a lot of things, I thought, but I clinked his glass nonetheless. He sat opposite me in a leather armchair. I scanned the walls which were lined with paintings. At least I hoped Richard thought that that was what I was doing. But in truth, I was scanning all surfaces to see if, perhaps, he'd left the Firbank correspondence on show, simply to tease me. But nothing was visible.

'Did you paint them?' I asked.

He laughed. 'I wish I had,' he said. 'That's an early Picasso.' He pointed to a still-life. 'It belonged to my father. He was a great collector. Most of the others are modern Italian.'

'And yours?' I said.

'I don't hang mine. Not on *my* walls anyway. But I keep some of them in the studio. Finish your drink, or bring it with you, if you like. Unless you're very hungry. Then we can see them later.'

'No, let's go now,' I said, wondering if my surprise was in the studio, for it was certainly not evident in the living-room.

Richard led the way down a long corridor to an annexe. The studio was an addition to the house and had taken over a large part of the garden. It was a galleried room and, from where I stood, I caught a glimpse of a counterpane on an outline of a bed. There was no sign on the floor of the studio of any work in progress. An empty easel stood in one corner, and by its side a table covered with a palette and neatly aligned paint-tubes, with jars of brushes alongside. A number of large canvasses were stacked against the walls, but with their canvas backs to the room. I was aware that Richard was staring at me as if it were my turn to say something. But he had shown me nothing to comment on.

'Are you going to show me some of your work?' I asked.

'Look behind you,' he said.

I turned, expecting the surprise he'd promised me. But instead, I saw two large portraits on the entrance wall, both of women, and though they were two different models, there was an indefinable likeness between them.

'They're lovely,' I said, for it seemed the obvious thing to say. Then I followed with the obvious question. 'Who are they?'

Richard went over to the wall and carressed the canvas nearest the door.

'This is Françoise,' he said. 'Sebastian's first wife. Rather beautiful, don't you think?'

I studied her carefully. Her body tended to plumpness, though her face was lean. Her most remarkable feature was a cascade of golden hair that dropped to her shoulders in a chaos of curls.

'She was a country girl,' Richard was saying. 'You can see it in the cheeks. She came from Brittany. Her father was a cow-man.'

Another of Sebastian's missionary pursuits, I thought. 'And she was illiterate, no doubt,' I added.

'Almost,' Richard laughed. 'But she was a quick learner. Almost too quick.'

'Is that why she left?' I said.

'No. Françoise didn't leave. Sebastian simply tired of her.'

A great old euphumism, I thought. A gross sub-title for a burial in the Bois de Boulogne.

We now moved on to the second victim, a brunette of equal beauty. But her hair was straight and short, with a hint of a kiss-curl on the forehead.

Richard stroked the canvas. 'Marie-Claire,' he said. 'A real beauty. A clergyman's daughter.'

That threw me a little. Such provenance implied a class that Sebastian was not wont to explore for marital purposes. It also suggested that missionary zeal had already been paternally at work. How much more could one mould Marie-Claire? In what area was she teachable?

Richard, as if thought-reading, provided the answer. 'She loved painting,' he said, 'though she knew little about it. But she wanted to be a painter herself. I offered to give her lessons. But she had no talent for it. But she was a wonderful sitter.' He carressed the canvas again. I had a feeling that, out of all Sebastian's wives, Marie-Claire was Richard's favourite.

'And what happened to her?' I asked.

'She got discouraged,' he said, 'and the rot set in.'

Her rot, I thought. Poor Marie-Claire's rot, side by side with Francoise's rot, she who was too clever for her own good. The French police had been very remiss, I thought. Clearly they had no priggish boy-scouts in Paris. 'They're both very beautiful in their own ways,' I said, but my heart was not in it, for I saw them as they now precisely were, gone to pastures new, in the Champs Elysees or Elysian fields hard by the Bois de Boulogne. Poor buggers. I'd had enough. I turned to Richard. 'I could do with another drink,' I said.

He touched my arm. 'Let's go back into the house,' he said.

He led the way and, once in the living-room, he refilled my glass. He must have sensed a disenchantment about me for, as he removed the decanter, he stroked his fingers on mine. He knew I would tremble, and that pleased him. I felt he wanted so much to make me happy.

'Aren't you going to ask what the surprise is?' he asked. He himself was flushing with excitement.

'I've been wondering,' I said. But I didn't want to push it. I knew my manners.

'Well, you need wonder no more,' he said. 'But you must excuse me a minute. First I must prepare our hors d'oeuvre, and then – well, you'll see. But don't move,' he said, laying his hand gently on my shoulder, and as he did so the fold of his dressing-gown fell slightly apart, and I saw the outline of his brown and beautiful thigh. I shut my eyes because I knew it to be the beauty of eternal damnation.

'I won't be long,' he said, and he left the room.

For my part, I wished him away and never to return, but I longed for him, too, murderer though he might be, and a triple one at that. I leaned back in my chair and kept my eyes closed. My mind was in confusion and my body trembled, I don't know how long I waited there, but when I opened my eyes, the room seemed darker, and I had a feeling that much time had passed. I recalled the hors d'oeuvre that I had imagined, that of quails' eggs, which I knew from experience took but a few moments of preparation. I sat up in my chair, for I was suddenly frightened. Then I heard a movement from the direction of the kitchen, and I was filled with a mixture of fear and relief. I stood up, in which position I felt better able to defend myself if so called upon, and in any case, in appreciation of the surprise he had promised me. Then I heard his voice.

'Are you ready?' he called.

'Yes,' I said, hearing my voice squeak.

'Then may I present,' I heard him say. Then there was a pause. 'May I present,' again a pause, 'Marion Firbank.'

And in she came. She was wearing the same red dress that she had worn for Richard's sitting. And she was indeed as beautiful. I was in a quandary. I was supposed to know her. And know her well. Not the woman of her, but those knobbly knees of her childhood, those dirty finger-nails, that now so careful hair that had once been Welsh-tangled and awry. Yes, I knew her as a child, I convinced myself, and I greeted her with all the memory of that knowledge.

'Marion,' I cried going towards her, for I was in truth overjoyed for, even though I didn't know her from Eve, I could see that she was alive and well and that my crusade was at an end. I reached her and put out my hand. But she did not take it, and I feared the consequence of all my lies and fabrication. I looked over her shoulder and I thought I caught the movement of Richard's shadow in the kitchen. He was eavesdropping I was sure. He had baited the hook superbly and he waited now, only to draw in his line.

'How are you Luke?' Marion said. Her voice was low and mellifluous and matched the sultriness of her expression. I could have loved her for playing her part. I wanted to whisper in her ear that she must continue the pretence of whatever she was pretending, or I would have some explaining to do to Richard. Then she took my hand and stroked my fingers with her own.

I trembled. If I didn't know that woman, and surely I did not know her, then I knew her touch by heart. I knew it in my bones where it had throbbed over a week ago, and had throbbed ever since with every thought of Richard. I stared at her, my heart pumping. I could not begin to understand it all. I was very confused, not knowing who was laying a trap for whom. But trap I knew it to be. I drew away from her, and then a little further, at the same distance as I had stood from Aunt Chrissie's wall, and again I saw that painting, that painting that had set me off once more on my crusade. But something more as well. The oils of the portrait were now caked powder, overblown rouge, and an exaggerated rose on the lips. The hair was a still-life, untouchable. Yet I dared to reach forward and touch it. As I did so, Marion took my hand. That touch again. And with all my fear, all my tremblings and with everything my heart dared not hope for, I said, 'Richard.' He nodded. Then I had to touch him. Touch was imperative, for a slight incredulity still lingered. My hand soothed the ruffle on the neck, the silk skirt on the thigh. I put my hands on his shoulder.

'There never was a Marion,' I said.

He shook his head with half a smile, and I, like a Paladin, pathetically wrong-scented, dismounted once and for all.

'And Françoise? Marie-Claire?' I asked. My voice trembled.

'Self-portraits too,' Richard said. 'Fantasy wives.'

'But Sebastian was *married*,' I spluttered. 'Aunt Chrissie showed me the photographs.'

'And Richard wasn't there,' Richard said. 'He was in New York. That's what they were all told. But I was there all right,' he laughed. 'I was the bride.'

'But how? The Registrar. The legalities.'

'Forged. Easy,' Richard said.

I backed away. I needed to sit down. It was all too much for me. I felt terribly cheated. And ashamed. I recapped on all that rubbish that I had invented for Marion; her Welsh pigtails, her miner father, even his crass silicosis death.

'You led me on, Richard,' I said.

'It was a game. We could play it some more.'

I trembled.

'Have another drink,' Richard said. 'You look as if you need it.'

I watched him walk to the drinks cabinet. It was, without doubt, a woman's authentic gait and an impressive one. It surprised me that, even after his astonishing revelations, my feelings for him were not changed. He returned with my re-charged Waterford.

'And you actually went to dinner with Aunt Chrissie,' I said.

'Yes. But only once. Sebastian and I got the giggles. Dear old Chrissie took it for shyness, but we never risked it again. It was easier in Paris. We did that sort of thing more often. When I was Françoise, Sebastian claimed that I couldn't speak French and that let me off the hook. As for Marie-Claire, well, I just sat there and looked ravishing.'

'But why?' I asked. 'Why any of them? And the letters?' As soon as it was out, I regretted it, for it was my self-introduction into the charade.

And Richard rightly took it up. 'How did you come by the letters?' he asked. Then he came and sat on the arm of my chair. 'You owe me that,' he said.

He was right, and I judged myself lucky that I had got off so lightly. But his proximity unnerved me, especially that one silk-stockinged leg that dangled over my own with freakish intimacy. So I rose, my glass in my hand, and stood with my back to the empty fireplace.

'It was a Tuesday,' I began. 'The day Sebastian died.' And thus I started on my tale, with full confession of my felony, and I have to own there was some pleasure in it. While I had been engaged on my Marion crusade, it had never occurred to me that my campaign was anything but natural and normal. But as I recounted my story, it struck me as being bizarre in the extreme. Occasionally, during its telling, Richard laughed, and I had to laugh with him, for it was clear that I was a detective of extreme ineptitude, with an acutely inaccurate nose for every false clue and red herring strewn in my path. When the tale was told, it was my turn once more to question him.

'But why the Marions? Why the Marie-Claires, the Françoises? Why the wives at all? And above all, why the post-mortem correspondence?'

'Come,' Richard said, leading me towards the table. 'I'll tell you over dinner.'

He sat me in my place and went to the kitchen for the hors d'oeuvre. I waited for the appearance of quails' eggs and indeed they shortly arrived and gave me no surprise. He took one of the small speckled ovals in his hands, and gently peeled it, then he laid it on my plate. Then he did the same for himself.

'Sebastian and I lived together for many years,' he began. 'When I first met him, I was a painter, just beginning to make my way as a portraitist. Sebastian was rich from a legacy from his grandfather. He loved paintings and was something of a collector. I was living in Paris at the time, and he joined me there. We were very happy together. But Sebastian was often melancholy. Guilt really. He was guilty about his money, and especially about its unearned source. Above all, he was guilty about what he was, and couldn't help but be. He had a great sense of the name of Firbank and its long dynasty. His brother's death had left him the only Firbank progenitor. He had fantasies about being a husband and father. But he knew it was impossible. A fantasy wife seemed to be the obvious solution. It just seemed to happen. It was fun, too, and it became an intrinsic part of our relationship. I don't know whether you can understand, Luke,' he said, 'but fantasies are perilous playthings.'

I gave a small smile. I, the master of illusion, practically the inventor of self-deceit, needed no lessons from Richard in the pit-falls of fantasy.

'Sometimes,' Richard was saying, 'the illusion seemed authentic, and at such times we'd go off to the Registry office and make it real. Madness. Sheer madness,' he said. 'But Marion was definitely going to be the last. Even if Sebastian had lived.'

'Why?' I asked. 'Why end it at all?'

'Simple,' Richard said. 'One fantasy tends to be replaced by another. Sebastian simply tired of being a husband. He preferred to be a widower. But that little illusion took as much production as the other.' Richard laughed and poured me some more wine. 'That's where the correspondence comes in,' he said.

I looked at him questioningly.

'Sebastian took his fantasies very seriously. To be a widower, you had to go through a period of mourning. You had to atone. You had to ask for forgiveness. One morning, out of the blue, I received a letter. We were living in Hampstead then. It was addressed to Marion, and I opened it. You saw what I read. It was my obituary. It seemed to me quite natural to reply. And so we wrote to each other. That, too, became a part of our loving.'

'But why Wimbledon?'

'We went there for my mother's birthday. You read about that. On the way home, we quarrelled. Marion had become too real. Like Françoise. Like Marie-Claire. They'd all come between us. I remember we were standing by the Common waiting for a cab. We were on the verge of breaking with each other and Sebastian said, "Let's bury her. All of them. Once and for all." And we did. I can't tell you what a relief it was. I used to go back every week to that same spot and post my letter. But I owe you, Luke,' Richard said. 'If it hadn't been for you, I'd never have received his last letter of forgiveness.' He touched my arm again. 'Poor old Sebastian,' he said, 'he didn't live long enough to enjoy his widowhood. Let's drink to him, Luke.'

He raised his glass and clinked mine. 'To Sebastian,' he said, 'you old and wonderful bugger.' He linked his arm in mine and we drank. 'Now let's get on with the serious business of eating.' He peppered and swallowed his egg whole.

I put my hand on his arm.

'May I call you Connie?' I said.

CHAPTER FOURTEEN

My name is Luke Wakefield and I am a man of routine. The seeds of my Marion-crusade had been sown on a Tuesday in the post-office, and I deemed it right and proper to visit that post-office once more, to draw a curtain, as it were, across that episode in my life. I no longer have the leisure I had enjoyed, or rather suffered, in my pre-crusading days. My life is full. Richard has taken up his quarters in my penthouse. Those rooms that once, in nightmare delusion, I had allocated to Connie and her son, are now host to Richard. He maintains his studio in Chelsea whither he repairs when the occasional need for the easel overtakes him. And I am glad of such arrangement, for both of us value our privacy. But most of the time we spend in each other's company. I keep him out of my kitchen for, though he is a more than passable cook, I do not encourage competition in that aspect of my life. We go often to the theatre and the occasional country weekend. I have not abandoned the telephone ruse. It has become a game that we share. I have introduced Richard to Sandra, Alistair et al, and he in his turn, has summoned an inordinate number of strange figures and faces to the other end of the line. My life is indeed full, but I remain a man of routine and, as to that post-office practice of mine, I would not dream of going there on any other day but Tuesday.

For it was on that day that the crusade had been born, and it was on that day that it must be buried. So it was that, on a Tuesday of a summer's day in May, I rose, showered and breakfasted on my terrace. I gave a cursory glance at *The Times*. For some reason that I cannot understand, and am not interested in fathoming, I no longer read the Deaths Column of *The Times*. I have no interest in it, whatever that may signify. After breakfast, I put on a dark suit, sutable for obsequies, and I set out at a brisk pace to the post-office. Since Sebastian's death, I had never once gone back. My simple communication needs were satisfied in an all-purpose shop run by Pakistanis in a street at the back of my building. Now as I took that route again, my stride brisk and firm, I thought of Connie and of all the anger and frustration and desperate sense of failure that, in those days, had prompted my every step. But now all that seemed to belong to another life of mine, a life dogged with shadows that at dusks would lead me to the south coast. Now I thought of Connie as a stranger, and I had to think hard to recall her companion's name.

When I reached the post-office there was, as I expected, a long queue. I joined the line, but without the patience of the old days. Now I was anxious to get to the grille with no time or inclination, and certainly no need, to engage strangers in conversation. I thought of Sebastian, and in my mind I recaptured his last moments at the grille. I had gone that Tuesday to the post-office, as I was wont to go on every Tuesday, in a desperate search for some meaning to my life. And now, by an arduous, devious and almost lunatic route, I had found it. And there and then I blessed Sebastian and the rich legacy he had bequeathed. So lost was I in my memories, that I did not notice how swiftly I had inched towards the grille. There was now but one man in front of me, on the point of collecting his pension. I could not help but wish him good health, good enough at least to last him out of the post-office. When my turn came, I asked for one first-class stamp, as Sebastian had done, and in his memory. I kept my fingers crossed as I slipped the money under the counter and took the stamp in exchange. On my way out of the post-office, I took one last look behind me. My obsequies were over. Thereafter, I would take my communications business forever elsewhere.

That week Richard had gone to Paris. He had asked me to accompany him, but I was wary of flying, and I was too shy to tell him so. So I had made some excuse of having to see my dentist. He would be away for two whole weeks and I was beginning to miss him. I was at a loss as to how to spend my time. I went out a great deal, walking and riding all over London, in and out of my penthouse, until one day my porter called me jack-in-the-box. But he no longer troubled me. I was counting the days to Richard's return.

A few days before the appointed time, I grew quite euphoric. I spent many long hours in the rose-garden, sniffing their scents like an addict. I picked seeding dandelions and blew away the days till Richard's return. And then suddenly it came. A Saturday. His plane was due in the afternoon and I had promised to meet him. I rose, showered, set my breakfast on the terrace and then returned to the hall to pick up my *Times*. Underneath the paper, there were a number of letters. Since Richard had come to live with me, my letter-box rattled with every delivery. There were invitations to art openings, travel brochures which Richard never tired of reading, and announcements of the new season at the Barbican and South Bank. An exciting post, with never a trace of Australian blue. I took those addressed to Richard and his sundry aliases, and put them to one side. I did not need to open them, for I knew that it was Richard's habit to share his post with me as we shared most things.

His plane was late and it was past supper-time when we returned to the penthouse. I had prepared a sumptuous meal for his return, and afterwards, over coffee and brandy, having exchanged our separate adventures of the past week, I crossed to the secretaire and handed Richard his post. Then I gave him my paper-knife and settled down for his reading. He perused the envelopes of each letter, guessing their contents, and then settled on one that seemed to excite his interest. He showed me the post-mark. Hampstead. First Class mail. I grew excited, too. He slit the envelope with one flick of the wrist, unfolded the single sheet and read aloud:

Dearest Connie, I have just returned from your funeral. I killed you my dearest, as gently as I was able, and I buried you where no-one will ever find you.

And so on. We have a great correspondence going, Connie and I. She writes to me regularly, from a Chelsea postmark, and I have to say that her spelling has greatly improved. So has her general manner. She does not argue any more. She agrees with almost everything I say.

Listen. Some may call it madness. Some may call it failure. Names, that's all they are. Names in the eye of the beholder. For my merry part, I don't look at myself any more.

REDHILL ROCOCO

Shena Mackay

High summer is flattering Redhill just now – it's gloriously hot. Life, however, has not treated Luke Ribbons so kindly ever since he made a major gaffe in the post office on pension day. So, rebuffed by Fortune, he's drifting away from parents, parish, old friends and – with luck – into the arms of Pearl Slattery . . . to sink into her alluringly fragrant bosom and be smothered in soft, blousy, sweet mother-love.

Unfortunately, Pearl doesn't share this romantic vision. Luke is dazzled by sunshine, the Slattery brood, the smell of freshly-cut grass, cheap perfume, warm beer, burnt toast and witch doctors' promises. It's as hard to live in Surrey as it is anywhere else.

'Witty, wistful and perceptive by turns, REDHILL ROCOCO is a marvellous entertainment' WOMAN'S JOURNAL

0 349 122171 7   FICTION   £3.50

Also available in ABACUS paperback: